BITTERSWEET SACRIFICE

NICHOLAS P BOYLAND

I0553762

BITTERSWEET SACRIFICE

NICHOLAS P BOYLAND

The moral right of Nicholas.P.Boyland has been asserted

First published in Great Britain 2013 by Rhino trikes Church Street Winsham Nr Chard Somerset TA20 4JD

www.rhinotrikespublishing.com

Published by Rhino Trikes

ISBN 978-0-9576285-8-8

Cover designed by Nico Designs

"All that I am or ever hope to be, I owe to my angel mother."

Abraham Lincoln

PROLOGUE

Stormy weather ahead

It was the autumn of nineteen eighty seven. The previous night, weather forecaster Michael Fish had told viewers: "Earlier on today, apparently, a woman rang the BBC and said she heard there was a hurricane on the way; well, if you're watching, don't worry, there isn't."

There was! It would go down in history as the greatest storm in three hundred years and the biggest blooper in television history, both tarnishing and sealing the reputation of the unfortunate weatherman for time immemorial!

CHAPTER 1

Prieten

The mood on the dimly lit Plymouth Street was decidedly tense. The severe storm had pounded the sea front closing most of the dockland area indefinitely leaving owners to count the cost and faceless insurance companies to wait with baited breath.

With money in their pockets and an uncertain future, the local dock workers had converged on a rough nightclub in the red light district to drown their sorrows. A bit of a ruckus had broken out between the rowdy dockers and a trio of Roma gypsy lads whose family had arrived a few days before the storm. The lads were already making their mark with the short skirted, bleached blonde scrubbers who passed off as the local talent; this didn't sit well with the grieving dockers.

Brian Dix had observed the commotion developing inside the club. The locals had a bee in their bonnet about the travellers parking up on an area of wasteland where they enjoyed a lunch time 'kick about', now the 'damn pikeys' had set about their women.

Brian Dix was familiar with the vernacular of the dock worker. Regular forays from Ireland to the mainland saw him enough of a 'salt' to assimilate into the group. Playing 'Devil's advocate', a few choice comments to wind up the chief protagonists, and things were soon heading the way Brian desired.

Tempers were frayed and scores had to be settled. The well-built Dockers outnumbered the notoriously tough Gypsies by five to three. Brian followed the scuffle as it spilled out into the street adjacent to the club.

"You fucking Gypos just don't know when to fuck off do you?" the shortest and stockiest of the locals cursed. "You come down here, poncin' off our fucking taxes, rip up our fucking footy field with your bloody four be fours and your friggin' pikey caravans," He turned to his mates, making sure they were all backing him up, "You march into our fuckin' boozer, all gold bling and bullshit," as he spoke each sentence, he violently shoved the biggest of the three brothers further into the street. "Now yer botherin' the birds! What next hey? You wanna nick the fucking copper pipes out of the bogs?"

The Gypsy lad had taken enough and landed a punch which would have seen a lesser man out for the count, but these lads were hard as nails and, had it been one on one, an even match for the travellers. Outnumbered as they were, the Gypsies were quickly on the back foot and the violence was looking like it could end in serious injury for them.

Brian Dix waited for his moment; he had no desire to become involved until all the protagonists had lost their edge. Crouching down by the edge of the kerb, he drained the last of the Guinness from his glass and carefully tapped the pint glass against the kerbstone, breaking off the lip in a jagged circle around the upper edge.

One of the dock workers had the first Gypsy lad held up, pinned with arms behind his back, while the stocky man was laying into him mercilessly with tight hammer blows to his face and chest. Brian casually walked up behind the guy and tapped him hard on the shoulder. Bewildered, he half turned. Brian jammed the broken pint glass into the side of his neck. Arterial blood sprayed in a wide arc across the road. The man let go with a pitiful half scream half gargle as he clasped a hand to his throat in a futile attempt to stem the geyser of precious life's blood.

"Jesus Christ. John? Jesus Christ man, you've fucking killed him! John? John?" The guy holding the Gypsy's arms screamed, let go of his captive, and ran to his friend's aid as he sank to his knees in the street, his consciousness fading fast.

By this time, the whole group and the crowd of bystanders stood aghast, rendered immobile by the shock and awe of the unfolding events. Brian turned to the Gypsy lads and shouted, "Run! What are you waiting for?"

With that, the boys snapped out of their stupor and ran as if leaving the scene of a crime was second nature. When they drew closer to their encampment, Brian signalled them to a halt.

"I'll catch up with you boys another time," he said. "The old Bill are going to grill you boys. You know nothin' so there's nothin' to tell. Best I go visit the missus; lay low for a bit."

The Gypsy lad who'd landed the first punch shook Brian's hand and said, "I don't know who you are, prieten. We won't forget what you done!"

Brian smiled, he didn't speak much Roma, but he knew that prieten meant pal. *Mission accomplished* he thought, then slipped away into the shadows and faded into the dark before the wail of police and ambulance sirens disturbed the sanctity of the night.

In the anonymous safety of Plymouth train station, Brian reached into his inside pocket to where the bulging money clip lived; always deal in cash was the motto of the army. No names, no pack drill. "Oh feckin hell!" he exclaimed. His pocket had been picked in the club, he was penniless!

CHAPTER 2

Stranded

The first sign of trouble ahead was the misfire, followed by a series of kangaroo hops, ending in a cough and splutter to the kerbside.

In the grand scheme of things, he knew he'd got off lightly but tragedy is personal and an ill-tempered Neil Curland was taking this tragedy very personally.

The petrol gauge said empty, in fact, the petrol gauge had read empty a half hour ago; now what it was saying was more akin to 'overdraft limit reached'.

The day had not started well. The country had woken up to scenes of devastation. Whole caravan sites had been picked up and thrown around with the compassion of an irate toddler. Rivers had burst their banks, seas had flooded inland. The town of Sevenoaks in the county of Kent had in one fell swoop become Oneoaks with the uprooting and destruction of most of its iconic trees.

On any other morning, the view from the Victorian box sash window of Neil's guest room would have been a picturesque, almost postcard perfect scene of a sixteenth century thatched cottage, slightly obscured by a two hundred year old oak tree. This morning however, the scene was more like a bizarre impressionist rendering of a gluttonous overweight child in a Hamstone onesie, devouring a stick of green candyfloss whole.

Neil had not slept a wink all night. In a gesture of community spirit, he had joined with his fellow villagers to aid the overstretched emergency services. Between them, they were attempting to clear the fallen masonry, glass and giant tree out of his neighbour's bedroom.

On the way to his car, Neil had narrowly avoided having his face taken off by a sheet of corrugated iron, freestyle hang-gliding across his path. Then he had endured a completely pointless day, due either to the phones being out of action or because there was nobody around to answer them.

Knocking off early, he had driven miles out of his way to avoid fallen trees and floods. Countless garage forecourts loomed along Neil's route, all of them closed. Everywhere he'd witnessed a post-apocalyptic air of devastation and abandon.

Cursing yesterday's lethargic decision not to fill the tank, he had willed the car this far along, but he had pushed his luck too far and it had come to an abrupt end.

If there was light at the end of the tunnel, it was the telephone box he could see a few hundred yards up the road, opposite a row of council houses, which was within reach, albeit with the promise of a good soaking.

Nearly colliding with the box in his head-down flat-out run for the sanctuary of the kiosk, Neil tore the door off the booth. Lungs burning with exertion, his olfactory senses were treated to a blast of ammonia, reminding him that the archetypal red box had two purposes, the second of which was a public urinal. *Time to give up the cancer sticks,* he thought, as he struggled to catch his breath. Picking up the receiver rewarded him with a ring tone.

Relieved, he fumbled his wallet from his soggy pocket and jumbled through the scrap metal collection, looking for the all-important tens, twenties and fifties.

Satisfied that at least the change god hadn't joined the conspiracy to destroy his day, he attempted to wedge a ten pence piece into the slot. A string of coarse expletives followed after he noticed the rock-hard chewing gum pushed into the slot.

He rested his head against the glass in a gesture of defeat. A clenched fist, rapping on the window of the booth, shocked him out of his miserable reverie. He peered through the Perspex panel, burned and distorted by local toerags and their Bic lighters. With said thugs in mind, Neil thought, *Oh hell, I suppose this is where I get a beat down for being on someone's turf.* He was pleasantly surprised to see a not unattractive female face looking up at him.

"Do you need a hand?" the face asked.

"I could really use a working phone," Neil replied. By this time, the face had acquired a body, long blonde hair and breasts. *Good size breasts too,* thought Neil, the typical bloke; no matter how desperate the situation, a healthy, single, heterosexual male will always weigh up the Good Samaritan as a possible conquest.

"I ain't got a phone mate, but I know someone who has. Come with me," said the breasts. Neil spent the best part of a second weighing up his options before deciding to throw caution to the wind and follow the stranger.

She ran up the first path they came to, past an old Vauxhall on blocks. Glancing around, Neil's privileged upbringing brought the snob in him to the surface. He couldn't help playing out a comedy sketch in his mind; his imagined application for obtaining the keys to a Local Authority house in an otherwise pretty rural location: *We, the undersigned, do solemnly promise that we will, within six months, deposit a worthless old rusty car in the front garden. Furthermore, we do agree to remove the wheels and replace them with four equal piles of house bricks,* he thought randomly.

As they approached the door, Neil could hear an unusual noise; a deep roaring sound which reverberated through the walls.

The woman rapped loudly on the door and shouted, "Tash, open up." The deafening noise stopped. After a few seconds, the scabby, paint peeling door opened. A woman stood in the doorway with a young child on her hip. She was dark-skinned and sultry, a brunette with long wavy hair, Hollywood smile, perfect, pert breasts and legs that, as they say, went all the way up. Neil's jaw bone collided with his chin. He was expecting what he considered a 'Universal Mum': short hair, chubby and black leggings; the sort that uses the excuse,

'I'm a mother now' to justify giving up on personal pride.

He scrutinised the two women as the blonde explained his predicament. The brunette deftly deposited her young offspring into a baby walker, bending over with her knees straight, giving Neil a tantalising glimpse of her skimpy knickers and barely concealed sex at the top of those magnificent tanned legs. True to say, on Neil's sex-ometer the rating curve had been raised so high that the Good Samaritan dropped off the scale.

As he surveyed the scene around him, it became obvious the source of the roaring sound was an enormous industrial sewing machine. Stacked in the corner of the room were bags and bags of what turned out to be golfing gloves, swatches of cut leather and bags of Velcro. It looked like a veritable factory. The woman interpreted his gaze as criticism and defended herself saying, "Sorry about the mess, it pays for me to run my car."

Neil thought it was high time he introduced himself and out of good manners, spoke first to the Good Samaritan. "Sorry, Miss Salvation, I haven't introduced myself." He took her hand in his politely. "My name is Neil. I live in the next village, a few miles down the road. May I ask you good ladies your names?"

The Samaritan burst into fits of giggles. "Ooh ark at him, in' 'e posh?" She replied, "Moi name's Julie, and she's......." she gestured towards the gorgeous creature, who Neil was now staring at open-mouthed, "she's Tash!"

Natasha looked up at him; her eyes sought out and made contact with his. His hand was still hesitantly resting on the door handle and she gently stroked her hand across his as she pushed the door to. It was as though an electric current passed through Neil's body. He could smell her perfume as she brushed past him, her hip gently disturbing the crotch of his trousers. She looked him straight in the eyes and discretely moistened her full red lips with her tongue.

Now Neil was feeling embarrassed; he could feel the rush of blood to his manhood and knew it would soon be straining against the wet material of his trousers. Without their eyes breaking off the connection, Natasha took Neil's hand from the door handle and said, "The phone is over here."

Neil stammered his gratitude and took the phone from her. The two women started to converse, giving Neil a chance to regain his composure. As he dialled the first number, he took the opportunity to have a long look at Natasha. *She's a rare find for these parts. Definitely has foreign blood in her veins. Probably Italian or Spanish, although her English hasn't the hint of an accent. It's an odd accent really, not local at all, like my own: Cosmopolitan. Maybe public school educated?* he questioned, rather vainly.

What Neil was most interested in though was her incredible body. She looked pretty tall for a woman. In high heels and with her big hair, she would be nearly the same height as Neil, who felt himself involuntarily whipping up on his toes.

Neil couldn't help but admire what she was wearing; a cropped, laced up front top, which ended just below her ample bosom. Her milky, coffee coloured breasts were straining at the laces, nipples clearly visible, poking out and up alluringly. Her chocolate-brown belly showed just the tiniest hint of post baby bulge.

Neil loved a woman with curves. Her skirt was the smallest little sliver of tartan which ended as abruptly as it started right at the point where Neil now found himself staring; the point where those luscious milky brown thighs joined. *Christ. If this was how the girl dressed when she was alone,* thought Neil, *imagine how she would look if she was dressed to impress."* He looked up from staring below her waist, to see her looking him directly in the eyes.

"Everything OK?" she asked, with a gently admonishing expression.

"Oh sorry," exclaimed Neil. *Busted,* he thought.

Natasha smiled coyly.

Oh my God, thought Neil. *I'm going to be in so much trouble in a minute.* The atmosphere between the two was certainly becoming charged.

Julie broke the tension by saying in a broad West Country accent, "Oright?" seemingly to no one in particular.

Neil now snapped out of his trance and continued on with the task of calling up assistance. His house-mate Colin was at his girlfriend Katie's house some twenty miles away and it would be some considerable time, given the weather conditions, before he could call round with some petrol to get Neil going again. Neil explained the situation to the two girls and said he had better go and wait in the car.

"Did you tell him where you were?" Natasha asked.

"Well yes," replied Neil, "I told him it was the house opposite the phone box so he will be able to find me. I'm right in thinking this street's called Copper Road aren't I? I saw a sign by the phone box."

"Yes that's right. In that case, you can wait here until he gets over. C'mon, off with those wet clothes, I'll stick them in the tumble dryer and make you a nice cup of coffee."

"This is a bit clichéd isn't it?" grinned Neil. "You sure you girls won't take advantage of me?"

"You should be so lucky," purred Natasha, just softly enough that Neil could tell it wasn't really a put down.

"I better get back next door," said Julie, "Mum will be stressing looking after Junior." With that, she said her goodbyes and sloped off.

"I'll be listening in on the baby monitor if you need a hand Tash," she sniggered as she left, just letting Neil know that she would not tolerate any funny business.

"I'll get you a dressing gown then we can have a chat over a steaming hot mug of espresso, how does that sound?"

Neil nodded. "At the risk of sounding incredibly corny, I have to ask, what's an attractive girl like you doing in these rather humble surroundings?" She looked a little surprised, Neil felt she may have taken offence and quickly moved to clarify, "You look like you'd be more at home on the catwalks of Paris or Milan."

She smiled then coloured up immediately from the effect of his flattery, and responded with, "Well, as it happens, I was born in Milan, my dad was Italian, my mum is English. I went to school over in Italy." Her face dropped and sadness glazed her eyes as she continued, "My dad died while I was still young, my mum brought us back to England, back to her family. I haven't seen Dad's family in years."

"Sorry about your dad," Neil commiserated, "I am blessed with both my parents in rude good health. I know I'd be lost without them."

Natasha nodded and said, "Make the most of them while they're around, you don't realise how much you'll miss them when they're gone."

"You're right there," Neil agreed. "So, you must speak fluent Italian, eh?"

"Non posso parlare fluentemente, ma posso ordinare il pranzo," she replied, smiling a little smug smile.

"Well," replied Neil, "I haven't a clue what you just said but it sounded pretty sexy to me." He rolled a sexy growl off his tongue!

She laughed, "I just told you I can order lunch, at least I think that's what I said."

Keen to show his linguistic skills, Neil countered with, "Madame Ich würde gern, Sie zu den Sternen bringen."

"Wow," said Natasha, "what did you say?"

"I said I would like to introduce you to the stars," he lied. In fact what he'd said was he wanted to *take* her to the stars!

"Oh right," she said, with a smile, "and I'm a Dutchman's uncle."

Natasha showed a keen interest in Neil's condensed life story. "So what brought you back to England after your colourful life abroad?"

Neil had a mind to say 'you' but resisted the temptation, as he was not sure how she would take such a corny joke. "After the army, I was offered a chance to open an advertising agency on behalf of a Swiss company I'd become involved with," he explained. "I established a UK limited company, offices and bank accounts and began trading on their behalf, before discovering that the Swiss branch of the company had become insolvent and the funds dried up. I bankrolled the venture myself for a while, looking for another backer for the idea, but in the end, the venture folded. Now I'm in the employ of a regional newspaper group, selling advertising space."

Natasha's eyes lit up. "Do you deal with the situations vacant?" she enquired.

"Yes of course," replied Neil, "better than that, I know most of the personnel officers well as I'm their rep."

"I don't suppose you could put a good word in for me out there could you?" Natasha whispered, "I would love a bit of independence."

Neil's face was a picture; this was panning out a treat.

"I can do more than that," he said, "you tell me what you'd like to do and I will fix you up with interviews."

The way Natasha was looking at him, Neil thought that he was on for a home run. Just then, he heard the child cry. Natasha responded instantly with a mother's instinct and the moment was lost. When she returned with the youngster and bottle in tow, Neil asked her what the story was with the child's father.

Natasha explained, "After my dad died, he was a strict Catholic and bit of a stickler for discipline, I went a little off the rails and fell for an older man, Brian Dix, Dixie they called him. He was what the Americans would call a 'Carny', he worked casual for the fair, travelled around the country with them." She looked down, examining her fingernails before continuing. "He was a real 'Flash Harry' riding high on the rides. He seemed so cool. Of course, all the girls fancied him but he wanted me. I got bullied quite a bit at school, developing a lot faster than the others and the not having a dad thing. Girls can be a lot worse than boys you know. It was quite a thrill to be the one getting preferential treatment on the rides. Then there was the alcohol. Brian was old enough to buy us bottles of beer and cider. The bullies became my best buddies to get their hands on the booze and fags. I was so flattered, I never thought about the age difference, didn't consider what kind of guy makes the moves on a fifteen year old girl. I suppose I probably viewed him as a replacement for my dad. Unfortunately, he was what my granddad would call a 'bad-un'. He was a bit of a drifter and a villain. An Irish Traveller. Anyway, he certainly wooed me with his charm and blarney. I let him take my virginity. It gets worse still, his kind like to really sow their seed. He convinced me that I couldn't get pregnant if he pulled out. God I was so stupid, so naïve."

Neil butted in, "Hey, you were fifteen years old, why do you think we have laws protecting children from predators like him? The man's a damn paedophile."

Natasha squeezed his hand in agreement. "Anyway, I don't think he ever withdrew, even though he insisted he had. God, when I think how gullible I was. I don't mean to sound crude, but it didn't take a genius to know he was lying by the state he left me in." She blushed beetroot red and giggled, "He told me that it was pre-cum and that it couldn't make me pregnant." She clapped her hands as if to signify, 'not to dwell on that', then added, "Anyway, a couple of months after my sixteenth birthday, I was 'knocked up', to put it crudely." She laughed. "I took my driving test with a baby seat strapped into the back of the car."

"So how old are you now?" Neil asked, adding, "If it's not rude to inquire as to a young ladies age." He had already guessed approximately, going by the child.

"I'm nineteen, nearly twenty," she replied. "How about you?"

"I'm an old man," Neil joked. "Twenty six next birthday."

"A girl needs an older man. You mature a lot later," she giggled.

Neil flashed her look of mock disapproval. She replied with a 'butter wouldn't melt' look.

"So where's this character now?" he questioned.

"Gone. He's drifted in and out of my life at regular intervals since Monica's birth. Her voice sounded pained, subdued. "He wasn't even around for the birth. My mum had to come with me."

"Why haven't you moved on and found someone else?"

Her eyes glazed over and she said, "I can't, he would kill me."

The atmosphere was somewhat cooled and it was opportune that Colin turned up at the door when he did. Still, a definite connection had been established between them and Neil was determined to see where it could lead. Natasha took the initiative and caught hold of Neil's shoulder as he went to leave; she gave him a smouldering look before turning his hand over and writing a telephone number on the back of his hand with a black Biro.

"My mum's number, if you want to contact me. It's safer," she whispered, squeezing his hand before letting it go.

Neil had long forgotten his car troubles and was thanking the God of deliverance for the good fortune he was now enjoying.

CHAPTER 3

Friends

Neil and Colin were back at the house they shared in a small village a few miles down the road from Natasha's house. Most of the debris from the earlier events had been cleared up. The neighbour's house now looked resplendent in its trendy blue tarpaulin roof with matching blue nylon rope accessories.

Colin and Neil had met by chance after Colin had stopped to help him fix a puncture in his Fiat sports car. Colin, seven years his junior, was driving his works van at the time but hastened to inform Neil that he too had a little sports model of the same marque. A few trips to the pub later, the two of them found they had a great deal in common. Neil felt he had outstayed his welcome at home with his parents where he had been staying since his return from abroad. Colin, the second-generation child of elderly parents, was feeling claustrophobic living with his. It seemed like a mutually convenient solution to rent a house together. So far, the situation had been ideal and the two men had become firm friends.

Colin admired Neil. To him, the older man was something of an inspiration. His siblings treated him more like a son than a brother. Neil, despite his obviously diverse and exciting life experiences, treated Colin as an adult, a man. He respected his friend and was somewhat in awe of his confident, extrovert nature. Neil, in turn, treated him as an equal in intellect and seemed to admire the 'Urban

Savvy' and gregarious personality which Colin possessed.

Colin's chin had dropped when he walked into Natasha's and saw Neil sat in the leather chair, dressed in some other man's dressing gown. Now they were back at home, he wanted to know all the details of how it had come to pass that Neil was relaxing in the home of this scantily clad goddess.

Neil briefly took him through the day's events, culminating in his arrival at the feet of Natasha and what he had learned of her since.

CHAPTER 4

Mother dearest

Neil found his interest in Natasha aroused, despite his reluctance to become involved in such a potentially volatile situation. Days were passing in a blur; he was having a hard time concentrating on work. Natasha had hijacked his dreams. Truth be told, in his mind's eye, Natasha's wicked body had found itself superimposed on the girly mag models he would peruse whilst he relaxed in a 'gentleman's way'.

Two weeks had passed when the opportunity arose to contact her. One of his employment agencies was looking to recruit a catering manager at a restaurant opening soon. It was perfect for Natasha and he felt she would be a shoe-in with his recommendation.

Neil tried to sound professional when he phoned Natasha's mum, as he had no idea what she had told her about him. He was taken aback by the friendly reception he received. Natasha's mum kept him yapping on for ages. She wanted to know everything about him. He got the definite impression that mum and daughter had been talking about him and that the discussion had been favourable.

Natasha's mum arranged for Neil to drop in for a cup of tea ostensibly so that he could talk her through the details of the job interview so she could pass the information on to her daughter.

On the arranged day, the sun was blazing down. Neil had spent the entire morning stuck in his car without air conditioning. After lunch, he decided to ride over to see Natasha's mum on his Chopper motorcycle. Neil had built it himself. It was a testament to his engineering abilities. The bike and his little red two-seater sports car were his pride and joy.

Being a typical single man, he hadn't kept up with the washing and the only clean items he could find were a tight plain black tee shirt and a pair of skin-tight white jeans. Failing to pull the fly closed, Neil shuffled out of the room. Standing on the landing outside Colin's room, he exclaimed, loudly, "You know Colin, I've discovered that if you spill enough pasty and doughnut crumbs on a pair of trousers, they definitely shrink!" Disturbed from the book he was enjoying, Colin opened his door to reveal an animated Neil, doing a little shimmying dance on the spot trying to close the impossible gap at his waistline.

"You donkey," Colin observed. "They're my jeans, yours are in the laundry basket. You can't fit two gallons of leg into two pints of trouser." He marched off to the laundry room, leaving Neil painfully bouncing around on the landing, trying desperately to reverse out of a pair of trousers. He returned with Neil's jeans over his arm, retrieved his own strides from the untidy mess Neil had left them in, and marched back into his room, mumbling expletives under his breath.

Neil looked at his reflection in his wardrobe mirror. He wouldn't have looked out of place in the Bee Gees' 'Staying Alive' video. Thanks to the daily lunchtime workouts he and his male colleagues indulged in, he knew he could pull off this look, but would have preferred to wear his business suit to make a good impression on Natasha's mum. After the hot sweaty morning he'd had, that wasn't an option. This would have to do.

Although Neil didn't consider himself 'ripped', there was not an ounce of fat on him. His shoulders were broad with fantastic muscle tone, more rugby player than footballer. Neil turned around to admire his best asset. He was by no means a vain man, but previous girlfriends had described his bum as 'peachy', so as far as asses go, he knew he had nothing to be ashamed of.

He parked the bike at the back of the house as Natasha's mum had instructed him to and walked through the gate, into the garden. Neil was surprised to see Natasha sat on the lawn on a blanket. No sign of her mum or the baby. She was looking absolutely stunning. Her long brown wavy hair was just about reaching to the blanket; the sun was catching it just right, accentuating the silky shine. She was sitting with her long legs tucked demurely to the side but her attire was far from subtle. She was wearing a tight white micro mini dress with rose petal motifs all over it. The skin-tight nature of the dress left little doubt that she wasn't wearing any underwear.

As Neil approached, Natasha turned towards him; her eyes were drawn towards the bulge in the front of Neil's white jeans. He was quite nervous, not expecting to be alone with Natasha and the sight of her was causing him some embarrassment as the bulge in his jeans was clearly conveying his excitement at seeing her. He sat down beside her and moved in to kiss her on both cheeks, as was the European custom. Natasha was obviously unsure of what he was doing but soon relaxed as she realised he was being the perfect gentleman. The pair just stared at each other for a while. They could both sense the quickening of each other's heartbeats. There was an atmosphere of illicit arousal, which seemed to build between them whenever they were together.

"I have found the ideal job for you," Neil explained, breaking the sexual tension. "It's a catering manager's position; I think I can pretty much say that the job's yours if you want it." Her eyes dropped and her shoulders sank in a gesture of sadness.

"Neil, I am so grateful to you for helping me out like this, but I'm afraid it won't be possible for me to take the job now."

Neil looked completely deflated; he thought he was getting a very polite brush off. It's funny how fragile a man's confidence is in the presence of a pretty woman. When Natasha lifted her eyes to look at Neil, he could see the tears welling in them.

"My partner is back." Her voice was quavering; her usual air of confidence was gone. "He will never agree to me working so I'm stuffed I'm afraid. I had kind of hoped he was gone for good this time." She looked away and dabbed her eyes with a tissue. "This is all so messed up." Natasha started to cry.

Neil put his arms around her and hugged her to him. She hugged him back tightly and sobbed her heart out.

Neil was in turmoil; Natasha had stirred feelings in him that were completely unfamiliar. Holding her so close he was in a state of sexual and emotional arousal. He wanted this girl so badly. He wanted her totally, not just in a physical sense but to connect with properly. He didn't want to even think the word, it scared him that much but deep down he knew he could fall in love with this girl.

They sat together for some time, just gently rocking back and forth until her crying subsided.

"Natasha," Neil said, "look, I really like you, I want to get to know you. I know it won't be easy but I want us to meet up and go on a date. Can we do that?" Natasha fluttered her long lashes and looked up in that heart melting manner which naturally beautiful women possess.

"I would love to go with you on a date Neil, I haven't stopped thinking about you since we met." She let that one hover in the air for a while. "You realise how careful we will have to be though? It's best we take friends with us so that no one suspects that we're meeting up. I won't be able to stay out very long though. I can't trust him to look after the baby. I'll have to see if Julie will watch her."

A rendezvous was arranged. Neil would have to press-gang Colin into coming along so the meeting would look casual if anyone came snooping. Natasha would bring her friend Sue.

CHAPTER 5

No news

Brian Dix ate his breakfast, sat on his throne at the kitchen table, in the home he had not contributed to but nevertheless considered to be his Kingdom. He'd had to work hard for his sex last night. He'd nearly given up after a while but after the threat of a slap, Natasha had given in and he'd taken what he wanted. He knew that she was a hell of a looker and he had to break a few heads here and there to make sure the local studs knew what to expect if they came sniffing round. *What I really need to do is get her knocked up again, that way she and her bloody interfering mother will have something to occupy their twittering brains and keep them out of my face,* he thought.

The television was buzzing with inane chatter in the background. Brian's attention was caught momentarily by a news bulletin about a violent foray in the Plymouth dockland area. The newscaster was reporting that the encounter had left a local dock worker on intensive care, fighting for his life. Brian raised an eyebrow and thought aloud, "Good for you mate, I meant to kill you! I must be losing me edge."

The news bulletin showed the police raiding the Gypsy encampment and rounding up the three lads who had been incriminated. Brian knew the filth had nothing on the lads and they had nothing on him, not that the lads would rat him out if they did. Gypsies were tight, just like Brian. *I'll wait around a bit for the dust to settle,* he thought. *Spend a little time on me other goal; getting the bitch up the duff again.* When the time was right, he would chase up his new Gypsy pals and put to them his little proposition.

Brian was irritable, he hadn't been back around this way for months and there were old oppos who he needed to touch base with. Natasha had slipped quietly from his bed early in the morning and had buggered off in her car before he could commandeer it. His bike was out in the shed, but the chances of getting it running without a fight would be slim. He hated to use the phone as you never knew who might be listening in, what with Natasha living on welfare; last thing he wanted was to get caught up in some stupid benefits investigation. *I'll have to chance it,* he thought. *I've no idea where the stupid bitch has gone or when she'll likely be back.* He lifted the receiver and dialled a number he had committed to memory. "Gunner, tis me, Brian, listen, I'm stranded here for it bit, I've had a bit of grief, tis not safe fer me to contact the army so I'm stuck here with no splash cash. Get yer arse over here and pick me up, we gotta get out and about and drum up a bit o' business. Fill yer motor up, I want to try and find us some action or maybe tap up a few friendlies, see if we can't find some wi' cash on the hip to help the cause." Despite being born and bred on a council estate in Derbyshire, Brian was of Irish Gypsy stock; he could, and would, lapse into a broad Irish brogue at will.

Gunner was a name from his past, a man who was always willing to raid a few sheds and break a few heads if there was a couple of quid in it for him.

Shedding was something Brian thought he'd left behind in his far distant past, but in times of need, a few lawn mowers and hand tools to the local auctions could always be relied upon to serve the terminally cash strapped.

CHAPTER 6

First encounter

Natasha and Neil's first date was set for the following Saturday. They would rendezvous at a local fleshpot and see where it led. Meeting up inside the nightclub as arranged, Natasha flashed Neil her trademark 'smoky eyed' coy look; head slightly inclined, eyes cast down to her feet, a subtle flutter of those long, gorgeous lashes. Neil instantly dissolved as he bravely put an arm around her waist and kissed her softly on the cheek.

"Wow," he said, casting an eye down the pink, cropped, tailored jacket and matching micro-skirt ensemble. "You look sensational." Natasha had brought along her friend Sue. Colin groaned inwardly at the sight of her. She was about sixteen stone heavier than him and was clearly more concerned with protecting Natasha from Neil's advances than becoming friendly with Colin.

Neil immediately took Natasha's hand in his and said, "Fancy a dance?" She beamed a toothy smile back at him and took his hand in acceptance.

On the dance floor, Natasha was captivating. Even with the confines of the crowded space, it was clear that Natasha knew how to move her sexy body in a positively mesmerising way.

Underneath the pink jacket, she was obviously not wearing a blouse or a bra. Neil was willing the straining buttons to fail. He couldn't keep his eyes off her breasts. The DJ was playing a selection of seventies soul classics. The pounding bass sounds and sultry lyrics were accentuating the sleazy sway of Natasha's hips. Neil was doing his level best to persuade his clumsy hips and groin to follow her lead.

"You are a cool dancer," Natasha lied, with a slight smile developing in the corners of her mouth, threatening to betray her dishonesty.

"Thank you," Neil shouted over the mêlée. "I think we both know who the dancer is here," he added, somewhat quieter.

"What?" Natasha shouted, leaning in to catch Neil's response.

"You are a marvellous dancer," Neil yelled.

"What?" Natasha shouted, leaning in further to him. Seizing the moment, Neil caught her cheeks between his hands and drew her lips to him, kissing her passionately. She was somewhat startled, but did not withdraw from the embrace. The fusion of their lips passed waves of pleasure through both their bodies, causing as fierce a reaction as opposite magnetic poles, sealing and combining their destiny with its chemical reaction.

The nightclub and its gregarious occupants forgotten, Neil's fingers danced across the exotic curves of Natasha's body. The electrical impulses passed between his fingertips and the nerve endings deep in her psyche, causing ripples of desire and stirring deep-set emotions.

The depth of their connection was clearly lost on Sue. The sight of her best friend and this usurper, flirting, was beginning to fan her discomfort. With the subtlety of a tank battle, she stormed across the dance floor and whisked Natasha off. The two girls disappeared, presumably on route to the loo, for a gossip and make-up touch up, as girls do.

Neil re-joined Colin at the side of the dance floor. "Thanks a lot mate!" Colin complained. "I didn't realise I would be on a blind date with Attila the Hun!"

"Stick with it for my sake Colin," Neil replied, "we are really connecting." He added, "Be strong!"

Colin shot him a grimace, "You are so going to owe me one."

"C'mon," said Neil, "I'll get a round of drinks in." The boys joined the throng, duelling to attract the attention of the bar staff.

After being served, the pair retraced their steps to where they had been previously standing. The girls were nowhere to be seen. Again, the nagging doubts began to surface. Neil was wondering if he had blown it. Had he come on too strong, shown his cards too soon? They hung about for a further half hour.

Feeling sure the girls had flown, Colin turned to Neil and said, "They've clearly cut and run mate!" After one more thorough scope of the club, Neil turned to Colin and said, "I think you're right, they've taken flight."

"Can't really say I'm sorry mate," Colin said, "that Sue was straight out of a 'Hammer House of Horror' script."

Neil replied, "Yeah, I'm sorry about that."

They drove the twenty odd miles home in silence. Neil couldn't believe he had got the signals so wrong, he'd really thought she had feelings for him. "Bugger," he cursed.

Neil and Colin had just poured themselves a couple of drinks when they heard a rough sounding car driving very slowly past the house. When they heard the car turn around and come back, Neil went outside to investigate. Natasha's sad old Fiat was rattling up the road towards him. "Christ," Neil murmured under his breath, "she's throwing caution to the wind." He jumped into the road waving like a madman.

The girls parked up, then shuffled into the house. Nothing was mentioned about the confused signals in the nightclub.

It later transpired that Sue was deliberately stalling and steering Natasha away from Neil's searching.

Colin, bless him, read the signs and invited (dragged) Sue into the living room to check out his video collection. Neil seized the moment and said to Natasha, "I just have to change into something more comfortable, come with me, I'll show you round the house."

They got as far as the landing. Natasha was just standing there, waiting. Neil couldn't contain himself any longer. He practically dragged Natasha off the landing and onto his bed, frantically kissing her and exploring the inside of her mouth with his tongue. Natasha did not protest as he undid the two straining buttons on her jacket and let her gorgeous full breasts spill free. His hands and mouth were instantly busy caressing, lightly nipping and pulling her big firm nipples. Natasha had sensitive nipples and she was quickly moaning and thrusting her pelvis towards him. Neil's manhood was rock hard. He was in a state of total abandon. He needed to feel Natasha's sex wrapped around him. He reached down between her legs, felt the smooth skin of her shaven sex. No knickers, clean-shaven. Neil had only ever read about Brazilian waxes in his 'adult comics'. He was sure he had died and gone to heaven.

Natasha's sex was soaking wet and Neil could wait no longer. He guided his throbbing penis towards her only to find her pulling his hand away and grabbing his shaft herself. She rubbed the head of his eager manhood up and down her entrance a few times, then, with his engorged head just nestling between her opening she caught his face in her hands, stared into his eyes and in a wanton voice, wholly disembodied from the cultured woman it emanated from, growled, "Fuck me."

As he slid inside, she parted just enough to let him slide in comfortably but held him tightly like a second skin. His phallus touched the neck of her womb just an inch or so before the base. He felt the skin stretch to accommodate all of him, the perfect fit. He felt his entire being building towards the most earth shattering climax he had ever known.

CHAPTER 7

Sleeping with the enemy

Sitting either end of the sofa, Natasha was putting distance between herself and Brian in the hope that he would lose interest.

"Come on Natasha, We haven't seen each other in ages, don't you fancy a little kiss?" Brian pestered, doing his best to sound sincere.

"Brian, I'm really not in the mood. You bugger off and leave me to cope with Monica on my own, you don't care if we have enough money to live on, just when we get settled, you breeze back in and expect me to fall all over you."

"Oh come on hun, you know it's the life, it's what I do. When my ship comes in, we'll be set up, then I'll take you away from all this, we'll get ourselves a nice spread over in Ireland and you'll live like a queen so ye will." Brian couldn't help himself slipping back into his Irish brogue at the merest mention of the place.

"Oh for goodness' sake Brian, you know I hate it when you start talking like an Irish tinker, you're a Northerner for God's sake! Why do you have to put on that daft accent? Anyway, I hated Ireland, such a backward place, I won't be going there and neither will Monica!"

"You cheeky fucking mare!" Brian grabbed her round the throat. "Since when did you get such a cocky mouth?" He dragged the screaming Natasha up the stairs by the throat, kicking the bedroom door open. He threw her onto the bed before jumping on top of her, pinning her arms and legs to the mattress. "What the fuck's going on, you got some other bloke, is that it? Got some other bloke keeping you warm? That's it isn't it? Why you don't want to sleep with your old man, you got yourself a fucking bit on the side! I'll fucking find the bastard and I'll kill him with my bare hands, and I'll make you watch me!"

Brian's fist was raised inches from her face, he was winding himself up into a rage, Natasha knew from past experience where this was heading and she knew what she must do to calm him down. She *was* his woman, and she *was* having an affair, and not for the first time. That's all it was; an affair. She belonged to Brian Dix and she always would. Sooner or later, Neil would tire of her, just like the others, and the liaison would end. She knew that she must keep her fledgling affair with Neil a secret, no matter what the personal cost.

Just a short spell in Brian Dix's company and Natasha's independent will was gone. She would do what she had to do to placate him, to mollify him. "Brian, I'm not having an affair, I swear. I love you Brian, you know you're the only one for me. Come here baby."

Brian Dix had achieved his first objective, now he just needed to locate her birth control pills and destroy them. All in good time.

CHAPTER 8

Thursday nights

Neil was trying hard to find ways to see Natasha. She ended up presenting him with a perfect opportunity. They met up one lunchtime at her mum's.

She held his hand and with breathless excitement said, "Thursday night is my college night. My courses finish next week then I have Thursday nights free. Brian knows that I stay away from home Thursday nights as I go straight from college back to Mum's and spend the night. If I can talk Mum into keeping on sitting Monica at her house, I can stay over at yours once a week." She was beside herself with excitement. "Every week!" she exclaimed. Neil was ecstatic at the prospect of having her for a whole night every week. He picked her up and spun her round in an embrace before landing a wet smacker right on her lips. Thinking with his head instead of his heart, Neil was especially happy as it meant she would have one night a week away from the nasty piece of work she shared a roof with. Their relationship seemed to be going from strength to strength.

Neil's best friend Colin had unfortunately lost his job and being unable to keep up the rent, had moved back with his parents until he could sort himself out. This gave Neil the opportunity to furnish Natasha with her own key to the house so that she could let herself in when he was working late.

Thursday was deadline day for his paper and meant he had to have all his ads booked in before he could leave for home.

When he arrived home, there was no sign of Natasha's car outside and the door was locked. Disappointed, he turned the key, walked in and slammed the door behind him with an annoyed kick.

As he tossed his keys on-to the tiled top coffee table, he smelt the overpowering and intoxicating smell of 'Paris' mixed with the unmistakable musky fragrance of arousal.

He rushed to the stairwell. The door at the bottom of the stairs was ajar. There sprawled out on the rough pine treads was Natasha. Apart from a pair of holed fishnets and a suspender belt, she was as naked as the day she was born.

Her hair was dishevelled. She was clearly quite intoxicated. The source of her intoxication was obvious. An empty red wine bottle was buried up inside her... up to the label.

"I've been waiting for you," she drawled, "you didn't come." Then she looked into his eyes with a wild, lustful look and said, "I've started without you."

CHAPTER 9

Lay with me, stay with me

Neil experienced the closest thing to an immaculate ejaculation as he had ever known. He nearly fainted from the sheer thrill of the spectacle before him.

His clothes dissolved and he was lying on the stairs attempting to usurp his glass rival. It was not going to work; there was no way to couple on these steep stairs. He leapt over the prostrate Natasha and dragged her bodily on to the landing where he roughly shoved her legs apart and buried himself balls deep into her. He knew in this state of arousal it would be all over in a few thrusts, so he pulled out of her and pulled her legs over the top of the landing so that her exposed sex lay over the top step. Positioning himself on the stairs below the landing, he cradled her thighs in his hands and started to lick the V of skin concealing and protecting her hard little nub. By now Natasha was in ecstasy. Neil sucked the lips of Natasha's sex into his mouth then penetrated her slit with his long thick tongue. He was sucking like a madman. There was no crevice or hole his probing tongue didn't explore but always he would stop just short of touching her swollen nub with his tip, instead, just circling it with wide sweeps of his moist smooth tongue. Just as Natasha thought she could not get any higher, he began a slow and gentle rhythmic assault on her, gently touching the point of her arousal with every stroke and building up the tempo until she dug her nails into him and exploded. Neil laid stroking her hair and gently caressing her until the shaking spasms subsided. Positioning his torso between her legs he gently entered her again, resuming long gentle strokes in and out of her sex with his rock hard manhood. Natasha was building towards her crescendo again when Neil's whole body tensed as his orgasm rocked up from the depths of his body and burst inside her, filling her empty womb. Neil's body jerked a few times as the last of his desire pumped out deep inside her. Abruptly, he withdrew, and buried his head between her legs again. This was too much for Natasha's constitution and her senses just exploded into a body tingling series of multiple orgasms, the like of which she had never experienced before.

The effects of the alcohol, sheer exhaustion and the afterglow of mind-blowing sex soon had Natasha's breathing softly slipping into the rhythm of deep sleep.

Neil kissed her and whispered, "Night night darling," then quieter still he ventured, "I love you Natasha." She was in the land of the fairies but something must have stirred deep in her subconscious and she responded by snuggling in close to Neil's chest. They fell asleep wrapped around each other as though it were the most natural thing in the world.

CHAPTER 10

A four-letter word

"Wakey wakey, sleepy head," cooed Neil as he held up a cup of coffee and a piece of toast.

"Oh Lordy Lordy, what time is it?" mewed Natasha.

"It's a little after eight thirty," Neil replied.

"Oh dear, I should be well on my way home by now, Mum is not going to be pleased." She tried to blink away the sleep unsuccessfully. "How much did I have to drink last night?"

"Well, from the looks of things when I came in you had drunk at least a bottle," joked Neil. "Although I'm not sure how much you had digested as it looked to me as if you were pouring it in the out," he finished with a knowing wink.

Natasha twigged the joke and went bright red from head to toe before burying her head in her hands and exclaiming, "Oh my God, what must you think of me?"

Neil slipped under the sheets beside her and taking her hands in his said, "Actually Natasha, I think I have fallen madly and deeply in love with you," he confessed, throwing caution to the wind.

Natasha looked into his eyes. "Please don't mock me Neil. It's not funny to play with someone's emotions."

"Natasha, oh honey, I'm not mocking you, I really have fallen for you, can't you see, I'm potty about you."

The look of surprise was quickly replaced by a flood of happy tears as she said, "Oh Neil, I love you too. I really do." They flung their arms around each other in a tight embrace. "What a mess," said Natasha before clinging even tighter to Neil.

"We'll make it work," whispered Neil. He meant it.

CHAPTER 11

Close call

With their love for each other formally declared, Natasha could no longer face 'doing her duty' with Brian.

"No Brian," she moaned, as Brian's dirty hands pawed at her again. "We can't, I've been bleeding non-stop since I stopped taking my pills, something's not right, *down there*."

Natasha was running a successful double bluff on Brian. He had destroyed her birth control pills, declaring that they were trying for another baby; however, in the months he'd been away, she hadn't been taking them, starting up again just a short while before she began seeing Neil. She had quite an adequate supply which he knew nothing about.

"Well you'd better get down and see the quack; I'm not fucking waiting for ever. You're not the only game in town you know!"

Natasha tried her best to look hurt whilst hoping that he would make good his threat and seek his comfort elsewhere.

Neil and Natasha managed to steal a few covert moments together throughout the week. Julie was playing her part, pretending that Neil was her new beau and inviting Natasha over for a coffee whenever he 'called round'. It was just to chat and hold hands though as Julie's house was always in uproar. Besides, Brian could just walk in to Julie's house without warning. Fortunately, that had not come to pass.

The following Thursday, Natasha said she would have to be more careful as she thought one of Brian's cronies may have suspected something and was watching out for her car. Neil decided she should park over in the next village, he would pick her up and they would drive away somewhere and go out for a meal. Natasha was wearing a short, red dress, which buttoned right the way up the front. She had her long curly locks curled forward over one shoulder and was wearing a red rose in her hair, matching the ruby-red of her lipstick. Her shoes were red patent leather with a heel of at least 5 inches. Neil, at her behest, was wearing his tight white jeans again with an open collared black shirt and a pair of Cuban heeled reddy-brown boots. They did make a damn handsome couple in anyone's book.

Neil turned off the main road and down a country lane, pulling up outside a posh little pub where Brian's kind would never be likely to venture. The pub catered to themed nights; tonight's theme was French. The function room was arranged with the tables in long rows giving everyone plenty of room for private conversation but sitting you close enough to your neighbours that you could join in a larger conversation if you wished.

Sitting opposite one another, Neil and Natasha couldn't keep their eyes off each other. Natasha had slipped her shoe off and was doing her level best to make sure Neil remained seated the whole time.

Neil beckoned the wine waiter over and ordered a bottle of Cabernet Sauvignon. After a few glasses of the rich fortified red, Natasha excused herself to go to the loo. Neil, the perfect gentleman, stood up as she left the table. She had just disappeared around the corner when Brian burst through the restaurant door. He scoured the tables, obviously looking for Natasha. Neil, quick as a flash, turned his seat towards the man sitting next to him and started up an awkward conversation. Brian didn't recognise Neil and, not seeing anything suspicious, turned around and left.

Neil ambushed Natasha at the entrance to the loo. "Brian was here," he exclaimed.

Her face distorted momentarily into a frown before she replied in a whispered growl, "Sod him!"

"Should we leave?" Neil questioned.

"Hell no," she replied, "I'm just starting to have fun." Natasha caught hold of his hand and dragged him back into the dining room, back to their table. Sitting down, her face flushed with excitement, she said, "Hold your hands out."

Neil, taken aback, replied, "What?"

"Hold your hands out," she reiterated, this time, more a command than a request. Neil did as he was told. Natasha held her hand, balled into a fist, above his open palms.

Poor Neil barely stammered out a, "Wha..." before her hand opened and a pair of red knickers sprang into vision like a released coil spring. Neil flushed scarlet and hurriedly stuffed the offending article into his jacket pocket. Before he could catch his breath, his wanton woman kicked something across the floor at him with a giggle. He looked down. Beside his chair, in the aisle between the tables and in full view of anyone who cared to look, was a ruby-red bra which up until very recently had the pleasure of holding Natasha's delicious breasts in check. Again, a flustered Neil, caught off guard, was grasping and fumbling to conceal the article before too many prying eyes grasped the significance of what was happening.

Neil shot Natasha a 'don't you dare' look. She responded with a finger in the corner of her mouth and countered his stare with a coy, 'butter wouldn't melt' expression.

Just then, the waiter crossed to Natasha's side of the table. She pushed her chair back as though to make room for him then slowly and deliberately let her spoon fall to the floor under the table. As the waiter knelt down to retrieve the spoon, she crossed and uncrossed her legs leaving ample time between the two manoeuvres for the waiter to re-surface blushing madly. Natasha's eyes didn't leave Neil's for a second. She was showing him that everything she did was for him.

Neil's heart was racing. His skin, moist with cold sweat and arousal, was powerless to control the situation. Natasha knew she had his full attention and that he was on the back-foot. She intended to fully press home her advantage.

As the dessert waiters made their way around the tables, distributing the pre-ordered sweets, Natasha seized the distraction to loosen the buttons at the front of her dress, making sure that a nervous Neil was well aware of her actions.

"Natasha," Neil winced, the condemned man, feeling dizzy from the intoxicating sexual tension.

"Yes Neil?" she replied, leaning into the conversation and thus doing affording Neil and the dessert waiter a tantalising down blouse view of her stunning assets.

"You are so for it when I get you home!" he groaned.

"Promises, promises," she cooed.

They continued to flirt and chat for the rest of the evening; the tension started to build as they went to leave. They sprinted across the car park like two fugitives before diving into Neil's car, practically crying with laughter. They met across the gear stick in a passionate embrace. Natasha's hand was stroking Neil's erection and he was probing her wet sex with a couple of fingers. "It's true what they say about fear being an aphrodisiac," said Neil, "let's get on home."

Neil parked the car around the back of his house in the old folks' parking area just in case they were being watched. "I'll go and check the coast is clear," warned Neil, "if all is OK, I will turn on the porch light and you come and join me. If not, do a runner back to the car and I will join *you*."

He let himself into the house without incident and turned on the porch light, which illuminated the pavement and street outside. He then waited outside his front door for Natasha to follow. When he saw her, his heart missed a beat. She had unbuttoned the dress all the way from top to bottom and was sashaying along the pavement in nothing but shoes and a smile.

CHAPTER 12

Natasha scores a home run

Neil awoke from a dream. As his tired senses came to life, he could smell the warm fragrant musk of Natasha's perfume. As her sleepy eyelids started to flutter into awareness, Neil planted a smacker onto each one before saying, "Morning lover."

"Mmmm," replied Natasha, smiling with warm contentment. "Oh Lord, what time is it?"

"A little after seven," replied Neil.

Leaping out of bed, Natasha's eyes scoured the bedroom floor, looking for last nights discarded clothing. Throwing on the creased up red dress, she grabbed Neil's wrist, hoping his watch was lying.

"Shiiiiit," she cursed, "I've got to fly." Something she saw outside the window caught her attention. "Oh shit, not good, not good," she exclaimed.

"What is it?" inquired Neil.

"One of Brian's cronies is sitting in the garden of that council house opposite," she whispered, "can I get out through the back way?"

"You can get into the neighbour's garden and out to the street through their side gate. I sometimes bring my bike through that way. He will still be able to see you as you walk up the path though. I'm afraid there isn't a back way out at all."

"Shit. Shit. Shit!" cried Natasha. "What am I going to do?"

Neil could see she was starting to panic. "Calm down," he whispered, "I've watched him for a while now, if he's looking out for you, he clearly has no idea which house you're in as his eyes are all over the shop. It's probably a coincidence; he may just be visiting a friend." Neil was hatching an elaborate plan. Most of Colin's clothes were still upstairs in his wardrobe; Neil reckoned he could knock up a convincing disguise so that even Natasha's own mother wouldn't recognise her.

The adrenaline was flowing through their veins again as Neil rummaged out the gear he needed from Colin's wardrobe. He chucked the stuff onto Colin's bed and told Natasha to start dressing. As he turned around, he saw her unbutton the red dress and pull it off over her head. The sight of her naked body was too much for Neil and he found himself practically throwing himself on top of her.

She responded by opening her legs as wide as he'd ever seen them and within moments Neil's erection was buried deep between them. The next moment saw them coupled, making frantic, spontaneous love on top of Colin's clothes. They were both so turned on that it didn't take long to reach a sweaty simultaneous climax.

"You are so, so bad," scolded Natasha, "look at the mess you've made of me. We're going to have to get a lock for that thing," she chastised, pointing at Neil's wilting treasure.

"Hurry up and get those clothes on before I have to do you again. I just can't seem to help myself when I'm around your naked body," laughed Neil.

Neil could barely suppress his laughter as Natasha unknowingly dressed in Colin's baseball suit; an authentic New York Yankees suit, complete with hat, baseball boots, bloomers and a baseball hat.

"Right." She tucked her long flowing hair into the collar of the baseball shirt, plonked the hat on her head and said, "Ready?"

"Just one more thing," chuckled Neil as he handed Natasha a signed baseball bat.

"You burk," chastised Natasha as she slung the bat over her shoulder Mickey Mantle style. "Show me to the side door y'all," she drawled in an awful Yankee accent. "I'll just darn well mosey on down to you folks' auto mobile, y'all join me when the coast is clear."

Neil was splitting his sides with laughter when he stopped her and said, "Wait, wait, you need a moustache."

Natasha screwed up her pretty nose in mock indignation and said, "Watch it Curland." It was the first time Neil had heard her say his surname, it sounded so right on her lips. It was at that precise moment that Neil knew; when the time was right, he was going to propose to her.

CHAPTER 13

Mum's the word

"What the fuck was your car doing parked overnight in Rockbeare?" Brian was livid; his crony had reported sighting Natasha's car in Neil's village. It would take some creative lying to placate him.

Brian reached forward to grasp a hand around Natasha's slender throat. Despite her obvious terror, she knew she had to be convincing and slapped his hand away. "I had a puncture. There was a tree down on the A30 so I had to cut through the lanes. Jesus, what's the matter with you?" She had him on the back foot and knew it. "If you didn't mess about in my car like you do, I wouldn't have so many problems with it! It's already been in the garage three times this month."

"Why the hell didn't you come back here when you were so close?"

"Why would I? Monica was at Mum's." Natasha stood her ground, defiant.

Brian stood motionless, processing the information.

Natasha was quick to press her advantage. "You're no damn help in an emergency, I phoned Sue, and she came out and gave me a lift back to Mum's. It's time you paid for some of the repairs to my car, you're always *borrowing* it. I bet you don't have your driving licence yet either do you? When are you going to stick around long enough to get things organised? Monica needs a full time dad, not someone who isn't even insured to take her out in the car."

Brian backed away, involuntarily putting his hands to his ears, the way he always did when a woman raised her voice to him. "*Shut up! Shut up!*" he screamed, clutching Natasha by the throat. "If I find out you're lying to me, I'll fucking kill you, do you hear me, I'll kill you and I'll make sure your fucking mother never sees that kid again." He gestured towards the living room where the innocent child sat staring at the television screen, blissfully unaware of the violent scenario playing out around her.

He pushed Natasha out of the way before grabbing her keys and rushing from the house!

Brian was already tiring of the situation with Natasha; right now he had a job to do. With the use of Natasha's car, and a tank full of fuel, it was time for him to put his domestic situation out of his mind, time to do his job. You didn't cross up Brian's masters, not if you wanted to draw breath in the future. You didn't cross up the IRA!

Natasha was in floods of tears as she told her mum what had happened, "Mum, I can't go on living with that maniac. I'm frightened all the time that he's going to attack me. I seriously wouldn't put it past him to use force to get his own way!"

"You think he would rape you?" Her mother was gravely concerned. "Do you seriously think that Brian would rape you?"

The expression on her daughter's face said it all.

"Oh Natasha, why haven't you said something before? Why haven't you left that idiot waste of space?"

"Can I move back home with you Mum?"

"Oh darling, you know what it's like with George, he can be so difficult. Can't you move in with Neil?"

"No mum, it's too soon. He's only just told me that he loves me, I can't foist Monica, and my baggage with Brian on him so soon, it'll scare him away for sure. I need to sort myself out, get clear of Brian on my own before I'm going to have a chance of happiness with Neil."

"Brian's not going to go without a fight though is he Natasha? You've tried to leave him before, he always gets you back," her mother reminded.

"If I can just make him realise there's nothing here for him, maybe he'll clear off to Ireland, his *spiritual* home, leave me alone and give me a chance to move on." Natasha was looking down at her feet, defeated.

"Chin up love, I'll square things with George, if he doesn't accept it, he'll face two miserable women making his life difficult. We'll work something out, I promise."

Natasha's mum drove them to the house she shared with Brian and moved all her and Monica's personal necessities back to the family home, leaving most of their possessions and the house to Brian.

If they thought this change in circumstance would make life easier, they were sorely wrong. With Natasha staying at her mum's, it would be increasingly difficult for her to meet up with Neil as Brian was tied to neither tide nor time and could be anywhere at any time.

CHAPTER 14

Reaching out

He drove off the main track, up a pot-holed scalping strewn stretch of tarmac and onto an abandoned WWII airfield. Left and right of the narrow strip of concrete, polished clean by daily traffic, were abandoned vehicles, partly stripped out, some burnt out to cover any forensic evidence. Brian smiled; these were *his people*, *his kinfolk,* warts and all.

He pulled up to the largest of the group of caravans, curtains twitched, Brian knew that his approach would have been monitored by a sentry high up in one of the airfields old lookout buildings. He was recognised as posing no threat, otherwise he would not have reached the caravans unmolested.

A man in his early thirties alighted from the van. "Dixie, ye' ol' fecker. Tis good t' see ye' so it is."

"Danny boy, ye old crook, how's the life of a scrap metal stealer these days?" Brian replied, thumping his friend in the shoulder.

"Ye' cheeky fecker," the man replied and thumped Brian back, pretty hard. "What brings you out here Dixie, I can't believe this is a social call, you're not a man to drop in unannounced, so ye aren't."

"Danny boy, I'm here with a proposition from our mutual friends and benefactors from across the water," Brian said.

The big Gypsy was shirtless and sun bronzed, every part of his muscled upper torso was covered in scars, tattoos, or bedecked in gold jewellery. He kicked a fold up chair towards his visitor and gestured for the rotund woman in the van to bring drinks.

"I see yer still wearing yer wealth fer everyone to admire Danny boy," Brian jibed. "got yerself a few new tats too I see!"

The huge Gypsy had the names of all the individuals he'd met in the bare-knuckle ring set in ink on his chest. A small symbol of a red cross suffixed the majority of the names, but a significant number were followed by an image of a cloaked reaper; the significance was obvious.

"Aye, still top of the heap Dixie. I reckon I've a few years yet before some fecker wears the reaper after *my* name."

"I'll get to the point Danny, our mutual friends have a very large consignment of Libyan arms, way more than is needed for the cause and far more than is safe to hide away in the arms caches. They need to convert the guns into currency."

"We'd have to put it to the Kampania Dixie, that's too big a call for us alone. We're not doing much in the way of armed capers, can't see us takin' too many of those off yer hands."

"I wasn't thinking of you taking them on yerselves Danny, I want you to reach out to our kinfolk up country, get some of the families up around the smoke in on the action. The army want us to reach out far and wide, tap into the Yardies, the Tongs, Angels, Outlaws, Yakuza, Mafia, street gangs, you name it."

"You want to reach out to the niggers Dixie, that's a big ask for our people. We don't trust the dark skins."

"We can bury our race issues for the right price Danny?"

"What's the game? Is it just for the love?"

"No Danny, not just about the wage, between you me and the gatepost, I think the army are wantin' to flood the land with Libyan guns, their latest plan to de-stabilise the British Government, soften 'em up, take 'em out!"

The Gypsy was contemplative. "You know I've no care for this Gajo Government but you get us caught up in a game like that, could end bad."

"The purse will make it worthwhile Danny, they're talking fifty fifty split on retail value."

"Who sets the retail, us?"

Brian laughed, "Market price Danny, they know the value of the merchandise and you know better than to try and con the army!"

"What's our play in this then Dixie?" Danny asked, nonchalantly scratching his balls which were hanging out of his shorts.

A large woman in dark clothing and a dark headscarf partially obscuring an even darker moustache scuttled out and placed two pints of beer on the makeshift table.

"Took yer time snu' what's yer feckin' problem?" Danny scolded, downing his pint in one huge gulp.

The woman cursed and scuttled away without even acknowledging their visitor.

"Bloody Mollisher, she grows uglier every day! I swear Dixie, a wedding ring has the power to turn a pretty Chavi in to a fecking Barri dog!

Brian laughed, he didn't speak the traveller dialect but he got the gist.

"So what do ye need from me Dixie?" Danny questioned seriously.

"I've reached out to a well-connected Roma clan who are on the road down near Plymouth. I've made sure that they owe me a hearing at least, you're my 'ace in the hole', with your rep' on the bare-knuckle circuit, I'll convince the 'Rom Baro' that you're a man to be trusted."

"Aye, the Roma will know Danny boy for sure, got some o' their best boys on me chest so I have, more than a few have met me reaper! There's no bad blood though, all fair fighting to be sure!"

"Well that's a plus Danny. These boys are connected to the horse and dog tracks all over the country and abroad. If we can get them on-board with these Libyan guns, we'll set the market, put the guns in the hands of druggies and gang bangers country wide."

"That's feckin' ambitious Dixie, lot o' love to be made, but feck it up and I see it'll be a couple of Irish Tinkers that wash up in the Irish sea!"

"Aye Danny, to be sure! So, are ye in?"

"Feck Dixie, what d'ye think? To be sure I'm feckin' in!"

"First things first Danny boy. I went and got meself dipped down in Plymouth, lost me whole float so I did! I need to run a couple of quick errands to fill me purse before I can get started."

"Yer lucky I know and trust you Dixie, else I'd be thinkin' you're full o' shite right now," the Gypsy laughed. "I s'pose you could use a crew, and I've got a couple o' 'lost' licences; you can use to hire some plant, that can be turned into cash down at the auctions quick."

"Aye, that would be grand Danny, I've seen a few gifts locally that I can turn a buck on, a loan of your boys would be a help so it would."

"All right then Dixie, let's make this happen."

CHAPTER 15

Cold feet

Sat in the comparative safety of Natasha's attic bedroom and enjoying the afterglow of a particularly enjoyable encounter of the physical kind, Neil was feeling confident. Brian had been off the scene for a while and Neil had arranged a few days holiday to attend a bike rally in Oostende, Belgium, with some friends.

"What about Monica, Neil? You know I can't just swan off and leave her." Natasha protested.

"Oh come on, your mum has already said she will provide a cover story if need be; you're attending a family wedding in London."

Natasha had family up in the smoke, so it wouldn't look suspicious; especially as Brian had never taken any interest in her kin.

"Yeah, but Mum really is away on that weekend, so who's going to look after Monica?"

"My folks have volunteered to step up to the plate, they really want to help!" Neil argued.

"They haven't met her even, come to think of it, they haven't even met me, nor me them. It wouldn't be right."

"It'll be fine Natasha, my parents are brilliant, they really want to meet you and Monica, they would love to be needed, and we can stop over when we get back, stay for a meal, then we get to kill all the birds with one stone."

"Are you sure it won't be too much of an imposition?" she enquired.

Now Neil knew he was winning. All that was required was the right amount of reassurance. "Of course not! If you knew my parents, you would know that they're at their best when they feel wanted and needed. You will love my folks, they will spoil Monica rotten and they will love both of you just as I do." With his powers of persuasion, Neil had sealed the deal!

"OK, it will be fun to meet all your friends; I've heard so much about them," she said, persuaded. "All right Neil, you set it up."

Neil smiled a little smug smile. "You're going to love it!"

Despite him still having no clue as to the existence of Neil, Brian was about to inadvertently throw an enormous spanner into the works.

CHAPTER 16

Unlucky for some

Neil spent the weekend prior to the trip working on his BSA Chop. Since he was riding his bikes a lot more, he had acquired a Ford Transit Luton van and was using it out in the street as a garage for his bikes, rather than having to drag them through the neighbour's garden.

He had been running up and down the street fine-tuning the carburettor to eradicate a dead spot and he felt he had it running spot on ready for the trip. He ran the bike up the ramp and into the truck next to its stable-mate, an old 750 Honda Café Racer; sadly neglected since he had built the Chop but potentially still a great bike. He threaded a length of stout chain through the front wheels and snapped the padlock shut. He then drew down the rear roller door and put the little hasp and padlock together.

Next morning, just as Neil was leaving for work, he noticed a piece of padlock lying in the road. His eyes were instantly drawn to the Luton. "Oh no!" he exclaimed. The padlock had been forced. As he lifted the roller door his heart sank into his gut. Both bikes were gone.

Unbeknownst to him at the time, Brian's recent quest for cash money had inspired him and his traveller cronies to pay Neil an opportunistic visit in the wee small hours and they'd had it away with both bikes. Neil was crestfallen; this was turning into a nightmare.

After a number of choice expletives, some tears and a temper tantrum or two, Neil got on the blower to the law. After a lot of shouting and threatening with negative editorial in Neil's paper, the local bobby reluctantly agreed to come over and examine the crime scene. Neil phoned into work, explained the situation and bought himself a little time.

The first thing the unhappy local bobby said when he arrived was, "I can only give you a half an hour. We don't normally come out to motorcycle theft at all. We don't have the manpower."

"That's reassuring," replied Neil, before adding under his breath, "just what I need, a PC Enis."

The policeman looked at the truck and the padlocks, shook his head and said, "Your bikes could be up in London by now and we don't have a hope in hell of finding them."

"Look," Neil spat, "we can at least try and find what direction they went in. The Honda had a flat battery and virtually no petrol in it and the BSA was unfeasibly loud. If they tried to ride the bikes away, someone would have heard."

"The bikes would have been loaded onto a van and gone whoosh," said the police officer as he made a surfing motion with his hand.

"Can we at least knock on a few doors?" said Neil, exasperated.

"OK," said the policeman, just to humour Neil, "get in the car and we'll take a little tour around the village and ring a few bells."

They drove straight through the village, the most logical route any fleeing villains would follow.

Neil was planning to stop at every junction and ask the locals if they had heard or seen anything. They didn't get that far as Neil spotted the Honda upside down lying on the bank of a nearby rhyne, a drainage ditch. Between them, they managed to pull the bike out of the ditch. Apart from the ignition lock the bike was pretty much undamaged. While they were busy, a local farmer rolled up in his tractor.

After observing them a while, the farmer dropped down from the cab of his tractor, strolled over and said in a broad Somerset accent, "Orright? I heard a lot of noise out here about three in the morning. Sounded like two motorbikes come up but only one of them went on. Made a right bloody racket it done too. What were it? Were they robbing?"

"Yes," replied the policeman, "they were stealing this gentleman's motorcycles."

"Bad job," replied Farmer Palmer.

The policeman went off to take the helpful gent's statement leaving Neil examining the bike. When he returned he informed Neil that he had stayed as long as he could and had other crimes to solve. Neil had already made his mind up to push the bike home rather than risking it being stolen again.

On the long exhausting push home, (uphill all the way of course) Neil was determined to get this bike roadworthiness tested, new battery, ignition and running again. Come hell or high water, he was going to make the weekend away with Natasha happen no matter what it took.

CHAPTER 17

Brass monkeys

It took some planning but Friday saw Neil on his newly taxed and tested Honda, with Natasha in his company car following on behind, making their way to nearby Crediton; the home of Neil's parents, and where Monica would be spending the weekend.

Friday afternoon was a bit of a hectic rush. Natasha was understandably apprehensive about leaving such a young child with these previously unknown people.

With Neil's reassurance and, mercifully, Monica's instant bond with his charming mum, events were finally beginning to go his way. Natasha's bag was duly loaded onto the bike with the rest of the camping gear. Neil and Natasha went upstairs to the spare room to change into bike gear. As always, the sight of Natasha removing clothing was getting Neil in an amorous mood and he started to paw playfully at Natasha's naked breasts.

She turned and embraced him. "If you think you're going to make me all messy before we even get started," she reproached. "Save it till we get there." She winked. "I have wet wipes."

Neil smiled at the promise then started pulling on his woolly fisherman's socks before pulling on a pair of Army long johns. Natasha was sniggering at the sight of her masculine lover shoving his thick muscular thighs into a pair of glorified tights. He was concentrating on dressing. After the long johns and thermal shirt, he followed up with a pair of leather jeans, a fleecy jumper and a fur-lined bomber jacket. Natasha too had donned a pair of nappa fashion leather jeans, and one of her signature tiny, cropped, lace up boob tops. Under the jeans she was wearing nothing but a pair of skimpy knickers and was pushing her feet into a pair of high-heeled ankle boots.

Neil laughed and remarked, "No. No. No. Very sexy but not the kind of gear you wear on a five hundred mile round trip on a motorbike in December. He borrowed a pair of his mum's woolly tights and a stout jumper for her. "What gloves have you got?" he asked. Natasha showed him a pair of ladies unlined leather gloves. The two just stared at each other before Neil burst out laughing.

"What?" she enquired. "What do you expect? I thought my biking days were over when I had the baby. This is all I could come up with."

Neil looked at her. She was all doe eyed and vulnerable, and thought how much he adored this girl.

"We will have to come up with something better than that," he remarked and proceeded to use his mum's phone to call his friends, Tim and Star, who were travelling with them. He replaced the receiver and turned to Natasha. "Star has a spare set of gloves. Her hands are tiny like yours. They should fit you fine."

"Star?" enquired Natasha.

"Hippies," replied Neil. "You know how it was with the sixties parents; all Earth, Sun, Moon, Star, etc. There was a bad side to all the dope and psychedelics they were doing, stupid names for their kids was one of them."

Tim and Star rolled up on a custom Shovelhead Harley just as Neil and Natasha were saying goodbyes to Mum, Dad and baby. A very quick introduction followed where Star handed over the gloves, a good, warm, fur-lined pair, to Natasha.

Star was an attractive slim woman, slightly older than Natasha and she hoped they would hit it off and become friends. Women tended to either love Natasha for the genuine person she was or write her off instantly as a threat. She thought Star looked like a confident woman who could hold her own.

"Where's the Beesa?" Tim enquired.

"Nicked," replied Neil, "long story. Tell you all about it when we get there."

Out on the road, Tim rode hard for a Harley rider, and it wasn't long before Natasha was feeling the cold, causing her to snuggle up closer to Neil for warmth. Neil was frozen solid and overtook Tim to pull into the next services. This turned out to be a wise move as the heavens opened seconds later, bombarding the intrepid voyagers with freezing sleet. Steaming hot mugs of weak coffee helped to take the sting out of the awful conditions. The girls wandered off together to the loo.

Natasha came out of the cubical first and stood at the sinks, brushing her long curls and touching up her make-up. Star soon followed and stood next to Natasha, her first opportunity to properly scrutinise Neil's new love. After a few moments she took a sharp breath. "Wow, look at you Missy, what a cracker, Neil's really fallen on his feet."

Natasha, embarrassed, said, "Puh-lease, I'm nothing special."

"No really," Star pressed, "you should see Neil's previous girlfriends; they were proper dogs." Natasha looked shocked. "I'm kidding." She hugged Natasha, laughing, "Take no notice of me love, I'm just pulling your leg. If you're half as nice as you are pretty, we are going to get on like a house on fire."

The boys were pondering over the best route to take to reach Dover soonest. The girls returned arm in arm, still laughing over Star's earlier joke.

"Start a rumour or share the humour," said Tim.

"Talking about you, not to you," replied Star. Still, the girls were certainly hitting it off.

"Next stop Dover," grinned Tim.

Neil grimaced.

They filled the bikes up with fuel and gunned them back towards the open road.

They pulled off the A20 and headed towards the docks. Neil's fingers were indicating that the temperature had dropped to somewhere between fucking cold and hypothermia.

CHAPTER 18

Four's a crowd

The ferry trip was between four and five hours. To Natasha's delight, Neil had booked a cabin so they could catch a bit of sleep and they parted company with Tim and Star who were not such frequent travellers and wanted to savour the entire experience.

Once inside the cabin, Natasha shed the leather jacket and chunky jumper. The cold had obviously had a lasting effect on her as her nipples were standing erect like a pair of acorns. As sure as the hounds will always smell the fox, a man will always spot a pair of erect nipples and Neil was soon standing behind her, massaging her breasts and sliding his hands inside her lace up top to massage her nipples between his fingers and thumbs. The pair began to passionately kiss as Neil lifted her top over her shoulders allowing her perfect full breasts to spill out into his waiting hands. Neil knelt down in front of his conquest and unzipped her leather jeans, pulling jeans, knickers and woolly tights down to her feet where her little ankle boots arrested any further attempt to disrobe her. Not to be outdone, Neil picked her up and threw her on the bed as she was before pushing her knees apart roughly, burying his head between her legs. Neil was distracted, enjoying the sweet taste of Natasha's sex and she too was otherwise engaged as the door flung open and two burly bikers burst into the room and flung their gear onto the opposite bunk.

"Way-hay!" exclaimed the nearest of the blokes as he plonked himself down on the bottom bunk.

"Entertainment included." Natasha leapt off the bed in surprise. As her feet refused to move due to the restriction of her clothing round her ankles, gravity took over and she fell flat into the lap of the prostrate biker. His eyes gestured momentarily towards the ceiling before shouting, "Thank you God."

Natasha was a picture. Naked in every sense of the word, lying face and breasts down in the biker's lap. Neil, fully clothed, was still in shock, watching the scene unfold before him as Natasha sprang up off the bunk, her breasts jiggling in a totally captivating manner before the restraints round her ankles kicked in again and sent her flying into the arms of the second biker.

The second biker was the perfect gentleman and helped her find her balance and pull her knickers up to cover her naked shaven pussy. Neil had awoken from his deep frozen inactivity and handed back her top.

"What the fuck are you doing in our cabin?" Neil demanded.

"We booked two berths," replied the guy whose crotch Natasha had recently been lying in, "this is where the Purser sent us. Cabin 14a."

Neil snatched his own tickets out of his pocket and scrutinised the booking. "Two single berths, Cabin 14a.........Oh cock!"

He looked at Natasha, whose face was now pillar box red. The four of them looked furtively from one to another before Natasha surprised everyone by bursting out laughing. With the ice broken the four of them roared with cathartic laughter before one of the bikers stepped forward, kissed Natasha's hand and said, "Madame, I can say without a hint of a lie, that it is a pleasure to meet you. My name is Donald, as in Duck, and my companion here is Gary."

Natasha did a little curtsy joining in the chivalrous farce and replied, "My name is Natasha, my knight in shining armour who has recently fallen from his horse, is Neil." She turned to Neil and screwed her nose up a little just to let him know he was not entirely out of the mire over this debacle.

"Now if we can take your order," said Donald, "I think the least we can do is go and fetch you good people a post coital alcoholic beverage."

"We were just getting to the coital when you burst in," mused Natasha, "but a nice glass of red wine would be appreciated."

"Madame, ever your servant. Your wish is my command," he replied.

Neil requested a rum and coke and Donald disappeared off down the narrow passageway towards the bars.

"What's the deal with you two then Gary?" Neil asked. "Where are you off to?"

"Oostende," replied Gary, "we're off to the St Nicklaus Treffen at the Velodrome."

"That's where we're going," said Neil, adding, "are you in a club or flying solo?"

"We are members of a medieval re-enactment society but as bikers we're not affiliated to anyone."

"You must tag along with us then," Neil insisted. "We're members of a bike club, 'The Booze

Brothers'; no shit, no attitude, just rock up and get pissed."

"That sounds like us," Gary replied, "where do we sign up?"

"You just did," Neil replied, "welcome aboard!"

With the help of generous measures of alkyfrolics which Donald returned with, the cabin, Natasha included, were soon in the land of the fairies. Just as well for her, as she didn't have to consciously suffer the snoring and farting which was an inevitable outcome of three burly men sleeping in close proximity.

"Oh heck," Natasha cursed as she tried to pull her now cold, soaking tights and leather jeans over her warm legs. "Not only is this uncomfortable, it's also impossible. How far do we need to go when we get off the ferry?"

Neil replied, "It's no more than two hundred yards from the terminal to the velodrome then we are inside a huge heated marquee. Why?"

"Well, I was going to surprise you with the sexy little outfit I was going to wear for you in the tent," she whispered, "but I'm going to have to wear it all the time now as I can't put those clothes on again until they've dried out."

Neil's heart was racing as Natasha went into the bathroom to change. The two lads had cleared off for breakfast but she was taking no chances on them returning unexpectedly.

The tannoy was just announcing for the drivers to prepare to re-join their vehicles as Natasha opened the door of the bathroom and stepped out. "How do I look?" she asked.

Neil's jaw dropped. She was wearing a cropped black leather bodice, laced down the front with pink ribbons leaving ample cleavage on display and a matching tiny studded leather mini skirt. The skirt was laced with pink ribbons up both sides leaving a two-inch strip of flesh showing all the way to the waist on both sides. Under the skirt, she was wearing a pair of hold up stockings with a thick two-inch band of black lace at the top. From the flesh on view between stocking tops and waist, it was evident that anything else under the skirt was the property of Mother Nature. To complete the ensemble, she produced a tiny pair of black high-heeled pumps from her bag.

Down on the car deck, introductions were made with Tim, Star, Donald and Gary. Natasha took Star to one side and explained her attire. Star replied, "You go girl, I've got my mini with me, I might just join you. Tim will think it's Christmas. Oh, it *is* Christmas. I'm glad Neil's found you, it's so nice to meet another girlie girl."

CHAPTER 19

Cycle slut

With the tent up and the gear stowed, Neil decided it was high time he too changed out of his wet clothes. He lay on his back on the floor of the tent to change out of his wet long johns.

Natasha, bored from standing around outside, called to him, "Neil, have you taken your tights off yet?" Neil ignored her the first time so she called out a little louder, "*Neil, have you taken your tights off yet?*"

Guffaws of laughter erupted around the camp, followed by an embarrassed whisper from Neil, "Yes thank you, I have."

This was the late eighties and Neil and his brethren were still conspicuously dressed in their 'originals': threadbare jeans and denim jackets, the dreadful bane of most mothers' lives as they fought with their young offspring to commit the cardinal sin of introducing them to the washer. By stark contrast 'biker chicks' were into dressing glamorously and in general they were still an above averagely attractive demographic, meaning that although Natasha stood out for her stunning looks, she didn't attract negative attention from her female peers. Star spotted Natasha, rushed over, threw her arms around her and hugged her hard. She too had changed into a skimpy short skirt and tight top.

She linked arms with Natasha and said, "C'mon girl, it's too cold to stand around outside dressed like this, let's go and find some nice warm men to stand by." To say the girls were attracting some male attention would be a gross understatement. Luckily for Natasha, the whole of the infield was concrete with ample concrete pathways leading from the marquee to the cycle circuit and the stands, meaning she could move about most of the site without sinking into the ground; crucial for someone walking about on five-inch heels, even more critical when the wearer was bereft of any underwear to protect her virtue were she to slip over.

Natasha was the epitome of the perfect 'biker chick'. Her long curly dark hair reached all the way down to her cheeky leather clad bum. Her breasts large and pert with upturned nipples, which would turn rock hard at the slightest hint of a draft or sexual excitement, were always in attendance no matter what she wore. Her legs were slim, long and tapered, from creamy thighs, down through slender ankles to petite delicate feet. Her legs were longer than should have been for her torso but combined with her large round breasts the illusion was one of absolute perfection. A body created with sex in mind. Sex was certainly on Neil's mind and on the mind of every red-blooded male that clapped eyes on his girl.

The girls made their way to the marquee where the bands were just warming up and the wine was on draught. Neil caught up and sidled into place beside his lady. Between them, the blokes looked rough as guts. In contrast, the girls looked stunning.

A couple of old faces hove into view in the form of Neil's former Army buddies and founder members of their bike club, 'The Booze Brothers'. Neil introduced Natasha to Jimbo and Goose. After a few appreciative words and slaps on backs, the drinking began in earnest.

The booze was flowing freely; the weekend was starting to look all warm and fuzzy. With a bottle of Malibu, which he'd won for best Japanese café racer, Neil was quickly becoming more warm and fuzzy than anyone else.

As the consumption of alcohol continued unabated, the girls' dancing became more uninhibited, as was the norm for the biker scene in the eighties. Rowdy shouts of, 'Show your tits', and 'Get your tits out for the boys', were soon rewarded with titillating flashes of flesh from the veteran and novice biker girls alike.

Natasha was dancing like a wild animal. Free from the restraints of baby, ex and kitchen sink, she was determined to make the most of her weekend away by seeing that she was 'last man standing'. Most of the bikers, exhausted from the long distances ridden, had retired to their tents. Neil was bravely trying to spin around and keep up with his girl. It was clear to her that Neil was not as accustomed to heavy drinking as he had implied and was well on the way to unconsciousness.

As she watched, Neil sat heavily into a chair before slowly tipping over to a point where gravity and his chair were at loggerheads. Gravity of course was the victor and Neil face planted the floor where he looked like he might spend the night. Neil was out for the count.

With Neil out of the picture, a group of Dutch muscle-bound meatheads moved in on Natasha. She was quite drunk and to be fair, was revelling in all the attention. She had been dancing and carrying on with these guys, and they in turn were keeping her pretty well plied with wine to the point where she was becoming oblivious to what was going on.

Neil's little sleep had allowed some oxygen to return to his brain cells and he had 'come to', after a fashion. He looked around with blurry eyes, taking in his surroundings and remembering where he was and who he was with. Looking around for Natasha, he spotted her. She was still with the group of testosterone fuelled body builders. They had some sort of bench-pressing competition going on. Neil's heart nearly stopped when he realised they were bench-pressing Natasha.

Neil's mouth hung open like a guppy fish. The current muscle man had one hand on his girl's thigh and the other in the centre of her back. The bow on the front of her bodice was undone and her gorgeous breasts were practically hanging out. Her tiny skirt had risen right up over her thighs and her sexy stocking tops were on display to all the lewd horny men gathered around watching the spectacle. Neil was experiencing an odd mixture of emotions. This was his girl. He was the only man that should be touching her and enjoying the delights which she had to share. Why was the sight of Natasha's body being used in this compromising way giving him a powerful erection?

As the current competitor lifted Natasha high above his chest, her back was arched, pulling her skirt high up her thighs. As the guy lifted her up with his arms fully extended, she wobbled slightly, causing her to open her legs in an attempt to balance. That was all the movement required to fully expose her shaven sex to the appreciative mob.

By now, quite conscious, Neil overheard a few of the Dutch guys talking. It seemed that the bench-pressing prize was to have Natasha. Neil had better intervene. He hadn't long been with her; nevertheless he figured that she wouldn't want this to happen, so he would rescue her. He strode over to the pretty dangerous looking crowd and spoke to them in English. He told them that Natasha was his wife and that their fun was over. To their credit, they were pretty cool about it, and when they saw that Natasha obviously wanted to be with Neil, they backed off and shook his hand, complimenting him on his gorgeous wife.

Neil had sensibly brought a head torch in his pocket. The strap was broken and he was using the same hand that was holding the Malibu bottle to steady the head torch, whilst Natasha, who had just entirely forgotten how to walk, or at least how to walk on heels, was leaning forward with her arms around Neil's waist

A drunken biker, hanging on to a floodlight pole as if it were the mast of a sinking ship, witnessed their journey from marquee to tent. Later he was overheard swearing to his leathered buddies that he'd seen a unicorn.

Natasha, obviously feeling somewhat frisky from *her* evening's exploits, undid Neil's belt buckle and zipper, pulled his semi hard manhood out of his trousers and was pulling on it like a set of reins.

They fell into their tent, quite literally, and started tearing the clothes from each other's bodies.

Natasha was like a woman possessed. Her heavy breathing was turning Neil on, testosterone clearing the residual alcohol from his brain and replacing it with pure unadulterated lust.

In a moment of desire-fuelled bravery, he whispered to her that he had been watching her 'playing' with the muscle men. She tensed up, expecting a jealous reaction. Neil held her face in his hands and whispered, "They were competing to decide who was going to have you. I was so turned on thinking about it; I almost let them do it."

Natasha lunged at him and her full lips were on his, her hungry tongue feeding off the inside of his mouth, sucking his moist tongue into her as if it were an extension to his penis. Neil had just one thing on his mind. He wanted to taste her arousal. He roughly broke off from the kiss and threw her down on her back on the sleeping bag before grabbing her thighs and wrapping her legs around his head. He was not disappointed. Natasha's sex was as wet as he had ever tasted it. He mentally thanked the Dutch guys for the thorough job they had done on their foreplay.

Natasha's hips were pumping her sex up to meet Neil's mouth, as if by sheer will she could take his tongue further into her. Neil was sucking the whole of her sex and her sensitive button into his warm soft mouth before stabbing his tongue deep inside her. His tongue was flicking this way and that, always just missing her hard little nub with every stroke. When she could take it no more, Natasha shouted, "Fuck me!" at the top of her voice. Neil's rock hard manhood was buried balls deep into her, his hips thrusting in and out of her sex. Full strokes, the full eight inches of his thick penis sliding all the way in before pulling all the way out. He kept up this technique until he could hold off his release no longer, then he sped up his strokes, making sure he ground the base of his penis against his girl's most sensitive spot with each increasingly short stroke. His climax built up from his toes, as his entire body tensed. Natasha's orgasm was also approaching. She grabbed Neil's head and screamed as her whole body shook with waves of pleasure. With a final thrust, Neil too found his release just moments after her and the two of them collapsed into a spent, sweaty heap.

The camp-site erupted into a round of spontaneous applause.

CHAPTER 20

Lots of luck, all bad

The following morning saw a camp-site full of hung-over revellers. A combination of full bladders and banging heads brought the bikers out into the morning sun.

"Oi, turn that searchlight off," moaned Neil. He aimed one frozen foot at his waiting bike boots, missed and tripped over the guy ropes, sprawling ass over tit onto the wet grass.

"Stop shouting," replied Natasha. They both looked at each other.

"*Coffee*," they said simultaneously. It was a statement not a question. They headed for the marquee.

After a couple of mugs of strong Belgian coffee, the world was starting to emerge from its blood-red haze. Natasha retired to the loo for hair and make-up repairs. Neil was being seduced by the smell of frying eggs and ham (the Belgians don't do bacon) and set off back to the bar for a nosebag. Natasha returned from the bathroom back on banging form, all the sleep and alcohol washed down the plughole. Neil's food antidote was having the same effect and before long they were both back in the pink.

The Belgian bike club were organising a marshalled ride out through the streets of Oostende and the old town district. After an enjoyable albeit cold few miles around the old town streets, one of the outriders cut in a bit quickly at a traffic island and Neil had to lock on the anchors to avoid a collision. One of the front brake pipes, damaged slightly when the bike was stolen and missed by the roadworthiness inspector, promptly burst, spraying the front wheel with brake fluid and causing Neil to have a buttock clenching moment trying to stop the bike with the rear brake alone. One of the English-speaking marshals had witnessed the close call and stopped to help. Despite the helpful marshal's local knowledge, they were unable to find a garage or workshop open with the necessary tools to fix it, so they limped back to the site with just the rear brake.

Neil and Natasha stopped off at an off licence on the way back to the site for a couple of bottles to drown their sorrows.

The only bit of luck in this unhappy saga was that the Honda had twin discs on the front; one of the many upgrades Neil had made to the original bike's specifications. Neil was trying to figure a way of blocking off one of the pipes. Despite his sound engineering credentials, he was finding it impossible to get a pressure tight seal on the pipe.

Natasha came to the rescue, proving that a pretty face could have a brain too. She suggested he take a length of tassel from her leather jacket sleeve and ram it into the pipe before crimping the pipe with pliers. He duly tried it and it worked a treat. Nice one Natasha. Bike jury-rigged. The wine was now cracked open to celebrate their ingenuity, rather than to ease their sorrows.

Well, Neil and Natasha now found themselves virtually alone on the site. After a quick change out of bike gear, Neil was back in his 'originals' and Natasha had donned her skimpy outfit from the Friday night in readiness of the Saturday festivities.

They could hear loud ska and reggae music playing and followed the sound to a dance tent, a much smaller marquee that they hadn't visited before. Inside, they found the place deserted but a little stage was set up with mirror ball and searchlights on the ceiling. Centre stage was a stainless steel burlesque pole.

CHAPTER 21

Patricia the stripper

Once again, the copious quaffing of red wine was having a profound effect on Natasha's inhibitions. She boldly strolled up to the pole just as a bawdy stripping song with a pumping base line started up. She wrapped one leg around the pole and started pelvic thrusts on the half beat like a proper pro.

Neil was gob-smacked; he was unaware that Natasha's two pre-pubescent obsessions had been gymnastics and disco dancing. As a young girl she had witnessed her father watching a burlesque show on late night TV. Fascinated by what she had seen, by the time she hit the wilful teens, and with movies such as 'Flashdance' as inspiration, she had learned to combine the two to devastating effect. Neil could do no more than sit back and enjoy the show. Natasha swung up the pole in a pirouette motion and was gripping with her thighs whilst hanging her torso out, slowly spinning back down the pole with the momentum from the pirouette. When she reached the floor, she gripped the pole between her thighs and lay back on the floor.

Her hands were at the laces of her top, loosening them right off. As the song tailed off, she stood alongside the pole and crossed one leg around the pole in the classic start position. Her hand fluttered to her laced skirt and subtly undid a bow on the side.

The next song came on; a sleazy number with a fast upbeat tempo. Natasha threw herself up and onto the pole. As she did, her skimpy little knickers, now bereft of their restraining bows, fell to the ground below her feet. Neil could feel the stirrings of yet another arousal in his loins.

Gripping the pole between her thighs, Natasha was swinging her upper torso left and right with the beat. In doing so, she freed her ample bosom from her lace up top, shinning up the pole a little before letting her upper torso lie back, flat against the pole, completely dropping her breasts out of her top and exposing them to the room.

Natasha was carried away in a world of her own. Her eyes were shut; she was enjoying the pulsating beats through her body.

Neil had noticed that the searchlights, previously focused randomly on the pole, were now following Natasha's movements and changing colour to suit the beats. Clearly, Neil was not the only person enjoying this little show.

As this song ended, the next song blended seamlessly, obviously now being DJ mixed rather than a random tape recording. As the beats pulsated, she unbuttoned her leather skirt and let it drop to the floor. Neil considered telling her she was being watched but thought better of it.

She took the sordid scene up a notch and started sliding her shaven sex up and down the pole.

Word had obviously filtered around the site that a show was taking place and late risers were beginning to filter into the tent. Natasha was completely oblivious; the searchlights in her eyes, the wine and the loud pumping music were conspiring to rob her of all senses but the throbbing between her legs. Still thinking her performance was between her and Neil, she gently thrust her pelvis back and forth, bringing her bare crotch into crushing contact with the cold steel pole. She was building to a climax, holding the pole with one hand, pinching and stretching her erect nipples with the other. The excited crowd were getting boisterous now but the noise did not seem to penetrate Natasha's lust filled bubble.

The DJ and lighting engineer were real pros and could see their performer was approaching a climax of a personal kind. As Natasha screamed out her crescendo, the music peaked and the lights were extinguished, leaving the tent in silence for a few seconds before the audience erupted into a rapturous climax of their own.

The house lights came up; spatial awareness was filtering back into Natasha's vision and consciousness. As the faces came into focus, she became aware of the shouts of, "More, more!" "Zugabe, zugabe," from the German contingent and the Belgian and French equivalent, "Une autre, une autre."

Natasha's face was a picture. Once again her lustful abandonment had got her into hot water. As the searchlight focused once more upon her, she stood in the centre of the stage blinking like a rabbit in headlights. Neil, once again slow to act to protect his lady-love, grabbed her clothes and her arm and ushered her off the stage and out of the marquee.

CHAPTER 22

In the cold light

Back in the tent and after a few sobering hours sleep, Natasha was reflecting on what she had been up to since arriving here with Neil. She was feeling quite upset and ashamed of herself for the way she had behaved. It seemed to her that the relationship with Neil was based only on lust.

"Neil, why didn't you tell me that there were other guys in the marquee? Doesn't it bother you at all that all those blokes were watching me?" Her mind was in turmoil. She felt she had been constantly upping the ante with Neil, trying to shock him or impress him with her sexuality. Their time together was so brief and precious, she was angry and upset by Neil's apparent indifference. However she approached it, it made her feel that he just didn't care that much for her, that it was just great sex for him at the end of the day.

"Oh come on Natasha, don't act the innocent! If I hadn't have broken it up last night, you'd have woken up in a Dutchman's tent without the slightest clue how many dicks had been in you during the night!"

"You bastard," she shouted in retaliation. "So why weren't you looking after me? This is your scene not mine. I had no idea what to expect. You wanted to bring me here, I've done everything I could to please you. You just don't seem to give a damn, you'd have been happy if I had fucked those Dutch guys, you practically said so last night!"

Despite it being an odd kind of logic, Neil felt that everything that happened between them was OK because what he did was just for her and vice versa. Last night's activities however fell into a different category, felt a little like a betrayal. All very foolish really when you consider that he had introduced the naïve and obviously inebriated Natasha into this horny male dominated environment and then abandoned her to her fate! However, such are the complexities of human relationships that insecurities, jealousy and doubt can soon cloud an otherwise clear spring. Sometimes the boundaries get a little blurred. Sometimes there are no boundaries at all. As is always the case in relationships, poor communication always leads to a lack of understanding and eventually an inevitable break down of trust.

If Neil and Natasha had only sat down at this point and talked it through, they both would have realised how deeply in love and committed to each other they were, but instead both went a little quiet and allowed the rift between them to worsen.

Neil turned around and walked away, clearing his head with a tour of the site. After watching the bikes return from the ride out, he returned to the tent and said hi to Natasha as she had woken up. "Coming up to the main tent? The first band is just about to come on."

"Not right now," she replied, "I'll come on up later; I'm not really up for it yet."

Neil felt her tone was a trifle abrupt but let it slide and shuffled on up to the main marquee, feeling a little subdued.

The bands were in full swing when Natasha came into the marquee. She was dressed in her leather jeans and pullover. Despite her attempt to dress dowdy, Neil still thought she looked knock-out.

He was sitting at the end of a long trestle table filled with bikers. "I've saved you a seat," he said.

"Thanks," she replied, keeping up the distinctly cool air.

Why didn't he just ask her what was wrong? Sometimes people need their heads banging together.

Natasha sat down and Neil thought, *Well if she's not talking to me, I won't bother talking to her.* And so the evening went on.

Natasha didn't for a second think that her cool attitude was contributing to the negativity between her and Neil. In her mind, this just reinforced what she was thinking. Come to think of it, Neil had not taken a lot of interest in Monica, Natasha's daughter. All he ever wanted to do was fuck.

She made up her mind that when they got home she was going to break away from Neil, and Brian, find a place for her and the baby on their own. "Damn all men," she swore under her breath.

Just then, one of the Dutch guys from the night before sat down next to Natasha and tried to engage her in small talk. Such are the stupid mind games that lovers play; she started flirting with him to provoke a reaction from Neil. She succeeded; he ignored her.

The Dutch guy rolled up a joint, took a long pull on it and handed it to Natasha. She, having no interest in smoking and even less idea of 'toker's etiquette', handed the joint to Neil. He then mischievously handed it to the next person. The joint travelled the length and breadth of the table. By the time it returned to its rightful owner, he didn't have enough left to fill a gnat's haversack.

He stubbed it out in his palm and stormed away, not a happy bunny. Neil laughed, Natasha laughed and he put his arm around her. The atmosphere warmed, but only a little.

The rally still had a few surprises up its sleeve, not least of which was when Natasha was voted sexiest woman at the rally and had to go up on stage for the prize giving.

The wet tee shirt competition was just getting started and Natasha was coming under considerable pressure to take part. She stoically refused but out of her earshot, Neil had to endure a lot of banter about her from guys who had been watching the pole dance routine earlier. How the mood had changed for them both in the space of a few hours.

That night was the first time they slept together without making love

CHAPTER 23

The longest night

The following morning started overcast and dismal. The motley crew of half-dressed bikers managed with some degree of difficulty to de-camp from their tents, unwashed, undressed and very probably unloved by all but their mothers. Dressed only in a pair of stained Y-fronts and German Para boots with the laces undone, one of the Dutch bikers managed to stagger out of his tent, standing bolt upright, taking the top pole out and getting tangled in the guy ropes before falling straight down like a felled tree on top of his neighbouring tent.

"Oi, you clown," came the exclamation from the neighbour who'd just been woken from his stupor by 16 stone of fat Dutchman landing in his lap.

Neil looked over at the ensuing carnage and remarked, "Twat."

The bikers suited up with the usual banter, hopping around from foot to foot as they tried to fit sleep swollen feet into nasty wet Army boots. Wet tents were unceremoniously bundled into kit bags and strapped to cold, damp seats. New friends and old said their tearful goodbyes, complete with promises not to leave it too long before the next get together.

The ride back home was miserable. It rained horizontal sleet from the moment they disembarked the ferry. Tim set his usual hare's pace. Neil and Natasha, frozen to the bone, decided they could no longer keep up the speed, so Neil waved to Tim to pull into the services. They pulled off the motorway to have a last coffee together and say goodbye.

"We are going to stay awhile and thaw out properly," said Neil, "you guys can press on without us, we'll be fine on our own."

"Are your brakes holding up OK?" Tim questioned, concerned.

"Yeah, brake fluid ressy is staying full and the single calliper is doing the job as well as can be expected. She'll be fine," reassured Neil.

"OK then, we do have a bit further to go than you, we'll press on for the M4 then and take the direct route home."

Star and Natasha said their goodbyes with hugs and a promise to keep in touch; Tim and Neil did that thumb grip hand shake thing, followed by a manly one-armed hug which terminated in a thump on the back. Typical overtly heterosexual biker gesture.

Neil decided to go splash his boots before throwing a frozen leg back over the bike. As he made his way into the otherwise deserted loo, he noticed the truck drivers' showers at the back of the loo. If he could manage to pull at least one towel out of their luggage roll they could warm up with a hot shower.

He went back out through the relentless rain to the bike without saying anything to Natasha and managed to extract one damp towel from the pack and scurried back in to the warmth of the truck stop.

"How do you fancy a treat?" he asked Natasha.

"What kind of treat do you have in mind?" she replied, one eyebrow raised sceptically.

He winked and explained.

"A hot shower? You are kidding me," she exclaimed.

Neil replied, "I have a towel ready, there is shower gel in the cubical. Seems to me it would be rude not to."

"And it won't be rude if we do?" Natasha smiled. "Hell why not, what's the worst that can happen?"

Neil went into the gents' first. "Coast is clear," he called to Natasha, "come on in." He had the cubicle door open. There was a small wooden bench just out of the range of the shower-head with enough room for both of them to undress and stow their damp clothes.

The water was scalding hot; the soothing warmth caused little goosebumps all over their bodies. As the skin on Natasha's breasts became taut in reaction to the temperature change, her nipples hardened up and grew to the size of cherry stones. Neil was massaging shower gel into her shoulders. She turned her back to him and he wrapped his arms around her in a tight embrace, bringing the urgency of his erection into contact with the cold flesh of her rear. Neil was massaging her nipples with his soapy fingers before following the waterfall of cascading warm water down to the valley of her sex. With his wet foamy hands he parted the lips of her sex and started to tease her pleasure spot with his long sensitive fingers. Natasha raised her arms and embraced him as his sensuous lips brushed gently across her shoulders and the nape of her neck.

"Make love to me Neil," she softly whispered to him. He responded with gentleness hitherto unseen in their lovemaking. Lifting her in his arms and gently resting her back against the tiled wall, he entered her.

Their lovemaking was slow and tender, charged for the first time with emotion rather than lust. There, in the confines of the small cubicle with the steam and the water flowing over their coupled bodies, it was an almost spiritual merging of bodies and emotions. The spasms of their mutual climaxes subsided, sobbing, their emotions cleansed, their love once again pure.

CHAPTER 24

Return to Gomorrah

Neil pulled the bike up outside his mum and dad's. Natasha dismounted and held the gate open for him to safely stow the bike in the garden.

The noise awoke Neil's folks and the downstairs and porch area burst into light.

As Neil's soaked and frozen fingers struggled with the bungees holding the gear to the seat fin, Natasha made for the door, eager to be reunited with Monica.

Neil's heart soared at the wealth of affection between Natasha and her child. Lesser men would have viewed the child as a threat but somewhere deep in his psyche, at an almost genetic level, his subconscious was scoring her as a perfect potential mother for his own offspring one day.

"Neil, you realise that I have to go back to my house soon don't you?" she questioned.

"No, I don't. Why the hell would you want to go back there?" Neil pouted.

"It's *my* home Neil, all my stuff is there, all Monica's stuff. I can't just stay on at mum's, living from a suitcase. Brian seems to have gone off again, nobody's paying the rent. I should go back home, otherwise I could lose the house.

Exhausted from the journey and the weather, they fell into bed and slept like the dead. The following day, after an enjoyable lunch with Neil's parents, they packed Neil's car up and said their sad goodbyes. It would be back to their ducking and diving again after having shared such close and intimate moments of abandon.

Despite taking so many steps forward, they seemed destined to have to keep going back.

Natasha's peace did not last long; a few days after the break away Brian returned, and seemed determined not to give her a moment's peace. He was around her like a rash. His attitude was more aggressive than she had ever known it to be. He would follow her from room to room, constantly try to trap her, grab her into his odious embrace. Even meeting at Julie's had become tense and fraught as Brian had taken to following Natasha to Julie's every time Neil's car was in the vicinity.

Neil had come face to face with Brian on one of these occasions; the man made his skin crawl. He either suspected Neil was more than just Julie's boyfriend or his ilk just didn't trust anyone. It was hard to know with a man like Brian. He didn't speak to Neil or even look him in the eyes. Nevertheless, whenever his back was turned, Neil could feel Brian Dix's eyes burning into him.

After they had been back about a week, Neil and Natasha managed to meet up at her mum's.

Natasha was noticeably shaken. She hugged Neil close and said, "Brian pinned me down on the bed today, he tried to force his hand between my legs. I swear if Monica hadn't woken up screaming, he would have raped me."

Neil was beside himself with rage, he wanted to go round there and beat the filthy bastard to death for touching the woman he loved, but she wouldn't hear of it.

"He threatened to take Monica," she cried. "Neil he means it. We have to do something. I can't let him take my child."

"What do you mean, take Monica? Take her where?" interrupted Neil.

"Back to Ireland," she cried. "If he takes her back to that bloody place, I'll never see her again. You don't know what it's like over there Neil. They're like a load of red-necks, he'll take her back to the bosom of his pikey relatives in the bloody wilderness and I'll never see her again. You just don't understand," she sobbed.

"What about the police?" protested Neil. "There are ways and means, injunctions, restraining orders."

Natasha interjected, "The police, puh-lease. Neil grow up, Brian's a traveller, the police won't even get involved unless they kill someone, even then, if it's not one of their own they won't give him up. Sorry babe but you really have no clue. If he takes her to Ireland, the police will have no power at all." Her voice dropped low, "I think he may have IRA connections."

"Oh good God almighty. This just gets better and better," Neil retorted.

Just as one door closes, another opens and a timely opportunity was about to present itself which would buy them some time, and offer a chance to cement their relationship for the future.

CHAPTER 25

Deliverance

"Natasha?" called Neil. "My lot are getting together for a family holiday up at Hunstanton. We would all love it if you would come with us?"

"Where on earth is Hunstanton?" she asked

"It's up on the East coast, near Great Yarmouth," he answered.

"I don't know Neil," she hesitated, "what is your family going to think of me, baby in tow?"

"They will love you just like I do. Trust me, it's all arranged, we don't even need a tent, we can stay in Mum and Dad's awning."

"Oh, I don't know," she procrastinated, "won't it be a bit weird?"

"Please, for me? We need this, it will give us time to decide our next move and get you out of that bastard's reach, at least for a short while," said Neil.

"I guess you're right. Maybe if I stay away from him enough, he'll give up and bugger off. OK I'll come." She giggled, cheering up immensely at the thought of being alone with Neil again.

Brian had been making himself scarce since his assault on her. She presumed he was back over in Ireland or on one of his many crime excursions around the country. In either case, it was easier for them to be together when he wasn't around so they counted their blessings. Brian had acquired a diesel van for himself, so at least she had her car back.

She drove to her mum's house where they transferred Monica and luggage into Neil's company runabout. After some cussing and swearing, trying to fit the huge wooden cot into the small boot, they set off in the direction of Hunstanton and the promise of some peace and tranquillity. Neil had neglected to tell her that she would be spending the latter part of the week alone with his family. He was obliged to drive all the way back to Exeter for Wednesday and Thursday to see his paper to bed. The earliest he would be able to return was Friday. He would give her this bad news once they'd settled in.

After enduring an excruciating five hour crawl in the Friday traffic, Monica, bless her, was sleeping like a baby should. Natasha, on the other hand, was becoming tired and irritable. "Are we there yet?" she moaned.

"'Kin' hell, you're worse than the baby," complained Neil. "Yes we are nearly there, or here, if you like. Geographically speaking, as we have just arrived."

"Thank goodness," she pouted.

Neil stretched his legs and strolled into the reception. "We're booked in staying with the Curland party?" The receptionist indicated to him where his family were on a large site plan mounted on the wall.

Neil and his adopted family rolled up to the little encampment his family had established.

Introductions were made. Neil's brother-in-law Brin, who was just heading off armed with rubber rings, lilos and three young, sullen looking girls, took an instant and obvious shine to Natasha. "He's harmless enough," Neil reassured her.

Brin said, "Hurry up and get set up, then you can meet us up at the pool. Let our girls get their hands on that baby, you'll have plenty of time to yourselves," he chuckled.

After setting up the bedrooms and the cot, having a cup of tea and a chat with Neil's mum and dad, Neil and Natasha decided to take Brin up on his offer and wandered up to the pool with their cossies. Monica was still sleeping soundly so Neil's mum offered to keep an eye on her while they went for a dip. With gentle persuasion from Neil, who was well overheated from the trip, they rolled their gear into towels and made their way up to the pool.

Brin was attempting to teach Neil to dive in, which basically meant he was calling Neil a wuss for not diving in. Neil responded with a half arsed attempt to get his uncoordinated body to enter the water without a huge belly flop, followed by a tidal wave and choking, drowning motions. Second attempt: Neil was breaking the surface, tears streaming down his face when he saw a vision entering the water from the side of the pool. Natasha was wearing a white swimsuit, flattering her taut voluptuous figure; her hair was tied back in a red ribbon. As she walked down the steps into the pool, Neil's eyes nearly popped out of his head. He swam over to Natasha and stood between her and Brin who looked as though he had seen a ghost. "Where did you get that swimsuit?" Neil barked.

"From East of Eden," she replied, somewhat confused. Neil pointed down. Natasha's eyes widened with horror as she realised the costume had become completely translucent when wet. Every man in the pool was staring at her with his mouth open. The bathing suit was so see through now that even the lips of Natasha's sex were clearly visible.

Well, the sex goddess look wasn't really appropriate for a family pool so without making eye contact with Brin, Natasha made a quick exit from the pool, giving the horny dads a long look at her pert, almost naked ass as she tried to hurry back to the changing rooms without wiggling. She returned a while later wearing a slightly more respectable bikini. Brin never said a word but she had gained a devoted admirer.

CHAPTER 26

First encounter

Neil decided, when he returned to Hunstanton, he would pop the big question to Natasha. He invited his friend and former house-mate Colin out for a chat and they spent a rather pleasant lunchtime in a local pub. It was a rare opportunity for Neil to relax. Time spent with Natasha was exhilarating and exciting but seldom relaxing, with him constantly looking over his shoulder.

"I'm moving in with Katie's parents," Colin announced, "it will be easier for me to find work over Bristol way. Can I pop over this weekend and clear all my stuff out?"

Colin had been dating Katie for about a year. She had stayed at the cottage many times when Colin lived there. She and Neil got along famously.

"I'm fixing to be away the whole weekend," replied Neil, "but you are welcome to come over while I'm gone. Here you go, take my spare key. You can use the van too if you like."

"That would certainly make life easier," replied Colin, "I'm not insured to drive a van though, shame!"

"Ahah," Neil grinned, "that's where you're wrong. In Germany, the vehicle is insured, not the driver. The van is registered for a few months yet, as long as you're license covers it, you can drive it!"

"That's a bloody sight more sensible than the system we've got here. Cheers Neil, I will borrow it."

"Oh and Colin, feel free to doss over if you like, you won't be getting much privacy at Katie's folks'," Neil said with a wink. "I'll catch up with you later Colin," he said, "I'd better get back to work. See you when I get back. Say hi to Katie from me." Neil hesitated for a moment, thought about mentioning to Colin what he had planned, then reconsidered, deciding to let him know when he had an answer.

When he was in his early twenties, Neil had been a member of the Army REME rally cross team. His knowledge of German and his good understanding with the local community had helped him to establish the use of a part disused aggregate quarry, just outside of the garrison boundary where they could keep their rally cars and get in a good deal of valuable practice. One day, representatives of 'The Regiment', as they were fondly known in those days, made an approach to Neil: Special Forces, SAS. They were over from the UK staying on garrison, taking part in an exercise and were looking to kick back and enjoy a bit of R&R before flying back to the UK. Of course, they weren't SAS, they were Sappers, bomb squad, whatever. You just knew.

They had heard about the rally cross team and were up for having a play in a quarry, that is, they would welcome the chance to hone their evasive driving skills. Neil was given the time off to escort them to the quarry and look after them while they were there. He wasn't complaining. They were a proper good bunch of guys with a finely honed squaddie sense of humour, so Neil didn't mind babysitting them a bit.

The moves they were pulling in the rally cars were truly awesome, proper stunt driving like Neil had only ever seen in the cinema. One of the moves they pulled was along one of the quarry tracks where there was a sheer cliff on one side and a flooded lake on the other. They drove two cars towards one another along this narrow stretch of track. Just before collision was inevitable and way too late to stop, one of the cars, travelling at considerable speed, turned into the cliff face. Neil expected the car to impact the cliff wall with devastating consequences, but instead it rode up the wall, and then turned back onto the track after the obstacle was cleared.

Neil was awestruck. "How the fuck did you do that?" Neil asked.

"Want me to show you?" replied the Jedi.

"Too right," replied Neil, throwing caution and common sense to the wind.

"It's simple," said his new-found hero, "nine times out of ten, the cliff or embankment will have a slight slope to it, as long as it does, you will be up and away. We do this all the time back in Hereford, scares the shit out of the locals. Two things to remember; watch out for storm drains, they will fuck you up and don't try it in a Rangie (Range Rover) as those softies will bounce right off and have you roof surfing right into your unsuspecting victim. Any motor with half stiff suspension will be OK though.

Ay up." He shouted as the world was suddenly on its side before softly dropping back to the track again. "Don't go too slow and don't stay up too long," he laughed. "Them's the rules."

They stopped and switched seats for Neil to have a go. Neil never suspected for a second that what he learned on that thoroughly agreeable day was to probably save his life one day.

Leaving the pub, Neil decided to take a short cut back to Exeter through the lanes. He was absent-mindedly rummaging through his cassette tapes in the glovebox when he caught sight of a beaten up Ford Escort filling up his rear view mirror; the guy was really tailgating him, a stupid way to behave in these narrow, steep-sided lanes, as you may have to stop suddenly meeting oncoming traffic.

No sooner had he thought it than it happened; a white Sherpa van, moving fast, coming towards him, braked across the lane in front of him.

Neil had pulled up quite quickly, leaving a gap between him and the Sherpa of about thirty yards. The guy in the van didn't look like he was going to reverse, so Neil glanced in his mirror to see what the guy behind him was doing. "Oh shit," he exclaimed as he saw Brian Dix stepping out of the Ford, carrying what looked like a sawn off shotgun. He raised the weapon to shoulder height. Without thinking, Neil gunned his company ride's engine, heading straight for the Sherpa van. The van driver, one of Brian's traveller cronies, confident that Neil was trapped, had got out of the van and was walking towards him.

The guy shit his pants when he saw Neil driving full chat towards him. At the last second Neil hit the embankment, and like a dream the Nova rode up the cutting past the traveller and his Sherpa van.

Two things went through Neil's adrenaline filled brain; don't stay up too long and watch out for storm drains. *Bang.* The shockwave coursed through the Vauxhall as it careered through the drain, leaving half its bumper behind.

He was fortunate to have made it over the storm drain and back down onto terra-firma without a puncture or worse. Now he had a chance to put some miles between himself and his assailants.

He drove straight to the police station in Exeter and explained what had happened. The desk sergeant took all the particulars then offered Neil his advice; "We will attempt to apprehend Mr Dix but, in the meantime if you could stay with friends or family: travellers have an uncanny ability to disappear at will and could prove extremely elusive."

"I'm staying up near Great Yarmouth on holiday for the week; hopefully you will have caught up with him by then." Neil furnished the Sergeant with his details and the name of the site he was staying on.

With all the excitement and tension, Neil completely forgot about Colin staying in his house.

CHAPTER 27

A decent proposal

"I've had a call from the police Neil," his advertising manager advised. "I think you should take a leave of absence until your adversary has been apprehended." Neil's boss, Yvonne, was aware of the volatile nature of his love life.

"Can I be spared at the moment? We're understaffed as it is, and I'm behind with my calls."

"You're not much use to us at the moment Neil; I think we can honestly say you're somewhat distracted."

"I don't want to go losing my job right now that would be the cherry on the cake, really blow my chances of getting Natasha out of this shit."

"I'll square things away with the shirts Neil, don't you worry. You're a popular member of the team, and you're a good salesman. The job will be waiting once you sort all this out."

"Thank you Yvonne, that takes a load off my mind." Neil didn't tell her about the car; that would keep.

He decided to drive straight up to Hunstanton that night. Determined not to allow Mr Dix to scupper his plans, he drove to a local 'fine wines' merchant and picked up a bottle of Moët & Chandon.

After a trepidatious visit home for a shower and change of clothes, an apprehensive Neil set off on the five-hour trip back up to Hunstanton and relative peace and security.

Darkness had fallen when an exhausted Neil pulled into the camp-site. The home fires were burning at the Curland encampment. Hearing his car, Natasha came running out to greet him. She wrapped her arms around him, tears flooding down her face. "I've missed you so much," she said.

"God, I've missed you too," Neil replied, "you have no idea how much."

Neil's parents were standing in the entrance of the awning, smiling at the obvious warmth shared by their youngest child and his new-found love.

Neil thought, *It's now or never,* and went down on one knee in front of his lady-love. "Natasha."

A look of total shock came over her face as it began to dawn on her what was about to happen. "Will you do me the immense honour of becoming my wife?" he croaked, his throat dry, voice failing just a little.

Natasha was staring at him with her mouth open in suspended animation.

He spoke again, this time calmly and with warmth and affection in his voice: "Natasha, will you marry me?"

The spell was broken, Natasha burst into floods of tears. "Oh Neil, I love you so much, of course I'll marry you."

Neil decided not to update Natasha on the Brian situation, at least not yet. He had decided, now she was his fiancée, she would be moving in with him as soon as they got home, come what may. They would look for a new home out of the area as soon as possible; get them out of Brian's familiar stomping ground and away from all his cronies. In the meantime, Neil had a little errand to run up in this neck of the woods.

Explaining to Natasha that he'd had a little incident with the car, he excused himself to go off and see if he could find a scrapyard for a replacement bumper. In fact, he was visiting his old armed forces biker buddy in nearby Wisbech who he knew would be able to help him out with a little 'personal security'.

Goose, pleased to see him, asked no questions when Neil explained his predicament.

"Here you go." He handed Neil a small black pistol. "Ex German Army, it's completely clean. If you use it, be sure to lose it. Eight rounds in the magazine, you know the drill."

As Neil went to leave, Goose said, "Buddy, you need help, you just give us a call, we'll be there for you, you know it." It was reassuring to hear. The military made real friends; the 'Booze Brothers' bikers were friends for life.

Natasha and Monica were Neil's family now and he intended to protect them, whatever it took.

When he got back to the site, Natasha had decided they should go out alone together to celebrate their engagement. Mum and Dad would mind Monica and the happy couple could spend a little quality time together.

They found a small pub with a large DJ, the guy must have weighed at least thirty stone. Poured into a tiny typist's chair behind a row of lights, he was obviously a local legend as the place was really rocking. The custom was to play slow songs at the end of the evening for couples to have a grope. Neil and Natasha enjoyed a great evening dancing, drinking and boogying with the crowd. When the music slowed, they stayed on the dance floor for a bit of smooching and grinding. Gloria Estefan's 'Can't Stay Away From You' came on the decks; Natasha started to softly press into Neil's broad chest.

"What's wrong?" said Neil, wiping a tear from her eye. "Why are you upset?"

"I'm not upset silly, I'm just happy, the words of the song remind me of how much we've been through. It's about a girl sacrificing everything for love."

Neil hugged her to him and listened to the words; the song described the emotional roller coaster they had ridden to get here. It was to be their 'special song'.

Walking along the promenade on their way back to the site, Natasha spotted a fortune-teller.

"Shall we?" she asked.

"You can, I've had enough of travellers for the time being thanks," Neil sniggered.

Natasha was in with the clairvoyant for about ten minutes. When she came out, she was smiling all over her face.

"Well, what did she say?" questioned Neil.

"Never you mind," she replied. "Nothing you need worry about, at least, not now."

Neil couldn't help but notice how Natasha seemed to be walking with a pronounced spring in her step.

As they lay together that evening, Natasha said to Neil, "Where should we go on our honeymoon? I've always fancied the Greek islands. Sand, sea and sex. Lots and lots of sex."

Neil replied, "Sounds like a plan to me, as long as we can hire a motorbike and take off into the mountains."

"Crete then, if you want mountains," she replied.

"Crete it is then, Crete on a motorbike."

The honeymoon seemed a million miles away from their present reality. Everybody needs a dream to cling to.

It was dark when they pulled up outside her mum's house to retrieve Natasha's car. Her mum rushed to the doorway and urgently beckoned them inside. Before they had a chance to share their exciting news, she said, "I have some grave news."

"What's up?" said Neil looking concerned.

"It's Colin," interrupted Natasha's stepfather, "he's in hospital, he's been severely beaten."

CHAPTER 28

The Holocaust cometh

"Neil's given me the keys to the cottage for the weekend," said Colin, "we deserve a bit of a break. What say we catch a movie, order a take-away, bottle of bubbly....." The last part of the sentence tailed off with a wink.

"Oh you think so do you?" Katie teased. Katie, slightly older than Colin in her early twenties, was one of those 'earthy' types who, rather than celebrate their beauty, tend to cloak their assets under a blanket of frumpiness.

Colin smooched around behind her and put his arms around her waist. With one hand lightly resting on her belly, just above her pubic mound, he rubbed his groin against her bottom and sang in his best sexy voice, "Sylvia?" acting out the Patrick Swayze and Jennifer Grey scene from the film 'Dirty Dancing'.

Catching on quickly, Katie glanced up and sang, "Yes Mickey?" They began to sing the boy-girl lines on cue.

"How do you call your lover boy?"

"Come here lover boy."

"And if he doesn't answer?"

Katie turned on her toes gliding away from him as she sang, "Oh lover boy."

Colin, totally immersed in his role, slid down on his knees and strummed an imaginary guitar singing, "Baby, oh baby, my sweet baby, you're the one!"

"Hey," Katie complained, "that was my line *and* you missed out a chunk!" She winked at him and cooed, "You'll have to do better than that this weekend if you want to seduce me."

Colin winked again and said, "That's it then, you're on a promise. I'd better go and get some bubbly."

It was the first time the couple had been alone together since Colin had moved in with Katie's family. Katie was a bit prudish and just couldn't bring herself to make love in her childhood home with her mum and dad in the next room. Secretly, she was just as eager as Colin for them to make the weekend go with a bang.

As Colin brought their bags in from the car, Katie opened the taps on the faucet and began running herself a luxurious bath. Hanging on the drier, over the radiator, was a collection of freshly washed sexy garments belonging to Natasha. Katie ran her hands over the silky smalls and a wicked thought coursed through her mind. *No, I couldn't, could I?* she thought, and then resolved to prepare a little surprise for her man.

The movie had been a 'chick flick' starring the usual suspects from the other side of the pond. Usual powerful storyline; boy meets geeky girl, girl hates boy, boy is horrible to her, she discovers that with some hair product she's beautiful, boy falls for girl, they go to prom. The tears of happiness were streaming down Katie's face by the end of the film.

Result! thought Colin, steering her back towards the car for his orchestrated night of seduction.

Colin disappeared out the back of the house, into the yard and brought an armful of dry logs from Neil's store. He busied himself setting an atmospheric log fire in the hearth. Katie had slipped past him in the doorway and gone upstairs to dress in something more 'comfortable'.

By the time she returned, Colin had a small smoky fire going.

Katie called out from the hallway, "Oh lover boy, come here lover boy," before thrusting a long, slim, stocking clad leg through the door and curling her thigh around the door in a sexy, provocative manner. She called from the hallway, "Put some music on, lover-boy." He was tempted to find something rude like 'Je T'aime' but in the end, decided the 'Dirty Dancing' compilation would be perfect.

As the sleazy music started, she exposed a little more leg through the door. Colin had never seen Katie act in a sexually aggressive manner before. She had gone the whole hog, availing herself of Natasha's make up and lipstick as well. She never wore anything more than a smear of lip gloss. The sight of his demure Katie dressed in stockings and suspenders, heavily made up like a geisha, nearly blew Colin away.

She had a trim little figure, not quite as tall as Natasha but with a firm heavy bosom and wasp thin waist. She filled Natasha's underwear impressively. Colin was suitably in awe and gently ran his hands over her curves before crushing her to him and hungrily seeking her lips with his.

They rolled around on the hearth rug, the yellow and orange hue from the fire threw dancing shades of light across their naked bodies as their desperate desire gathered pace before erupting into a noisy climax of repressed sexual energy.

Colin stroked Katie's hair and remarked, "Wow! That was a bit quicker than I expected."

She smiled up at him contented.

"You're a wild woman; I don't think I know you at all."

"Would you like to get to know me better?" she purred.

"Oh God...Would I?" He scooped her up in his arms and took the stairs two at a time, throwing her down on the bed. Either she was possessed by some devilish demon, or the previous lack of privacy and excessive consumption of champagne had brought some hitherto concealed wanton slut to the surface.

Colin was young, his batteries re-charged in seconds. Lying on the bed in front of him, wide open, willing, dressed only in suspenders and stockings, was a complete stranger, a stranger who wanted him. The best part was, his girlfriend wouldn't mind!

The banging on the front door was loud and insistent. Colin couldn't believe the bad timing and cursed Neil for not telling everyone that he was away. His attempts to jam his erect penis into his boxer shorts had Katie in fits of laughter. Colin cursed again, hoping this hadn't blown the mood. "You just hold that thought," he said. "Don't you dare move a muscle, I will get rid of them and be right back to sort you out properly,"

She giggled, "Hurry back, lover-boy." She licked her lips and thrust her naked pelvis up to show him what he was missing.

"Aaaaaargh!" he exclaimed before skipping down the steps, this time, three at a time!

As he turned the lever on the Yale lock the person on the other side had already turned the door handle and the door hit Colin square in the chest, knocking the wind out of him. Before he could react, he was struck in the face with a blunt object.

The light was already fading in his eyes when he heard his assailants shouting, "Smash his fecking balls in." He smelt acrid tobacco smoke breath as one of his attackers brought his face down to his and growled in an unmistakable Irish drawl, "This'll teach you not to put your mucky little paws on what's not yours."

One of the other thugs said, "When we've finished with you there won't be anything left to stir your tea with."

Mercifully, darkness had engulfed Colin's consciousness as the first sickening blows rained down.

Two of them took turns laying into Colin as the third one ran up the stairs.

Katie was in a state of shock as Brian Dix, dressed in a ski mask, burst into the room. Paralysed with fear, she was still lying on the bed, waiting for Colin's return. Only, her expression had changed from lust to abject terror!

Brian paused as he surveyed the terrified woman, lying on the bed naked. Katie feared the worst but could not move a muscle. He obviously reconsidered his first reaction, deciding he wasn't here to rape. Nevertheless, he drank in the moment of absolute control he had, standing as he was baseball bat in hand.

Remembering what was taking place downstairs, he turned and ran for the stairs shouting, "Oy, he's the wrong bloke. Let's get the feck out of here. We've got the wrong buffer."

The two thugs in the living room stopped their assault on Colin and stood back. Showing no remorse at all for their innocent victim, one shouted into Colin's deaf ears. "You just got fecking lucky mate, so you did. I was just about to shove your fecking ball bag back inside your belly. Tell your buffer mates to lay off our women!"

Still pumping with adrenaline and aggression, Brian burst into the room. Seeing Colin lying prone on the floor, he took a mighty swing with his steel toe-capped boots between Colin's legs before turning and strolling out of the door.

It was a full ten minutes before the power of movement returned to Katie's terrified body. She gingerly pushed the open front door shut. As she turned, she saw the reflection of Colin's inert, prostrate body in the mirror above the hearth. Katie's scream was enough to bring the neighbours running.

CHAPTER 29

Damaged

"What?" exclaimed Neil.

The colour drained from Natasha's face. "Brian," she whispered with a resigned tone.

"Oh my God," said Neil, "I'd better get to the hospital."

Katie was at the hospital with Colin, she was unharmed but sedated.

Katie's dad, obviously livid and in a state of shock, recounted the story to Neil. "Clearly Katie wasn't who they were expecting to find and they took off out of the front door."

"How is Colin?" questioned Neil.

"He's bashed up quite badly. They broke a couple of his ribs and nearly smashed in his windpipe." Katie's dad's gestured for Neil to follow him into a day room. "They assaulted him so badly Neil, there is so much bruising to his genitals, the doctors won't know if he will recover fully until all the swelling goes down. His tone became serious. "What's going on Neil?"

"I can't explain right now, it's complicated. I'm so sorry that Colin and Katie have been dragged into it."

"The police are going to be eager to talk to you Neil; you had better get your ass down the police station and face the music," Katie's dad finished.

Neil phoned the police in Exeter. After a long-winded conversation he put down the phone and said to Katie's dad, "I have to go to the police station tomorrow and make a statement."

He called Natasha, who had stayed at her mother's with Monica. He glossed over the seriousness of Colin's injuries, sparing her that.

"Is it OK if we stay over at your mum's tonight? I am too tired to face going home now."

"God Neil," Natasha cried, "that could have been us. Poor Colin, poor Katie, it must have been terrible." She could hardly speak for sobbing. "Neil, this is all my fault, they didn't deserve this."

Neil could feel the anger welling inside him as he replied, "We don't deserve it either, your ex is a fucking mad dog, he needs shooting." Then he added, "This changes nothing Natasha, we are still getting married, I just hope that bastard gets what's coming to him." There was a pause in which Neil could hear Natasha sobbing. "I'm staying here at the hospital for a bit, I want to be here when Colin wakes up. I need to be with you tonight. Could you wait up for me? I need to hold you." Neil was close to tears.

"I love you Neil."

"I love you too, wait up for me…. Please." Neil replaced the receiver and returned to his vigil beside his best friend's bed.

CHAPTER 30

On the lam

Thanks to his assault on Colin, Brian was now facing serious assault charges. The police are notoriously reluctant to pursue travellers but Colin's parents were well connected and pressure was being brought to bear from higher echelons.

This time, Neil was shown into a private room at the police station. The authorities were obviously taking things more seriously now.

The detective walked Neil to his car with a grave look on his face. "So, you say that this man may even be connected to the IRA in some way. Well we definitely have actual bodily harm on your friend which we can pick him up for, we'll speak with the intelligence   services and the RUC in Ireland, see if we can dig anything up. We can also contact Interpol and see if he has anything outstanding in the Republic. In the meantime, I will have to interview Mr Dix's wife, see if she can throw any light on where he will have gone to ground. She may be able to give us some info on his associates in Ireland. The Garda may be persuaded to help if he has any priors over in the Republic. They do work with us against criminals you know," he reassured Neil.

"She's not his wife, she's my fiancée," Neil corrected.

"Sorry, of course. Perhaps you could bring the young lady in tomorrow, the sooner we take this character off the streets the better." Neil shook his hand. "Look Neil," he added, "we can't offer you much in the way of protection against this guy, he seems like a serious player though, so off the record," he hesitated, "I would take some precautions to protect yourself, in case he comes gunning for you."

"What do you suggest?" asked Neil.

"Officially, I would try to make like a tree."

Neil raised an eyebrow. "Bark?" he questioned incredulously, obviously offended by the inappropriate remark.

"I meant leave," the detective added, somewhat embarrassed by his own insensitivity. "Sorry Neil, I realise this is no time for humour. Try to make yourselves scarce. Look, this guy you're messing with is a serious criminal, possibly even a terrorist. Unofficially, I would get myself some personal protection." To cover himself, he added, "And I didn't say that."

Neil left the police station feeling somewhat less confident than when he had arrived.

CHAPTER 31

Scuppered

"It's all to cock Danny boy," Brian Dix complained. "The feckin' missus is messin' with some buffer an' I've lost me feckin' safe house, not to mention me feckin' kid and me warm bed." The caravan rocked as Brian thumped a fist into the table.

"Sort the feckin' Gajo out boy! Off the fecker!"

"Aye, Danny, but the timing's all wrong to be sure. Now I'm about with a bounty on me head an' I've still to reach out to the Roma down in Plymouth. This puts the feckin' cat among me pigeons for sure Danny so it does."

"Ye didn't kill the lad Dixie, the law won't be lookin' too hard for ye. Just keep it low, let's us get on down to Plymouth and do the business, then you can sort out yer domestic. If all goes tits up, be away back to the homeland till the shit dies down."

"Aye Danny boy, I'll sort out the slut's feckin' lover boy before I duck out, ye can be sure o' that. Shit Danny, I'm between a rock and a hard place on this now, that bitch was me feckin' cover on the mainland, without her I'm lookin' over me shoulder from here on in."

"Ach, Dixie, there'll always be a place fer you to hang yer hat here by us, don't ye' be worryin' yerself," Danny assured him. "Now let's get on and take care of the business with the Roma so's we can get this thing movin' on and see us some love flowin' into our pockets."

"Aye Danny, this other thing will have to wait."

The run down to Plymouth went off without a hitch

The Roma family had moved again from their pitch down at the docks, but were not difficult to track down.

As luck would have it, they nearly drove headlong into a white pick up truck containing the brothers Brian had helped in the street outside the bar those months hence.

The window on the pick up slowly wound down. "Well I'll be," the largest of the three lads exclaimed. "It's our farmec norocos!"

All three of the lads broke into smiles and chatter in their native tongue as they recognised Brian Dix.

"I don't speak yer lingo lads but we share a heritage, can we go somewhere fer a little chat?"

"I said you is our guardian angel!" the boy re-iterated, in English, offering his hand through the open window for Brian to shake. "I'm Bo, these are my brothers Pit and Stevo

"Ach, the name's Brian, this here grizzly bear is me man Danny," Brian dismissed, shaking each of the eagerly offered hands in turn. "I was just in the right place at the right time. Them Gajos needed takin' down." Brian put on a serious tone, "Lads, can you take us to see yer Rom Baro, we got a little business proposition to put to yer family, if you'd be so kind as to make the formal introductions.

The meeting went better than could have been hoped for. The Rom Baro was an elder, well connected at the races and the horse fairs up and down the country. With him on board, the Provos would get their wish; the Libyan weapons would hit the streets in a big way, from the Yardies, the football 'firms' the feuding Angel and Outlaw gangs down to the common street hoods. The English would drown in a wave of violence which could potentially rock the Government in Westminster, stretching their resources and weakening their presence in Northern Ireland, thus strengthening the cause. Brian's work was done, now he could move on to his other issues.

CHAPTER 32

Crisis

Neil decided to move Natasha and Monica in with him while they looked for a suitable home out of the area. Everything had taken on a more sinister air as the gravity of the situation was beginning to sink in with Neil. He now realised where Natasha's earlier desperation came from.

The stress was beginning to tell on Neil. His lunchtime gym sessions were becoming intense.

Neil's work colleague, Phil, was sat on an exercise bike next to the free weights where Neil was pumping well over his usual weight. "What's happening with your routine Neil? You dropping the cardio vascular completely? I haven't seen you on the machines in ages, you just power lifting now?" his friend asked.

"Just trying to bulk up a bit mate, that's all," replied Neil.

"Not meaning to teach Granny to suck eggs mate, but you shouldn't lay off the cardio vascular completely, that's a recipe for disaster. Everything in moderation mate," Phil cautiously advised.

"I appreciate your advice Phil; it's just this whole Brian business has got me so psyched out. I don't know what the bastard is going to try next. I feel like a sitting fucking duck. Working out is the only thing I feel like I'm in control of."

"Well try to keep it together mate, punishing your body in here without proper warming up won't help your cause, you should know how it works; develop your breathing and stamina in harmony with bulking up otherwise you will burn out."

It was advice that Neil knew chapter and verse but he wasn't going to take any notice, his working out had taken on an obsessive intensity, fuelled by what he felt was an impending, inevitable showdown between him and Brian.

The emotional relationship between him and Natasha was going from strength to strength. It was clear that the three of them as a family was working. If only they could get Brian Dix out of their lives, they would have a chance of happiness.

Their love life was suffering despite the feeling of complete fulfilment Neil would feel with Natasha asleep beside him every night, lying in his armpit. He couldn't drift off. He hadn't had a good night's sleep since they had returned from Hunstanton. He was hiding his car some distance from their home so that he couldn't easily be observed coming and going. The constant stress, trying to second-guess Brian, coupled with the sleep deprivation meant his health was beginning to suffer.

In the gym, the sweat was dripping from every pore as Neil pumped over eighty-five kilos, rep after rep. As he stood in the shower he was remembering that wonderfully innocent night on the way back from Oostende, it seemed a lifetime away. Suddenly, the tiles rushed up towards him. A heavy blackness engulfed him. The next thing he felt was the cold wet floor against his cheek. He didn't remember much about the trip in the ambulance as he drifted in and out of consciousness.

Natasha was stood next to his bed as he properly came to for the first time in hours. She was gently stroking his face. Neil could see that she'd been crying.

When she saw he was awake, Natasha's face lit up with relief. "Oh God Neil, what happened?" she asked, her voice fraught with worry.

"I've no idea what happened, I was in the shower, then I was in an ambulance," he stammered. "I must have collapsed."

The doctor came to Neil's bedside, "Nice to see you awake Mr Curland," he observed. "I am Doctor Rees, I was the doctor who examined you when you were admitted."

"What's the matter with me?" Neil enquired.

"I was hoping you might be able to throw some light on that," the doctor replied. "Your fiancée has filled me in on your unusual home situation. Basically, you came in in a state of total shut-down: your heart was racing, you were burning a temperature and were drifting in and out of consciousness. We sedated you to give you a thorough examination. We've run a series of tests on you, your heart is fine but your pulse is rocketing from eighty beats a minute to one hundred and forty beats a minute at the blink of an eye. Something is triggering your fight or flight reaction. I can only describe it as a sort of major panic attack." He went on, "Have you been having trouble sleeping? Problems with your routines perhaps or are you overworking?"

Neil asked to speak to the doctor alone, he didn't want to burden Natasha with what was happening to him in case she blamed herself.

After a few days in observation, Neil was discharged with some tablets, which would help him with the stress, and some medication to help him sleep. He was also prescribed some counselling.

Knowing the NHS, he would probably be lucky to see that in this lifetime

CHAPTER 33

The lull before the storm

After his scare, life began to calm down a little. Neil was taking a mild anti-depressant, which was taking the edge off the stress, medication to help him sleep, bed rest and a few weeks off work; doctor's orders had helped to make him feel much more like his old self.

The police were keeping them updated with how the search for Brian was progressing and so far he had not re-surfaced. It turned out that he was wanted on both sides of the Irish Sea so it would only be a matter of time before he was apprehended. Laughter had returned to the house

Sex with Natasha was back on track. A fancy dress birthday party invitation saw Natasha dressed as a sexy St Trinian's girl with Neil dressed as Vivian from the TV program 'The Young Ones'.

The sight of his lady-love dressed as an über sexy schoolgirl complete with pig tails, fishnets and see through blouse was sending the pulse racing. Despite his cocktail of medication, Neil was feeling damn frisky. At the end of the evening, as they were leaving, they had to walk through the local rugby ground. Natasha tried to steer a well tipsy Neil towards a small copse behind an electricity pylon. "I want you to take me out here in the open," she purred.

Neil, feeling a little conspicuous replied, "You're joking, there are people walking by." They continued to walk up the lane.

Natasha, sashaying along with an exaggerated wiggle, lifted her skirt and removed her knickers in one deft movement before kicking them into the air and throwing them in Neil's face. "I didn't realise you could be such a bore," she taunted.

Neil grabbed her between the legs and powered her towards an outside urinal. The toilet was just an open concrete cubical; the rank ammonia smell was overpowering. He shoved his hand up between her legs and was viciously fingering her sex. She was kissing him with a flaming passion, desperately trying to get his manhood free of his trousers.

"Lift up your leg," Neil commanded, trying to shove his half erect penis inside her. After a few unsuccessful attempts, he lifted one of her legs up and pushed her back against the wall. One of her black stiletto heels was lodged in the stained stinking trough as his organ found her entrance; he shoved his swollen erection inside her, scraping her backside against the filthy wall as his thrusts lifted her off the ground. Natasha loved the depravity of the situation and was moaning louder than she ever had in bed.

He pulled his penis out of her and ordered, "Turn around, I want to have you from behind." She obliged and found her face pushed down towards the stinking mass of cigarette butts and stale urine. He pumped her like that until he felt his orgasm welling up from deep within his groin. His left hand was pulling and stretching the nipple of her left breast. With his right hand, he was alternately fingering her swollen clitoris and shoving fingers into her sex alongside his swollen head. Both of them were approaching a noisy climax to a rough, almost violent sexual encounter. Voices were approaching as Neil made one final vicious assault on Natasha's sex before filling her womb with his hot seed. As the endorphins flooded his brain, he practically collapsed against her back, almost pushing her face first into the sticky, stinking mess.

First to compose herself, Natasha heard the voices coming closer. "Quick," she whispered, dragging the almost prostrate Neil out of the stall and out into the night just in time as a group of young guys walked towards the stalls. They had only just avoided being caught.

About a hundred yards away from home, Natasha could feel the fruits of Neil's passion running down her stockinged legs. She rummaged her hands through his pockets for her discarded underwear.

Back in the trough, the three young guys were emptying beer filled bladders; the stream of urine soon filled the trough and splashed back up onto their Nike Air Jordans. A pair of skimpy lace knickers lay caught in the pipe, blocking the drain.

CHAPTER 34

Gun ho

Neil and Natasha returned from their house hunting expedition. Neil manoeuvred the pushchair and baby through the door while she returned to the car for the shopping and estate agents' flyers.

Neil had just plonked the sleeping Monica in her cot in the spare room. Busting for the loo, he dashed for his en-suite bathroom. Just as Natasha was pulling the door to, Brian burst through the door and punched her full in the face, knocking her flat on her back. He shouted, "Where is he?" Pushing on past the prostrate Natasha, he leapt up the stairs, two at a time, and glanced into the rooms. He overlooked the en-suite, probably mistaking it for a cupboard. He saw Monica in her cot, flew into a rage and rushed back down the stairs. Natasha had run out of the front door and was seeking refuge in the post office.

Neil quickly grabbed the gun from under his pillow and ran down the stairs. The estate agents' leaflets scattered all over the floor momentarily distracted Brian. Comprehension was obviously flooding his brain and he spun round, heading back toward the stairs, obviously intending to make good his threat and snatch Monica.

Neil burst out of the stairwell screaming a hail of abuse and grabbed Brian by the throat, propelling him back into the sitting room. Brian, with his traveller roots, knew how to fight. He managed to fend off the attack, sidestepping and swinging the stronger and bigger built man into the fireplace. As the two of them crashed into the grate, the gun was knocked out of Neil's hand and into the ashes of the recent fire. Neil, using his superior weight and strength, managed to wrestle Brian back into the fire and had him pinned against the back of the huge open-hearth. Brian was trying his damnedest to stick his thumbs into Neil's eye sockets, his trademark move. Neil was using both his hands to ward off the assault on his eyes. He felt Brian's teeth clamp down round his ear and knew he had to act fast to avoid being maimed by this mad dog. He slammed the other man hard into the hearth, loosening the grip of his teeth, giving him a split second to seize the upper hand. He could feel the poker under his thigh; it was a stout wrought iron antique and weighed a fair few pounds. He swung it hard at Brian, once, twice, three times. He struck him in the head and face. Brian fell back into the hearth. Neil caught his balance and stepped up and out of the fireplace. As he turned, Brian burst into life, barrelling past him and out the front door. As Neil caught his breath, he realised that Brian's plan had changed. He was going after Natasha.

"Where's that fucking gun?" he cursed aloud, as he searched through the embers. He felt the cold metal of the Walther P1 pistol against his palm. Scooping it quickly into his pocket, he ran out of the door, towards the village centre where he assumed Natasha and Brian had headed. Neil was running full chat towards the village pub when he saw Brian trying to drag a terrified Natasha out of the post office.

Some of the villagers had obviously tried to intervene; the postmaster was sitting on the floor, blood streaming from his nose. One plucky lady gripped Natasha's arm, pulling her back into the post office, she shouted, "Leave her alone you bastard."

Neil caught up to the commotion, pulled the gun from his pocket and stuck It in Brian's face.

"Back off you fucking animal," Neil screamed.

Brian pushed his face into the barrel and spat at Neil, "Shoot then you fucking cunt." The Irish traveller brogue fading with the intensity of his venom.

Someone leant out of an upstairs window and shouted, "I've called the police." With that, Brian took off like a scalded cat and disappeared in a cloud of tyre smoke.

"You'd better go too Neil," the postmaster said. "The police will think it was an attempted raid and will turn up mob handed."

Neil and Natasha ran back towards the cottage. Neil's neighbour Gordon met them at the door. "Give me the gun," said Gordon. Neil began to protest. "There isn't time," said Gordon. "Just give me the gun. I'll explain later." Neil handed the gun over. Gordon handed him a black US police officer's torch and said, "When they come, and they will come, tell them that it was this torch you threatened him with, otherwise you can kiss goodbye to your liberty." Neil was shocked, he considered his elderly middle class neighbours to be pretty stuffy, and their outlaw attitude was a real revelation.

As sure as night follows day, a SWAT team were soon tearing around the village. Neil waited in the street rather than have his front door smashed in.

He was arrested and taken to Exeter police station for questioning. It transpired that the woman who had phoned the police said Neil had a gun; the postmaster told them he hadn't seen a gun. The women in the shop weren't sure what they'd seen, the whole incident had been so frightening and dramatic. Neil explained about the torch. A thorough search of Neil's house revealed nothing. After a trip to the infirmary to have his ear stitched up, Neil was released with a caution. Brian, of course, had vanished again into the ether.

That night, Gordon and Sandra, his attractive wife who was about 10 years his junior, came over to Neil's. Natasha had done a sterling job of sorting out the mess made by the fight and the inquisitive marauding plod. Natasha brought them up to speed about what had brought on the earlier crisis.

Natasha and Neil were in a sort of shocked but euphoric daze. The shit had hit the fan; everything was out in the open. They could start living together properly as a couple now. At least for the near future they knew they were safe. With the recent events added to his charge list, the hunt for Brian had intensified. He would be 'on the lam'. With any luck, he would be all the way to Ireland by now.

Sandra took Natasha out to the kitchen to impart a few 'older woman' wisdoms to her regarding Brian.

"Since when did you become such an expert on police procedure then Gordon?" asked Neil with a wink. "I thought you were a retired librarian or something."

Gordon, who looked the spitting image of Roger Whittaker, replied, "Well, there are a few things you don't know about me. As we are now partners in crime, I guess it's safe to let you in on our little secret."

Gordon had been a bit of a rogue in his younger years. Neil was gobsmacked. It turned out that after his quiet, intensely private and reclusive neighbour had spent a short while on a forced holiday at Her Majesty's pleasure for the forging of official documents, Gordon had discovered a hitherto hidden talent for art forgery and was responsible for most of the fake art in the West Country. His favourite genre was that of the 'Primitives'. Neil was no art lover but he had been around auction houses most of his life due to his uncles and cousins being in the antiques trade. His dad was also smitten with auctions; they were the car boot sales of the sixties through to the eighties. Neil had to chuckle as he'd often witnessed these absurd paintings, facsimiles of ancient cave paintings depicting out of proportion farm animals, many selling for four figure sums.

The vision of Gordon crouched in his attic, painting these 'Old Masters' was hilarious.

Gordon reasoned that these less expensive paintings were a gold mine because there were no records of who had them so they could regularly change hands without attracting too much attention. Much safer and more lucrative long-term than copying well-known artists.

CHAPTER 35

Exit strategy

In the comparative safety of the traveller camp, Brian Dix was holed up, licking his wounds and recounting his recent run of 'bad luck' with his Irish Gypsy comrade.

"Feckin all gone to shit Danny boy," he was beside himself with rage. "I'm fecked over to be sure Danny. The slut's feckin' Gajo soldier boy's to blame for all this, so he is. I'll do for the sorry bastard when I get hold of him, so I will."

"What's this mean to our deal Dixie?" Danny questioned.

"Oh bollocks Danny, I'm in too deep here, so I am. This puts the whole mission in jeopardy. I'll have to run back to Ireland with me tail between me legs, so I will.

"What about the sit down with the tribes?"

"Can you tie up the loose ends Danny boy? Make the moves stick?"

"I don't know Dixie. I'm a scrapper me, I'm no big thinker, you're the brains, me? I'm just the muscle. I don't know Dixie, to be truthful. 'Tis a big ask for a man like me."

"Feck Danny boy, this will fall badly for me if it all goes tits up. I could lose me feckin' ride with the army even."

"I'll do me best Dixie, you know I will, but 'tis a lot to put together, just gettin' the tribes to sit down to talk will be a big get, let alone getting 'em to work together."

"Just my feckin' luck Danny; me feckin' ship's comin' in and I'm away at the feckin' airport."

Typical of men of Brian Dix's ilk; no undesirable situation is ever of their own creation.

"I'm bankin' on you comin' through Danny. The army might just off me otherwise."

"Ah, Dixie, it'll not come to that. I'll do the best I can for you, so I will."

"I need to sort out a motor for me getaway, have you got somethin' plain knockin' about Danny, swap for me van?"

"Aye Dixie boy, I got an old Astra in the yard, won't stand out too much. Got a good sound motor under the bonnet she has, see you right."

"I'll have to get off Danny boy, got to touch base with me army contact, sort meself out a passage back home and a place to lay me hat when I gets there. I'll tell you what though, I'll leave that feckin' slut with somethin' to think about before I check out Danny, ye can be sure of that!

CHAPTER 36

Rocking out

Neil walked in the door excited. "Mum and Dad have rented a mobile home in Hale for a week. It's only a two-hour drive down, we can stay with them from Friday, come back Sunday night, what do you think?"

"Sounds like fun," Natasha answered.

On the way down to Cornwall, Natasha said to Neil, "Monica needs a comfort stop, can we find some services?"

"Sure," Neil replied, "there's an independent diner near Newton Abbott, we'll pull up there."

Neil, in a world of his own, nearly missed the turn off.

"Neil. Services!" Natasha shouted.

"Jesus," exclaimed Neil as the sudden scream caused him to swerve the car abruptly onto the out ramp. Neil checked his right hand mirror to see he hasn't caused anyone any grief. "Christ," he shouted, "did you see that blue Astra, he nearly lost control trying to make the pull in."

As they parked up and exited the car, Neil wondered whether the Astra just made the same error as him or if the car was following them. He decided it was probably the former and put it from his mind.

Friday night saw the family relaxing in the clubhouse. Monica was in her element; the club had its own Redcoats. They embodied a combination of enthusiasm and confidence, bereft of talent or shame. Armed with a plethora of silly 'dance along' records by artists like Toni Basil and Kylie Minogue, they soon had all the kiddies screaming and laughing. For the adults, the entertainment was cringe-worthy at best, but the comfy chairs, booze and freedom from kids made up for it. The mums and dads were having a great time.

After a wonderful Saturday spent lounging on the beach watching his parents dote on Monica, Neil came upon a flyer, advertising a Queen tribute band who were playing in a club in Hayle, the nearby town. He cheekily suggested that they leave Monica with his mum and dad, and nip out to check out the band.

Natasha got dressed in a tiny little black skirt with a zip up the front, a pair of black stilettos and a short black blazer jacket.

"Just you wait until you see what I'm wearing under the jacket," she teased.

Fortunately, there was ample parking close to the venue. It was just starting to get dark when

Natasha striped off the blazer and chucked it onto the back seat. Neil's eyes popped right out of their sockets. Natasha was wearing a tight white Lycra laced blouse. Her breasts and nipples were completely exposed through the lace. She caught Neil's lustful stare and said, "Then there's this." She dropped her hands to the front of her tiny short skirt, pulled the zip all the way up and showed him her shaven sex underneath. "You likey?" she purred.

"Yes Ma'am," panted Neil, getting his wandering hands slapped down as he tried to grope a handful.

Inside the club, the group were awesome and after a couple of glasses of vino Natasha was having a whale of a time. "C'mon, let's work our way to the front," she shouted, dragging Neil behind her. Natasha was dancing, wiggling her sexy ass to the music. The venue was a seedy sixteenth century inn, full of dark alcoves. There were people sitting on sofas around the edge of the stage. Pressed up against the people around the edge, Natasha's sexy ass grinding was attracting some attention from the horny, mainly male rockers in the audience. Neil slipped his hands around her hips, grinding his hips against her ass as his hands slid further down, lifting the front of her micro skirt and sliding his fingers between the lips of her moist exposed sex. Natasha was starting to really get in the groove; great music, red wine and now fingers in her wet sex. Could life get any better?

The excitement was reaching fever pitch in Natasha; she was grinding her pelvis against the thrust of Neil's fingers; the close proximity of other men; the stage show; the overtly sexual 'Queen' front man, chest exposed, gyrating, his muscular sweaty torso just feet away from her sexually charged body. She was approaching the point where nothing mattered but that point inside her, controlling every fibre of every nerve. She leant her head back and whispered to Neil, "Take me." Neil, acutely aware of everything going on around him, was nervous. Being that he was driving and by necessity, sober, he was not feeling the alcoholic abandon his fiancée was embracing.

With a dry, tense throat feeding a raging thirst, Neil tapped her on the shoulder and made a drinking gesture with his fingers and thumb. Disappointed, Natasha dropped abruptly from her euphoric cloud, nodded and offered up her empty glass.

Sometime later, she felt the hand return to her groin and parted her legs involuntarily as the warm creamy feeling returned to spread upwards from her throbbing sex. It appeared that Neil had found his inner courage. He was really excelling himself now as she felt his fingers pushing up inside her. He replaced the fingers with the head of his manhood and started rubbing it up and down the crease of her rear. He twisted her micro skirt around so that the open zip was at the back. He was actually stroking it up and down, trying to discretely enter her sex from behind. She consciously pushed her feet sideways, parting her legs wider and started to push back against him, desperately hoping he didn't take fright and give up; her need was all-consuming. She gasped a little with surprise as the head found her entrance. His warm shaft slid into the welcoming folds of her sex. He didn't pump for fear of being observed, but thrust his penis all the way in and then ground his crotch against her with short energetic little pumps, a way she had never experienced before. The heat, the proximity of people, the alcohol and the depravity of their actions had Natasha on the edge of a powerful orgasm. The room was spinning with the stage lights, the disembodied flesh in her sex, the lead singer, pounding out a power ballad, grinding his obvious bulge up and down the mic stand in time to the beat. Natasha's eyes closed as she gritted her teeth and rode out the mutual explosion of sensations throbbing from the fullness between her legs. As the pulsating spasms subsided, the spent member slipped from between her legs. She opened her eyes. Just as the band finished their first set, the house lights came up. Natasha spotted Neil across the other side of the club returning from the bar carrying two drinks.

As he drew level with her, he handed her a glass of wine and said, "Sorry it took so long, queue for the bar was horrendous." Comprehension flooded into Natasha's brain and she excused herself to use the ladies' room.

Sitting on the seat in the ladies' loo Natasha's mind was in turmoil. Her tormented body was shaking as the guilty pleasure slowly leaked from her sex.

"Oh God. Oh God. What have I done?" she sobbed into her hands. She reasoned that she thought it was Neil so it wasn't being unfaithful. "Oh God, how could I not realise?" In the back of her mind she was racked with guilt, not so much about what she'd done, but the fact that it was the single most erotic encounter she had ever experienced. Even in the wretched state she was in, her body was still convulsing with the aftermath of her passion. Her sensitive bud was still in a pulsating engorged state and she knew to just stroke it would send her back over the edge. The temptation was overwhelming. She pressed a finger into her sex; the warm viscous ejaculate coated her fingers. She touched the forbidden balm to her quivering spot. Her second orgasm of the evening exploded into a pyrotechnic eruption of her body and nervous system.

When the fever subsided Natasha was left feeling desperate with regret. She knew that she must return to Neil soon otherwise he would suspect something was wrong but she couldn't leave the cubicle until she'd cleaned herself up. Oh how she regretted the decision not to wear any knickers.

Using loo paper and water from the flush, she managed to clean most of the mess from herself. Trust her mystery lover to be such a heavy comer.

The band was still on a refreshment break when Natasha returned to Neil's side.

"I thought you'd fallen down the hole," Neil quipped.

I wish I had, thought Natasha. She looked around her. The house lights were up; the room was filled with men, young and old. It could have been any one of them. She stared at a couple of guys. They noticed her staring; some stared back, some averted their gaze, some winked, or mouthed a hello. Nothing, no clue as to who had shared her without invitation. She considered pretending she felt ill so Neil would take her home. No, she decided to tough it out, enjoy the rest of their night. She sidled up to Neil and cuddled into him. He turned his head down to face hers. Tilting her head up, she kissed him full on the lips, opening her mouth slightly, drawing his tongue into her mouth. She wrapped her leg around his waist. As the band waded into another set, the house lights dimmed. Neil stroked his finger along the length of Natasha's sex before sliding his fingers inside her. "God, you're so wet," Neil remarked, nuzzling her ear.

"I know, I am so turned on," she purred back to him, inwardly smiling.

"Someone's going to have a damn good time tonight," Neil whispered in his lady-love's ear.

If only you knew the half of it, she chuckled to herself, confidence returning.

As the band wrapped up the evening with a couple of lively encores, Natasha had well and truly got her 'second wind'. She begged Neil to find somewhere else to carry on the party night. Neil remembered seeing a lively hotel 'fun bar' back on the seafront which looked like it would fit the bill, so they rocked up there with Neil straight to the bar to top up Natasha's 'wine buzz'. In the middle of the dance floor were pillars, rising up through the middle of tall round tables with equally tall bar stools pulled up to them. While Neil visited the bar, Natasha plonked herself onto one of the stools. Within moments, she had an admirer standing beside her, chatting to her. Neil glanced over; he thought he recognised the guy from the venue earlier.

Natasha's companion spotted the silver chain around her neck and started making a big thing about the motorbike charm suspended from the chain. Neil could clearly see he was using the charm as an excuse to get his hands and eyes very, very close to Natasha's gorgeous ample breasts, which were clearly and blatantly visible through the tight Lycra lace top. The lighting in the bar was far less subtle than in the venue and Natasha's big erect nipples and large dark areolae were plainly on show.

Neil returned with the drinks and introductions were made. The guy's name was Pete; he had a mobile home in one of the beach side parks. He was obviously not at all embarrassed to thrust himself on a couple in this manner. Neil and Natasha were touchingly naïve to the idea of 'swingers'. With Natasha's provocative attire Pete obviously believed he'd hit the jackpot.

Neil had to excuse himself to use the little boy's room as a matter of urgency. While he was gone, Pete asked, "What kind of bike is it?" Turning the little bike charm around, allegedly to examine the make and model, he accidentally detached the bike charm from Natasha's necklace and dropped it on the floor between her legs.

Natasha sat forward on the stool and looked down towards the charm. Just as she uncrossed her long legs and opened them slightly to extend her reach, Pete crouched down, ostensibly also reaching for the charm. His new position brought his eyes exactly into focus with Natasha's slightly parted legs and her recently used sex. Pete let a whistle of appreciation escape his lips as he drank in the sight of Natasha's beautiful shaven sex. She blushed slightly, but took a little longer than necessary to close her legs. Pete retrieved the charm and rested a hand high up on Natasha's thigh before slowly rising to his feet.

As Neil returned from the restroom, Pete took a very long time to replace the charm onto the chain, his hands resting on Natasha's breast as he exaggerated the effort required to crimp the ends of the loop ring back together.

Watching his clumsy, obvious endeavours to touch Natasha's breasts and the way her heavy, seemingly laboured breathing caused her ample bosom to swell to his touch had an aphrodisiac effect on Neil and his manhood began to stretch the fabric of his trousers.

Pete decided the loop needed some stronger pressure and took the chain between his teeth. His face was now obscenely close to Natasha's breasts. Neil couldn't help but notice the zip on Natasha's skirt had worked its way open, right to the top.

Pete leant across to Neil and said, "If we're lucky, we might just get a lock in." Normally, last orders were religiously called at half ten with most pubs chucking out the stragglers no later than half eleven. Sure enough, the landlord announced, "Lock in the snooker room." The curtains were drawn, doors locked and those lucky enough to be on the inside got to stay drinking for a little longer or until they'd had enough.

With the whole pub crammed into the snooker room, the atmosphere became charged, more like a nightclub than a pub. The snooker table was pushed back against the wall and the parquet floored area under and around it became a dance floor. Pretty slick.

"Dance Natasha?" Pete asked. "You don't mind do you Neil?" Neil shook his head and they took off to the dance floor bumping and grinding to some funky seventies beats. After a while, Neil decided to join them and the three of them had a laugh on the dance floor with Neil and Pete taking it in turns to 'bump' Natasha around the floor.

Pete took his cue to get a round in while Neil and Natasha had a little smooch on the floor. There was no DJ, so the songs were coming in a refreshingly random order, not typical for a disco, which normally tended to follow a tired old routine of dance first, followed by slow later. Pete returned with the drinks and the three of them retired to a table for a break.

Pete dragged Natasha back onto the dance floor, causing her to spill her red wine over Neil's shirt in her haste to place her glass back onto the table. Pete was soon rewarded as the fast tempo song came to an end, followed by a slow smoochie number. He took a few liberties with the quite inebriated Natasha. Neil looked on with a mixture of apprehension and excitement. He knew it was wrong on so many levels but he couldn't help finding it exciting to see other men appreciating his Natasha.

The music suddenly came to an abrupt end. The landlord shouted over the noisy crowd, "The Old Bill are raiding us. Everybody out."

Everyone rushed to exit through the kitchen entrance. The trio scrambled out into the car park. Neil unlocked the car doors.

Pete suggested, "Hey Neil, any chance of a lift back to my caravan?"

"Of course mate, no problem, you'll have to direct me, I'm not too familiar with Hayle." As it happened, Pete's mobile home was within walking distance of the camp-site the family were staying at. Pete invited them over for a nightcap.

"Do you fancy stopping for a quick one?" Neil asked Natasha.

"Hell why not," she answered, the alcohol she'd already consumed exaggerating her jovial reply.

"I'll drop you guys off, then I'll whip the car across the road to our site so it's on hand for tomorrow," Neil said as he pulled up outside Pete's caravan. Within five minutes, Neil was back at the door of the caravan. "I'm wearing my drinking shoes," he declared, "wait for me to catch up, you two!"

CHAPTER 37

Bust

The caravan was a fair sized model, a double. It transpired it was a legacy from Pete's former marriage. "She got the house, kids and car, I got the caravan," he remonstrated.

"Neil, what wets your whistle?" Pete asked, opening an impressive drinks cabinet.

"Ooh, vodka and orange?" Neil replied. Pete poured a very generous measure of vodka into a pitcher before adding a splash of orange juice.

The atmosphere was decidedly mellow; Pete's selection of music echoed Neil's with Dire Straits mingling with Bob Marley and The Who to provide an evocative backdrop which had the guys engrossed in a musical who's who.

A slightly swaying Natasha had to break the spell by drawling, "I'm bored, put on some dancey stuff." Pete responded with a selection of sleazy disco numbers kicking off with some sultry Donna Summer.

The three of them gyrated around for a bit before it became clear that Natasha was a little too worse for wear to be moving so energetically. Sitting down before she could fall down, Natasha asked Pete, "Don't you have any games we can play?"

"Hmm," Pete considered, "I've probably got a pack of cards tucked away somewhere. Might have had 'Mousetrap' kicking about, but I think the kids took it with them when they were last here."

Natasha screwed her nose up. "Shall I dig out the cards?" he asked.

"Oh go on then, s'pose we can have a giggle with a pack of cards. Old maid anyone? Snap?" she teased.

"We could make it a bit more interesting," he interjected.

Natasha raised an eyebrow.

"Well, if you're both up for it, what about a drinking game with a twist?"

Neil and Natasha waited for him to elaborate.

"We play a game of Pontoon. One of us plays bank, deals out the cards..."

Neil interrupted with, "We both know how to play Pontoon, what's the twist?"

Pete continued, choosing his words carefully. "Well, we bid on cards with a credit, at the end of the hand, the winner collects the credits from the losers."

"And the credits are?" Neil prompted.

"An item of clothing or a drink forfeit."

Natasha and Neil looked at each other. Natasha said, "I'm game if you are, sounds like fun."

"OK," said Neil, "who's going to play bank?"

"Five rounds each, starting with me." Pete dealt out the cards.

A few rounds hastened by, the luck was shared and so far, the forfeits had been distributed evenly. The three of them were starting to feel a little tipsy. Losing the next hand, Natasha broke the pattern by taking her necklace off.

Pete protested, "That's hardly a garment of clothing."

"I'm wearing less than you two," she slurred. As the next hands fell, both Pete and Neil ended up without their socks. Natasha's luck began to fail. Whether down to the amount of alcohol she'd consumed or the boys were playing in cahoots, soon, both her high heels were lying in the discarded clothes pile. Another couple of hands fell; Neil and Pete were now sitting in tee shirts and trousers.

Again, Natasha found herself sat with a pile of useless cards in her hands counting the spots; "Twenty one, twenty two..............Bugger, bust." She took a deep breath, looked at the near empty wine bottle in front of her, reached over her head and wriggled out of the tight Lycra top, allowing her full breasts to fall free into clear view.

Both the boys let out a little gasp of approval. Pontoon is a game more of luck than skill and the next few rounds saw Pete disrobed to his boxer shorts. Inevitably, Natasha's luck ran out. The boys were staring at her as she picked her glass up and drained the last of the drips of wine from the bottle. She looked up to Pete to provide another bottle so she could pay her penance.

"No more wine I'm afraid, I can offer a gin and tonic?" She contemplated changing her tipple at this late stage, decided against it and sat down; she unfastened her skirt and threw it to the side. She crossed her legs to preserve her modesty.

Pete protested, "No I'm sorry, that won't do, we should get to see our winnings."

Neil didn't argue, so with a blush turning her face scarlet, Natasha slowly uncrossed her legs, sat on the floor 'Ghurkha' style, bum resting on her heels, and exposed her shaven sex to the admiring gaze of the two horny men. "Do we play on?" Pete asked. "The stakes are going to get a little higher if we do."

"We only go as far as Natasha is prepared to go, no pressure," Neil added.

"OK, what say we offer a forfeit as a bet, we all agree on the bet before we proceed. Natasha plays as bank then collects or pays out all forfeits? Don't fancy having to do any homo stuff," Pete said with a wink.

They all agreed on the rules. "Right," said Natasha, taking charge. "I win; you both have to give me a full body massage, naked. You both naked that is. I get to keep a towel for my modesty. I lose, and I'll let you both feel my breasts?"

"Your pussy," Pete corrected, "we get to feel your pussy. Until we decide to stop."

Natasha glanced at Neil. "OK, straight in at the deep end." The hand played out. Neil cautiously stopped with a nineteen, Pete played on, he was holding four cards and his count was eighteen, an ace or a two would see him with a five card trick, the bank would require a pontoon to beat. "Twist," said Pete. Natasha dealt out the last card face up. It was an ace. The room started to sway as Natasha was feeling decidedly light-headed, she knew where this was going and although she was very turned on, her heart and head were locked in a turbulent struggle.

She turned over the first card. A queen. Feeling that she may yet be saved, she turned over the next card; a three. She had lost the hand.

She looked at Neil, he was so turned on. She needn't look to him to help her. Resolute, she stood up, walked over first to Neil. She opened her legs for him; his fingers worked their way up inside her wet sex. He played about for a while; his heart wasn't really in it. She knew he wanted to see Pete finger her. Neil withdrew his fingers from her and sent her over towards Pete. He caressed her long curly hair, trying to relax her; she parted her legs in submission. Pete took his time; he stroked her clitoris for some time, causing her legs to tremble with excitement. His long fingers stroked up inside her sex, first two fingers, then three and then four. Neil came up behind her; he started kissing her, stroking her neck, softly caressing her breasts. Pete got on the floor below her; he was starting to work his hand up inside her wet sex. Natasha felt a sudden sharp twinge of pain as Pete tried to insert his whole fist into her sex. The situation was rapidly spinning out of control. She softly moaned, "Stop," followed by a commanding shout of, "Stop." Neil and Pete instantly froze as Natasha said, "Neil, I want to go home...Now."

Pete looked angry.

As they were leaving, Neil stopped on the caravan steps and said to Pete, "I'm sorry mate, if Natasha's not comfortable then it's no go. Sorry if we've led you up the garden path, we've never done anything like this before."

"Don't worry mate, been there and done that," Pete sneered, looking Natasha straight in the eyes. Neil just looked between them, puzzled.

Natasha knew at once that they had met already, earlier in the evening

CHAPTER 38

Sober thoughts

Walking back to their camp, Natasha was clearly upset. "Neil, you say you love me and you want to marry me, yet you don't seem to care when other men touch me and take liberties with me."

"I'm sorry darling, I get so carried away, and I get so turned on by you. I let things go too far I know. I really do love you; I want to marry you more than anything in the world. I just get so carried away. I don't know what comes over me," Neil protested.

Natasha decided not to chastise Neil too much in case Pete let the cat out of the bag. Besides, truth be told, she got just as turned on as he did. She just got insecure as she was used to being in an abusive controlling relationship and she was reluctantly seeing tell-tale parallels between this one and that. You could control someone in many ways; money, violence, sex... even love. She snuggled in close to his chest and said, "It's OK, I had a lot of fun tonight, I just need reassuring that you still love me. I'm not used to all this risqué stuff; it's messing with my head. Let's just find a quiet spot down on the beach and make love, just the two of us."

"Sounds like a plan," Neil replied, as he steered her towards the dunes.

The sand dunes at Hale beach were vast and plentiful, you could have any number of courting couples making out there without disturbing each other. Soon, Neil and Natasha were getting down and dirty in their very own private beach.

Neil started to kiss Natasha's belly, he kissed his way down towards her sex. She considered it for a second, then chickened out, pulled him up her chest and said, "I just want you inside me."

"Crikey, you're so wet," Neil remarked as he slipped his hard penis into her sex, "I can't feel you."

Natasha's eyes were closed, she was enjoying the thrusts of Neil's ample manhood, but her thoughts were on the uninvited intruder she'd enjoyed earlier.

What would Neil think if he knew just how wanton his unfaithful little slut really was?

CHAPTER 39

Reality check

Sunday morning saw the start of a beautiful day in Cornwall. Neil and Natasha awoke to the glorious smell of fried bacon and eggs courtesy of Neil's mum. "How do you have your eggs Natasha?" Neil's mum questioned.

"Fertilised," Neil whispered so that only Natasha could hear. "If last night's anything to go by," he added with a laugh.

Natasha slapped him with a pillow but thought to herself, *If only you knew.*

"Eh?" Neil's mum commented, hard of hearing.

"Nothing Mum, scrambled please, she said."

After a hearty breakfast, they strapped Monica into her seat for the drive home and said goodbye to Mum and Dad.

A couple of miles down the road, they left the town and set off across the moor on their route home.

"Jesus Christ," Neil exclaimed as a plain blue Vauxhall Astra suddenly appeared as if from nowhere. The car rammed into the side of Neil's work's Nova. The smaller Nova swerved violently and left the road. Neil valiantly struggled to steer into the spin but the little car hit the verge and flipped over onto its roof.

Driver and passenger were unhurt but disorientated and dazed, hanging upside down. Caught up by the seat belt, Neil was powerless to act as the rear door was wrenched open by a thug wearing a ski mask and armed with a box cutter. He sliced the straps holding Monica's car seat and within a few seconds she was gone, whisked away into the Astra, which accelerated away with a squeal of tortured tyre rubber.

Nothing could prepare a man for the depth of anguish a woman feels when the infant she has given life to is torn from her breast. Natasha's pitiful screams carried out across the moor.

For the first time in his life, Neil felt totally helpless.

CHAPTER 40

Brotherhood. 'Goose'

Along with the gut wrenching confirmation that their worst fears had come to pass they had to endure the police going through their usual inept motions.

Natasha's mum arrived to console her daughter and to offer them the practicalities of transport home. Neil was hurting too, he hadn't realised how much little Monica meant to him. She was a part of Natasha and therefore a part of him. He knew he had to get her back. He felt it was his fault that these events had been set into motion and it fell to him to put things right.

The police were out of their depth and would be more hindrance than help.

Neil spoke to Natasha's mum; "We need to go after Brian now before the trail goes cold. He has connections with the Republican movement in Ireland; do you know what that means?"

Natasha's mum shook her head.

"He's had involvement with the Provisional IRA for a few years now; his little excursions have involved 'fishing' trips between the mainland and the Republic. He's wanted over in Ireland too."

"What can we do?" she questioned.

"I think I may have the connections to track him down," Neil replied. "We need to move fast before the bastard goes to ground."

The police were, as Neil had predicted, slow to mobilise. Brian was Monica's paternal father, and as such, they were reluctant to take her abduction as seriously as if he were a stranger. Neil was interviewed but the police had enough history on Brian to have him down as the only serious suspect.

Neil rang Goose and told him what had happened. "Jesus Christ Neil, why didn't you call me sooner? Before it came to this. We could have avoided things getting this far," Goose shouted, out of a mixture of anger and frustration. His analytical mind was looking at all the angles before he cut off Neil's call. "I'll get back to you bud, I need to round up some skills and I need to do it quickly." He put the receiver down.

Neil met Goose when they were both servicemen's kids, attending school on a garrison camp in Germany. Goose was a gifted pupil, excelling in the emerging subject of 'Control Technology' and a handful of sciences. He was something of an enigma. A visiting Royal Air Force careers officer had discovered him and recruited him straight out of school for some sort of 'special duties' which he never spoke about.

After only eight years of service, Goose was discharged, allegedly on account of a non-specific nervous complaint. It seemed his time in the blue uniform had left him with enough cash to live a comfortable life, and a unique address book full of contacts which were worth their weight in gold.

A couple of hours passed before the phone rang again. "Right Neil," Goose commanded, "I have put a call out to some well-connected boys serving in Northern Ireland, if he is north or south of the border they will get us the intel on your man. They can't offer us much practical help once we get there but they can get us across to NI without anyone getting wind we're there."

"Excellent," said Neil. "Goose, I'm going to owe you a debt I can't ever repay."

"Neil," Goose interrupted, "if this guy really matters to the Provos, he'll be untouchable. You'd better hope he's not too special. We don't have the might of the British Forces behind us anymore." "We don't have our hands tied by them either," added Neil.

"Neil, we need to get there first so that when the intel comes in we are ready to move. Including you, we will be a four-man team. We need money to move and we will need an exit strategy, which includes the little one. We need to provide a passport with her on it otherwise any shit storm we kick up will catch up with us. Better still, false papers for all of us, at least to cover us for spot checks. Bugger, it's going to take me time to organise that. Time is something we can't afford. Every minute we waste gives him longer to cover his tracks."

Neil thought for a second, remembered his neighbour the 'forger' and said, "I think I can swing that, you'd better get photos of all the protagonists to me ASAP."

"Consider it done mate. In that case, I'm on my way down to you now. I've got a box of our old forces photos and any others we need will have to be with my Polaroid. Let's make this happen."

Neil turned to Natasha's mum. "I'm going to need money. Can you help?"

She looked down at her feet for a minute then said, "I have Natasha's dad's life insurance pay out. It's quite a substantial sum."

Neil replied, "I need cash, we can't visit the bank in Armagh, we're not supposed to be there remember. I'll have to take whatever you have in cash plus whatever I can get from the cash machine."

Natasha's mum left the room. A while later, she was back with a whopping great wedge of cash in her hand. "Will ten thousand be enough for now?" she asked. Neil looked at her with new-found respect. "I don't trust banks," she answered, to his unasked question.

Neil left the still distraught Natasha at her mum's and shot back to see his neighbour Gordon whom he had already brought up to speed on the phone about what had gone down.

"Gordon, can you still forge documents?" Gordon whistled through his teeth, and with a grin he beckoned Neil up to his attic 'studio'. After rummaging through a few old boxes, he laid his hands on a clutch of paperwork.

"Passports, ID cards, ration cards, driving licenses, birth certificates. What do you need?" Neil smiled.

By the time Goose arrived with Jimbo and the photos, the ink was just about dry on the papers they would need.

"Stay strong bud," Goose said, patting Neil on the shoulder and joining hands in the universal biker handshake. Jimbo embraced Neil in a hearty hug. He had forgotten what a man mountain his mate

Jimbo was. He couldn't help but feel reassured when Jimbo was around, even though he knew Goose was the brains behind the operation.

"What happened to the fourth man?" Neil questioned.

"The fourth man is Lost Bob; he's setting off on his bike. We'll pick him up at Clevedon services. If we can find him," boomed Jimbo. The three of them burst out laughing; a cathartic release, despite the seriousness of the situation.

CHAPTER 41

Brotherhood. 'Lost Bob'

If Goose was the 'brains' of the bunch, then it would be true to say that Lost Bob was the 'brawn'.

In the Royal Air Force, units trained their servicemen to the level of tradesmen with qualifications recognised in the civilian world. Nevertheless, the RAF also needed an infantry, men who could be deployed to fight and to move things. If those things didn't fight back, or move, they would paint them. When they had painted them, they would guard them. This unit was the RAF Regiment. The men, who proudly wore the 'crossed rifles' insignia, were known as 'Rock Apes'.

'Lost Bob' was one such 'Rock Ape'. Strong in arm and soft in brain, he had accepted early redundancy in the forces' cut backs. With his gratuity, he had bought himself an ancient, iron lifeboat, which had been converted to a luxurious houseboat at enormous cost.

Bob was partial to more than the odd drop of cider. With work for an unskilled ex-serviceman not always easy to come by, lack of steady earnings coupled with an appetite for regular cider was a recipe for disaster.

To keep costs down, the houseboat was berthed in a harbour, in the mouth of the river Avon; a tidal river. Twice a day, the tide would come in, and twice a day, go out, meaning the boat spent half its life floating and half its life sitting on the bottom, sometimes at a precarious angle. Bob had ingeniously solved this little dilemma by sleeping on a blow up mattress hung from an old garden swing, suspended from the roof. Whichever way the boat leaned, he would sleep flat.

In a moment of pique, a penniless and sober Bob sold the twin Perkins marine diesel engines, which were the pride of his boat, deciding that as he never sailed anywhere he didn't need the engines. With the considerable earnings, he paid his overdue harbour fees and went on a month-long bender.

As sure as night follows day, the money and cider ran out. Down the pub, an unscrupulous opportunist made Bob an offer for the now redundant transfer boxes. Bob surmised that, as he had no engines, he could live without the transfer boxes. A deal was struck and Bob's flagons replenished.

That night, a very merry Bob crawled through the galley of his home and onto his cleverly suspended bed for a well-earned sleep, looking forward to the business of serious drinking, which would begin again in earnest the following day.

Bob woke up with a start. "Christ I've wet myself again," he thought. There was no doubt he was lying in a pool of cold water. He threw himself off the airbed in his accustomed manner, designed to clear the frame, before it started swinging to and fro. "What the fuck?" he exclaimed, moments before his open mouth filled with cold salt water. Panic burned the residual alcohol from his brain as he clawed his way back to the surface, clinging to the airbed while his rationale responded to the situation.

He was floating on a lilo, somewhere in the Severn Estuary.

His home, devoid of gearboxes, propeller shafts, and those seemingly insignificant little shaft seals, which prevent seawater from occupying spaces where, in the normal scheme of things, air should be, was at the bottom of the harbour.

CHAPTER 42

Brotherhood. 'Jimbo'

Neil and his companions left their motor just on the outskirts of Liverpool and were picked up in an Army Bedford four tonne truck and given army overalls to wear over their leathers.

The driver greeted Goose and said, "When you get on board, cover yourselves up with the camo netting and stay quiet. There's water in the hosepipe, you'll have to piss in the flat-bed. You'll have an eight-hour crossing so try to get some sleep. Don't get caught."

Jimbo, not the most flexible of the crew, dropped heavily down to the bed of the truck. "Ow. Fuck," he cursed, "what the fuck have I just sat on, felt like a fucking coconut was trying to deflower my fucking ring." He felt down under his arse and scooped up a scruffy open-faced matt black crash helmet. "What the fuck is that doing there?" he shouted.

"Sorry mate, that's my helmet," Lost Bob confessed, with obvious embarrassment.

"What the fuck have you brought that for? You doughnut," Jimbo shouted, rubbing his sore ring.

"Dunno," Bob replied, "I just forgot to forget to bring it, so used to always carrying it."

"You are such an old hippy, Bob," cursed Jimbo, "just keep the fucking thing away from my arse would you?"

Despite his massive, imposing bulk and fearsome manner, Jimbo was a real 'gentle giant'.

He was the only one of the group who had been married. His now ex-wife was a real ball breaker.

She had left the sensitive Jimbo a broken man. It was down to Goose to pick him up, dust him off and bring him back to the land of the living. With the noose and all the trappings of his former life behind him, Jimbo now lodged with Goose and his mum, an arrangement which perfectly suited all parties.

In common with Neil, Jimbo was ex-army. Goose and Jimbo met when the latter's artillery regiment mobilised as a support regiment to RAF Gütersloh in Germany. Both men had a penchant for six cylinder engine motorbikes. A firm friendship soon formed, which continued on after their repatriation to civilian life.

All the men had met up in the post forces years as members of the motorbike club 'Booze Brothers'.

CHAPTER 43

Gypsy blood

"Mr Doherty. It's Brian Dix," he announced into the receiver. "I've got a bit of a problem here Mr Doherty, I'm a bit compromised. I've got the 'Tans' crawlin' all over me so I have."

"Are they on to the mission Brian?" Doherty asked, concerned.

"No Mr Doherty, nothin' to do with the mission, that's all but locked down here. It's just collateral. I need out Mr Doherty. Can you get me off the mainland; get me somewhere safe for a while, at least till the heat dies down."

"Brian, get yerself to Bristol, I've an address of a safe house where we can talk further. I'll see what I can organise for you."

Doherty read out an address, instructed Brian to commit it to memory. "Get yerself to Bristol Brian, and then we'll talk."

"Mr Doherty, thanks."

"Don't fuck up Brian, just stay calm, we'll get you home."

The anonymous sympathiser called Brian to the phone. It was the call he was waiting for, Doherty. "Mr Doherty, what have you got for me?"

"I've got a little job for you, south of the border Brian. Seems that some of your traveller kinsmen have decided to play hardball with our little enterprise. We have some influential tinkers here, threatening to veto our plans to unite the clans."

"What do you want me to do?"

"Do what you do Brian, get in, win their trust, see if you can straighten them out, if not, roll with it and wait for us to give you further instructions."

"Mr Doherty, there's a small complication this end I'm afraid."

Doherty sighed, "Isn't there always a complication Brian?"

"It's me girl Mr Doherty, I've got me little girl with me."

"That's your concern Brian, as I said, roll with it. We can move her with you, how you work her in is your affair."

"Thank you Mr Doherty."

"Brian, keep it low key and don't make any loud noises until we tell you to, is that clear?"

"Crystal clear."

Passage from Bristol to the Irish coast just off Waterford was hurriedly arranged and within a few hours, Brian and a subdued Monica were sneaking past the coastguards on a tiny fishing boat which looked wholly unsuitable for crossing the open water of the Irish sea. Appearances can be deceiving, and underneath the peeling exterior of the boat's hull was a pure thoroughbred vessel which would be the pride of any Cornish smuggler.

It seemed that the wind was blowing the right way for Brian.

He was doing what he did best; leaving everything to his wits; his feral instincts. Loosely following his superior's instructions; he was to infiltrate the group at Cherry Tree Farm, and win their trust.

His impulsive decision to kidnap Monica before making his escape from the mainland had proven a winner with his adopted brethren, on the run with a stolen infant in tow it gave his cover story kudos, especially when he explained that he had liberated her from her 'settled' or non-traveller mother. When he requested sanctuary, any suspicion they harboured was quickly dispelled. He was welcomed into the bosom of the community.

Nicholas P Boyland

CHAPTER 44

Incognito

After a torturous drive through the pouring Northern Ireland rain and several tense moments at army checkpoints, the rescue party rolled up at the barracks in Armagh. Ensconced in an unused briefing Portacabin, hanging, waiting for the call was the most torturous time for Neil. Up until then, things had happened apace. Now time was ticking monumentally slowly.

Goose's contact in Armagh, an NCO, walked into the briefing room. "We've hired you a motor from a unit we use for covert ops here, they are trustworthy, the motor looks like shit but it's totally A1 mechanically, so nothing to worry about. It's a 2.8 Granny the Rads discretely moved back and it has thick steel plate under the driver's side floor so it should be tough enough to get you into and out of trouble. If you have to ram, try to use the back end, they are built like brick shit houses and will keep going no matter how hard you hit them. Now you can't risk crossing the border and checkpoints heavily tooled, but you can't take these boys on with just your dicks in your hands, so," he handed them a gym bag each, "in these bags you'll find paint-ball masks, pads, gloves, overalls and most importantly, boxes of CO2 sparklets for paintball pistolas." The boys shuffled around nervously, exchanging incredulous glances. He continued, "Under the first two rows of sparklets you'll find your proper ammo." He smiled. "My idea, excuses the weight you see. I had to think on my feet a bit as you mustn't be caught with any obvious army issue kit! Your pieces are Russian. Provo stuff, you'll be familiar with them, I'm sure," he winked. "They're fully loaded to go in an emergency. Chuck them right down in the bottom of your bags." He laughed, "I've stuck some barrel bungs in them for authenticity. We have thrown in some other pressies too, there isn't much, a couple of smoke bombs and some thunder-flashes, it's BAOR assault course training stuff, the sort of thing you could easily acquire openly if you had a mind to. Nothing sensitive." He added, "Oh and lads, when you get south, try to sound like you are all from the same area, affect an accent if possible; West Country perhaps, that's an easy one. You need to lose the forces' accents. The Micks are not experts in colloquial speak but they recognise generic Squaddie.

Goose raised an animated eyebrow; the boys cracked up with laughter.

The NCO received a paging and abruptly left the room. Within a few moments, he was back at the door. "You're good to go, we have an address in Waterford. He's on a traveller park in Cherry Tree.

Cherry Tree Farm. It's a relatively soft target, no real fortifications. Unless he is holed up in the farm itself or farm buildings." He showed a couple of photos to Goose depicting a classic arrangement of farmhouse, yard and surrounding outbuildings. The caravans were arranged outside the gates of the farmyard in an adjacent field. He continued, "The farm and outbuildings are stone with heavy tiled roofs. You can see from the photos that the yard is gated but it's a conventional farm gate. If this was a Provo stronghold, I would expect the entrance to be fortified." He handed the photos to Neil. "You might just get lucky. You will encounter a checkpoint as you leave South Armagh so I hope your papers are in order, once you leave here you are on your own, nobody but the people in this room know what's on, so treat all as hostile, but don't hurt the friendlies, if you know what I mean." He turned to Goose and added, "Check in with us before you hit the target in case any last-minute intel comes in. If you get stopped by friendlies, try to talk your way out, but don't make a fuss. Go quietly and get them to call us. We can get you out of the shit if you get compromised before any action, but we'll have to close down the op. If you get stopped by either the Garda or by our boys after the gig, you're on your own. Is that clear?"

They all nodded the affirmative.

He continued, "You all know the deal with the Garda; they're supposed to be singing from the same sheet as us, but they're sympathetic to the Provos' cause, so expect no quarter from them. There's a drop off point for car hire firms at Rosslare, leave the car there. If it's dirty you will have to torch it." He turned to Neil. "Good luck." As the lads were about to leave, he turned as an afterthought popped into his head. "You boys are blessed this weekend. There's a motorbike show on in Waterford, should give you the perfect excuse for being in the Republic. You can say there's an inter-club paintball match on if anyone gets too nosey!" He pointed at his forehead and exclaimed, "Genius," before bursting out laughing. "Lose the pieces when you're through. They're clean but don't even think about taking them home!"

Neil fired the engine of the Granada and quietly engaged gear, leaving the safety of the army compound behind. Now it was for real. The tension in the car was tangible.

They didn't have to travel far before the first military checkpoint had them held at gunpoint. The boys were left to sweat for a while as the conscientious guard checked their papers.

The Corporal leant into the car, looked at Jimbo's tattoos and said, "Nice ink. Where were you stationed mate?"

Jimbo smiled and replied, "All over mate, Fallingbostel, Munster, did a couple of tours here in Armagh."

"What about the rest of you, all Squaddies?"

"Fuck off," spat Goose.

Jimbo laughed and pointing at Neil added, "No, we are, other two are ex Crabs."

Goose butted in with, "Fucking Pongos, do we look like you mouth breathers?"

"Away with you, you fucking knobs," laughed the Corporal lowering his weapon and returning their fake papers, "go and raise some fucking hell boys. Watch yourselves, you hear. Even with the civvies and long hair you still look like a bunch of fucking Squaddies, worse still, you might get mistaken for Regiment."

The four leather-jacketed bikers didn't attract any further scrutiny; the closer they got to Waterford, the more they blended with the local wildlife.

The farm was not difficult to find for men trained in combat orienteering. A safe vantage point was found where the car could be discretely parked but still accessible.

"Stay put," said Jimbo, "I'll just go for a recce piss. You keep out of sight Neil; you're the only one of us that's recognisable." Jimbo just walked up to the bushes surrounding the outskirts of the farm.

"Just as well he's such a big bastard; he can look right over the bushes," Goose laughed.

Jimbo nevertheless chose a part of the bushes that was sparse enough that anyone observing him would see that he was innocently emptying his bladder. On his return, he filled the others in on the intel he had gathered.

"Right," said Goose, "we'll go and find a telephone box so we can touch base with the Armagh Int Corps boys, then we'll get some field glasses out and start a recce proper.

In a stroke of luck, a phone box was located just outside the village, so the boys didn't have to make their presence known to the village.

Goose left the car and shut the door of the box. After a short exchange, he was back in the car with an ashen expression on his face. "There's been a development." He paused, searching for answers. "I don't know quite what to make of this: Cross border intel has it that the Provos may have caught an inkling of something going down. The Garda may be planning a raid. It would appear that these people are criminals, not IRA. They must have stepped on the wrong toes. Your little girl's caught up amongst some pretty nasty, desperate people. If we are going in, we have to move fast and we have to be discrete. We can't risk getting caught between two sides otherwise we could find ourselves the common foe." He glanced around the car at the expressions of the others. "My enemy's enemy is my friend?" he offered as an explanation.

"How much time do we have?" Neil asked.

"An hour or two at the most, we haven't the time to wait for cover of darkness or to recce the site properly, that gives us only one option; someone has to walk in the front gate and find the baby, fast." Goose delivered the final statement with an expression of grave concern.

"I've got it..." exclaimed Goose.

"Care to share?" interjected Neil.

"Where's your lid Bob?"

Bob reached into the foot-well and pulled out his jet helmet to a grunt and a scowl from Jimbo. "Can it Jimbo," Goose snapped, "this little sucker could be our deliverance."

Goose wandered into the field. Strolling over to the caravans, he knocked on each caravan in turn calling, "Hello, hello, anyone home?" At each van he was rewarded with total silence. At the third van, the one closest to the bushes, separated from the road by only a small sparse copse, he knocked on the door, receiving no reply; he noticed the mortise style lock securing the door. A twitching curtain attracted his attention. Glancing in, he saw a young baby in a travel cot, lying on the bed; it was her hand reaching out and grasping the curtain that had alerted him. He recognised Monica immediately. Anxious not to alert Brian and his cohorts to his discovery, he quickly slipped into the farmyard and with the borrowed helmet on his elbow, walked up to the farmhouse door and rapped loudly on the knocker. "Hello, anyone home?" he shouted. Goose was an experienced enough soldier to feel the crosshairs trained on him.

The door opened a crack. A woman, old past her years, questioned, "What d'ye want?"

Goose delivered his practised speech about breaking down on route to the bike rally and could he possibly use her phone to summon assistance.

"No ye cant, we've not got a phone so we don't," she drawled in a heavy Irish traveller dialect with perhaps a hint of marijuana slur. "There's one outside the village so there is, nobut a mile on from here. Now away with yuh, feck ahf." She slammed the door in his face.

"Charmed, I'm sure," Goose added for effect. He returned quickly to the car and relayed what he had learned.

"Do we have a tow hitch?" Neil asked.

"Hey?" Goose replied, trailing a little behind Neil's thinking.

"Do we have a tow hitch? Never mind," he said, getting out of the car to see for himself. "Right," he said, getting back in and shutting the door, "we drive straight through the hedge backwards, through the copse, we will be hidden from the observers in the farmhouse by the caravan itself, as long as we stay forward of the van. We haven't time to wind up the legs so we'll need Jimbo's strength to lift the draw-bar in situ. We know that the van is locked so rather than waste time trying to get it open, we will have to hook it up and fuck off before anyone has even twigged what's going on; bish bosh."

Goose looked contemplative. "It might just fucking work. Let's get it done."

CHAPTER 45

Snag

From the outside, the pub looked as drab and ordinary as any drinking man's boozer. The fagnolia and wood panelled walls gave away not the slightest hint of the strategic importance of the building. This was an IRA safehouse. Deep within the Catholic area of West Belfast, many influential decisions of the 'troubles' had been planned on these premises; some of the most controversial executions, and paramilitary operations has started out as ideas mooted at the oval table ensconced in the massive concealed underground bunker below the pubs outer walls. Tonight was a special occasion; tonight, local warlords were hosting one of the most notorious leaders of the paramilitary wing.

Doherty was not part of Sinn Fein; he was a soldier through and through and was widely held as the true leader of the Provisional IRA.

With the introductions over, the assembled activists began the meeting. First item on the agenda was the impending marching season and the catholic communities proposed response.

Doherty was well aware of how important for morale these risky visits were to the soldiers and volunteers who operated within the Northern Irish cells. Normally based in the comparative safety of Dublin, he was free to lead a life which would not have been too far removed from a minor dignitary on the English mainland, in stark contrast, his

Northern counterparts fought a daily battle against the protestants, the British forces, the Royal Ulster Constabulary, and the emerging loyalist paramilitaries for survival on the streets.

His own cell was briefed not to disturb his Belfast meeting unless the call was of the utmost importance. Well the call came, he knew he had to take it and excused himself from the table.

"Patrick, this better be bloody important!" he barked into the receiver.

"Can you get to a pay phone sir, I've got something important in and we need your response."

"Jesus Patrick, give me five minutes, I'll need to organise an escort."

Despite the associated risks, it was safer to use a random public phone box than to trust any house phone.

Within a few minutes, Doherty returned the call. "OK Patrick, you have my attention, what's the emergency?" he said with more than a hint of impatience.

"We've received a call from our friend in ERU.[1] They have had a tip off which suggests that the

---

[1]

Garda special forces

British are planning something involving your undercover man with the Gypsies."

"Planning what? Do we know what they are planning?"

"Some sort of a raid for sure, we don't know what or when but it's supposedly underway."

"Do we have a cell down Waterford way, ready to respond?"

"We've a few soldiers and some volunteers training down that way, not an organised cell but loyal men who'll lay down their lives for the cause."

"Get them down to the farm; get my man out of there." Doherty took a contemplative pause. "Listen Patrick, tell them to extract my man alive if they can, but if it's not practical, they're to drop him; is that clear?"

"Perfectly clear Mr Doherty," Patrick replied.

"If they do manage to get him out alive, I want them to spread the word that he was killed in action, make sure that our friend in the ERU shares that information with his colleagues. This could be a good break Patrick, so it could."

It was a smiling Doherty who returned to his place at the planning table. The British could inadvertently do him a favour by reporting Brian Dix as KIA[2] thereby expunging his criminal record, his

---

[2] Killed in action

identity, and placing the survival of the stateless Mr Dix entirely in his hands. A powerful weapon indeed.

CHAPTER 46

Retribution

Lost Bob and Goose were stationed on the road beside the hedge; they were both armed with handguns and spare magazines, ready to act as back up if things went wrong. Neil and Jimbo got themselves ready in the Granada. Neil, the more skilful driver, gunned the engine while Jimbo crouched in the passenger seat ready to move as soon as they reached the van. Goose gave Neil a three-finger countdown then thumbs up. He dropped the clutch and the armoured Granny tore through the hedge and into the copse. Within seconds, Neil was bumper to tow hitch with the caravan in an almost perfect manoeuvre. Jimbo leapt out of the vehicle and unceremoniously dumped the draw-bar onto the Granny's hitch before leaping back into the passenger seat. "Go, go, go!" he shouted, adrenaline pumping. Neil powered the car back out the way they came in, leaving two deep train tracks as the protesting caravan was dragged onto the road on its legs.

All hell broke loose in the farmhouse. Bodies armed to the teeth spilled out into the yard. Goose and Bob were doing a sterling job keeping them contained by spraying them with small arms fire. It was only the element of surprise that kept them on top though as they were heavily outgunned. As the Granny burst out of the hedge onto the road, Jimbo dived over the back seat and got the rear doors open. Flinging a smoke grenade with all the force he could muster, Goose threw his body into the slowing vehicle, with Lost Bob following suit, laying down a good cover of smoke between them and their assailants.

Neil gave the Granny full beans, praying to himself that Monica would be safe in the travel cot. A few good bumps saw the caravan legs bent up and away and the van running on its wheels.

With immaculate timing, the fugitives rounded a corner and encountered a convoy of dark transit vans coming the other way. The occupants had their features obscured by balaclavas.

Judging by the ensuing fireworks, the two forces must have practically run into one another. It couldn't have been timed better if they had planned it.

"That baby has a fucking guardian angel," Goose shouted over the revving of the engine and the whooping and hollering of the victorious heroes.

As soon as they felt it safe to do so, Neil pulled off the road into a secluded field. Smashing the window and climbing into the van, he was relieved and delighted to see that Monica, despite her entire cot being on the floor, was standing up, dummy in mouth, holding her arms out for Neil to pick her up.

Despite the urgency of their escape, Neil picked up the baby and hugged her to his cheek. Her arms were tightly held around his neck.

"Should we torch the caravan?" Neil asked.

"You were wearing your gloves weren't you?" Goose questioned, looking at Neil and Jimbo. They both nodded the affirmative. "In that case, I don't think we need to attract the attention. We'll just leave it be, I doubt there'll be too many questions raised about the movements of these characters."

The sky had turned dark with storm clouds. Within minutes, the heavens opened with an almighty storm. "This'll help to cover our tracks." Goose walked around to the rear of the Granada, and with the help of the rain, rubbed his hands across the bodywork, examining the paintwork for damage sustained in the recent encounter with hedges, trees and even bullets. "Amazing," he exclaimed, "you'd think we'd been out for a Sunday drive. Barely a mark on her."

Jimbo pointed out a sizeable dent in the rear left wing.

Goose let out a derisive snort. "That'll wet flat out."

Jimbo punched him on the arm and barked, "Twat." The pair laughed out loud, jumped back into the car and they sped off.

CHAPTER 47

Friendly shores

The drive east to Rosslare passed off without a hitch.

Neil and Monica both had dicky tummies on the ferry trip to Fishguard but it was a very contented crew that arrived back on the mainland safe and sound with their mission accomplished and precious cargo intact. As they disembarked as foot passengers onto Welsh soil, the fake papers, which Gordon had made only twenty-four hours earlier, passed the scrutiny of the customs officials.

They walked out of the ferry terminal, past the long stay parking spaces.

Lost Bob, who had barely spoken a word in the last two days, suddenly found his voice to ask what was probably the all-time stupidest question. "Lads, where the fuck's the car?"

Goose put a fatherly hand on Bob's shoulder. "Liverpool mate." Goose, Neil and Jimbo cracked up into delirious laughter; the perfect antidote to the stress of the last few days.

"Fuck Bob, you really are lost aren't you?" Jimbo chuckled.

The pace of the operations success was requiring a fluidity of planning. Goose had checked back with his Int Corps buddies in Armagh.

Following complaints from locals of a running gun battle playing out in their village the Garda had locked down the area. The farmhouse and surrounding property was a scene of carnage with fallen combatants from both sides. The Provos had won the day. Brian's body was not found among the dead.

"He's either really dead, or nearly dead! These boys don't mess about. He'll turn up on the side of the road with a bullet in his head. That or he won't turn up at all. Depends if they want to send a message or just close the book!" Goose's contact said.

It was sombre but welcome news. This development further complicated how Neil was to just turn up with Monica, without explanation of where he had found her. Goose, ever the strategist, came up with an unpalatable but unavoidable solution.

Goose began walking back to the ferry terminal with renewed purpose.

"Where are we going?" Neil questioned.

"Hertz Rentacar," Goose replied.

Using their fake papers, the boys hired a car from the ferry terminal. After the hyper excitement of the last forty-eight hours, they were glad of a fairly uneventful four-hour, cross-country drive across Wales heading back to the Severn crossing. Driving back over the bridge, they pulled into Clevedon services.

"Now you know what to do don't you Bob?" Neil questioned, handing the sleeping Monica over to Bob's care.

"Duh, I walk into the cop shop at the services, if there are no coppers there, I look for some filth in the car park. Failing that I find a security guard. I hand the baby in, saying I found her abandoned by the wheelie bins outside the garage." Neil looked far from comfortable with this plan but it was better than anything he could come up with.

"Don't fuck up Bob otherwise we're all looking at some difficult questions to answer," Goose cautioned.

Neil gave Bob a serious look and said, "You stick with her Bob, no matter where they take her, don't you let her out of your sight. I don't want to lose her again."

He suspected that the Old Bill would not fall for this hook, line and sinker but hoped that the positive outcome would convince them to let things lie.

"The Old Bill will take the baby to hospital to make sure she is OK before handing her back to Mum. Once she gets to hospital Bob, you can take your leave. The coppers will probably give you a grilling, just don't go calling us up or anything. You're supposed to be a complete stranger so just get on your bike and go back home until the grateful mum contacts you. Sorry you'll miss the celebrations but you'll get yours later." Goose finished with, "Good luck."

Neil made his sad farewells to Monica, before heading into the services to phone Natasha.

Goose stopped him. "Sorry bud, you can't do that. Your missus may have Old Bill around her, watching her. Her reaction is our money shot. We've got to stay away now until after they call, then we can slip back around. In all the ensuing commotion, no one will notice us appear."

The remaining three rescuers jumped into the hire car and set off towards Liverpool to retrieve their car. During the ride home, they decided it'd be safer all round if they didn't give Natasha all the details until the dust had settled, just in case the police decided to poke around in what was, in essence, a rather large shit pile.

The plan worked like well-oiled clockwork. The Detective Inspector breaking the good news to Natasha was left with no suspicion that he was witnessing genuine joy and relief on the face of a tormented mother that had just been given the best possible news; that her baby had been found alive and well and was on her way home.

"It's over," Neil whispered into her ear, "he's gone."

Natasha pulled from his embrace, looked into his eyes and said, "What do you mean, he's gone?"

"Brian, he's gone," Neil reiterated, making sure she comprehended what he was telling her.

"Did you?"

Neil interrupted, "No, not exactly. He must have crossed up some of his former allies. He messed with some pretty heavy players." Neil held her hands up to his chest, looked into her eyes and said, "Please just trust me, let some water run under the bridge. When the dust has settled, I will explain everything. Until then, you must just trust me."

She looked deep into his eyes and said, "I do trust you," and added, "I love you Neil."

CHAPTER 48

Final solution

The hotel was a grand affair; situated in the centre of Dublin the panoramic glass front of the penthouse office suite offered a beautiful view out over the Irish Sea and towards the Howth peninsula. Doherty stood at the smoked glass, field glasses pressed to his eyes. He was observing a round of golf at the prestigious Howth club. Playing an imaginary swing using the glasses as a club, a grin formed in the corner of his mouth; if the British thought the heads of the IRA skulked about in foxholes, they were sorely mistaken!

The buzzer sounded from somewhere below the expansive desk. Doherty pushed a concealed button and the solenoid on an outer door clicked open.

The man stood behind the bullet proof glass outer door, his face wore a concerned expression. Doherty smiled from behind the one way glass and pushed the button a second time to allow the visitor to enter.

"Patrick, what news?"

"Not good Mr Doherty, Dix led our men straight into a firefight, we lost some good soldiers."

Patrick explained to him how the day had gone awry. When he had finished Doherty asked, "And Mr Dix, what of him?"

"Oh, he's just in the pink Mr Doherty, that bloody Jonah would survive any Biblical curse the good Lord could visit on him."

"Indeed Patrick, indeed."

"The Gypsies lost a lot of their folk too Mr Doherty."

Doherty paced up and down the expanse of his office, nervously contemplating the potential gravity of the developments, "Damn, Patrick, this will jeopardise the arms deal for sure!"

"We should take care of Dix, Mr Doherty; he's a bloody liability, so he is."

"You may be right Patrick, you may well be right. Leave it with me; I'll have a think about it." Doherty turned away and sat down at the desk. A look told the soldier that he was dismissed and he let himself out of the penthouse without further ado.

Doherty sat at his desk for a while, head in hands, deep in contemplation. Brian Dix had been instrumental in bringing this deal together but, once again, his hot-headed unpredictability threatened to kill the plan where it stood. After a time, he made a decision. He picked up the phone and dialled a number over the encrypted line. The next words he spoke would decide the future of the troublesome Brian Dix.

CHAPTER 49

Hero worship

Life settled back into a comfortable routine. Neil and Natasha were interviewed by the police, the DI visited a few times to see little Monica. Natasha implored him to give her the name of the person who had found her.

The DI called back a few weeks later. "We've been in touch with the gentleman who discovered Monica, he is happy to meet up and would like to come and visit you. To be honest, he had been on our case from the start. Seems he's taken quite an interest in the little girl's welfare. We had to practically arrest him to get him to give her up," he laughed. Neil smiled.

Natasha laid on a banquet fit for a king. Jimbo and Goose were down for the weekend. If Natasha thought it odd that they had come down, she didn't mention it. She was beside herself with excitement as the motorbike pulled up outside. She whisked the sleeping Monica, resplendent in a white christening gown, up into her arms.

Neil opened the door, Bob walked in. The four burly lads embraced and shook hands with easy familiarity. Jimbo punched Bob on the arm and said, "You found the place alright then, 'Lost Bob'." The four off them burst out laughing. Natasha stood back, a look of total confusion on her face.

Neil put his arms around her and said, "Sit down Honey; we have quite a story to tell you."

CHAPTER 50

To the victor, the spoils

Things settled back down surprisingly quickly. If little Monica had any memory of her harrowing experience, it didn't show at all.

The police mothballed the book on Brian; if they had any unanswered questions, they seemed happy enough to leave them that way. Neil and Natasha decided to move house to a rented property in a nearby village, where they could start over afresh. Their new home had a beautiful mature garden that Monica could enjoy and which would allow the family to expand if they so wished. The village was even more picturesque than their previous domicile. Monica was attending the local kindergarten and Natasha became involved with the pre-school administration. She was becoming a popular figure around the village.

Unbeknownst to her, she acquired a nickname by the local young farmers, certainly a name they never used to her face. If someone referred to 'Nipples' it was generally accepted that they were referring to Natasha.

Neil had decided to quit his job with the newspapers and start his own business, building custom motorcycles. It was early days, but so far the business was doing OK.

A week before Christmas, Natasha announced to Neil that she was on her period and would be off limits over the festive period. Neil was crestfallen; despite her liberated sexuality, Natasha was adamant they didn't have sex during her period.

Neil had invested in some considerable money's worth of sexy attire for his fiancée and was gutted he wouldn't be sampling it on Christmas night.

Imagine his surprise when on Christmas Eve, after Monica was settled in her cot, Natasha took his hand and led him into the bedroom. She took off her dressing gown. She was wearing the black, silky, backless, low cut dress he had bought for her; the dress he thought was still wrapped up and concealed behind other gifts, under the Christmas tree.

"Period?" he enquired.

"Elaborate ploy," she answered. He put his arms around her waist and moved to kiss her; she blocked his move by swiftly dropping her elbows down, grasping his hands. "Open your gift first," she pouted, handing him a tiny, delicately wrapped box.

"What is it?" Neil questioned, tearing the ribbons and bows from the wrapping in his haste to get to the prize inside. She didn't answer, just waited while he lifted a solid silver chain from the box. "Here, let me," she said, undoing the clasp and placing the chain around his neck. Hanging from the chain was a tiny silver key. "This belongs to you now," she whispered. Before Neil could question her, she kissed him with ferocious passion. "Now I'll show you the rest of your present." She pulled the hem of the short little dress up, revealing the suspender belt and black stockings he had bought for her. She coyly allowed her raised thighs to gently part. A look of confusion danced in his eyes before he focused on the rest of his gift; there, to the left of his fiancée's most precious place, was a fresh tattoo of a little red devil, complete with horns and a trident which reached up and above what would be her knicker line if she wore any. Around the devil's neck was a silver chain; the chain was joined to a tiny little silver padlock, fastened via a piercing passing through both sides of her clitoral hood, effectively locking her clitoris away, giving the device physical as well as symbolic relevance.

The devil had a tail, probably a forked tail. Neil couldn't tell as the tail disappeared between her legs.

"Natasha, you never fail to impress," Neil whistled through pursed lips.

Natasha looked into his eyes and her coy expression was replaced by a look of pure lust. "You hold the key Neil, and you can let the devil loose any time you like."

CHAPTER 51

Call my bluff

Despite the extra demands on their time, the couple were still managing to enjoy a fairly exciting sex life. The long dark nights stuck at home without babysitters on hand had inspired them to use a little imagination in their sexual relationship.

Neil had first instigated their shared penchant for writing down their fantasies in wild and fantastical stories. They would both try to top the other's fantasy, going further and further to achieve their distorted version of sexual one-upmanship. As sure as day follows night, when they got the opportunity, they would try to play out these fantasies.

One of Neil's favourite scenarios involved Natasha and a particular venue and outfit. One Saturday night, during one of the balmy nights of spring, the couple had been out enjoying a boogie at a local Exeter venue. Natasha had consumed more than her fair share of alcohol, and was feeling quite drunk, uninhibited and horny. On the way home, Neil commented that Natasha was wearing the outfit from his favourite fantasy and that they would be driving past the venue on route home.

The fantasy involved Natasha walking up the well-lit drive of a local nightclub, a proper seedy place where she had worked behind the bar during one of Brian's protracted absences, and where she was still quite well known. She would walk through the doors, past the doormen and into the nightclub, all the time wearing just the jacket and skirt, minus the blouse and bra. The jacket was a long Bolero style, barely covering her breasts at all, and not designed to be fastened; in fact, it had no buttons or clasps to secure it, even if one wished to.

Natasha picked up the baton and said, "OK. I am game if you are." With that, she removed the bra and the blouse from under the pink jacket and short skirt ensemble she was wearing.

"You wouldn't dare," commented Neil.

"Try me," Natasha replied.

Neil took the key from his necklace, still playing brinkmanship; he made a big show of symbolically removing the padlock from Natasha's clitoris, an action with further inflamed her passions.

Neil was shaking with excitement as he drew the car up outside the 'Red Hen' nightclub. He could see the two burly bouncers standing guard at the entrance. "You have to walk with your arms by your sides. No holding the front of the jacket," Neil dared her.

"OK," she replied and stepped out of the car.

If Neil thought she would chicken out, he was wrong. She sashayed towards the entrance as if she hadn't a care in the world, doing her best to walk the line, despite the amount of alcohol she had already consumed. He could see there was no way she was concealing her breasts. The bouncers stepped out towards her, whistling. They opened the doors to let her in. Just before she stepped over the threshold, she turned to face Neil, leaving him in no doubt that her breasts were completely on show.

One of the two doormen escorted her inside. A little way up the road, Neil managed to park up. With an understandable degree of impatience, he tried to gain entrance to the club. The sole remaining bouncer was having none of it. By now, a queue had formed. Neil, as a seemingly single guy, was low on his list of priorities and would have to wait until at least as many blokes had left as were in front of him. Neil protested, telling him that his fiancée was inside.

The doorman joked, "Mate, lots of fellahs' fiancées are inside."

As it happens, Natasha had walked straight into the doorman, Dave, who had fancied her like mad back when she had worked there. He had missed his chance the first time around through lack of confidence. A few years down the line and given what Natasha was wearing, he was not about to miss out again. He grabbed her arm without a word and led her into the staff restroom.

Fuelled by the alcohol and the rush of doing something so incredibly daring, Natasha's fidelity was seriously at risk.

Once ensconced in the back room, Dave wasted no time in seducing the inebriated Natasha. Within a matter of seconds she was up on the coffee table, legs apart, and he was feeding his erection into her hungry sex.

Before her befuddled brain could focus, he was taking her, using her hard. What was supposed to be an extension of their harmless fantasy had turned into a full on adulterous session.

Natasha was so turned on; she wrapped her legs around Dave's waist and urged him on to use her harder.

Neil was still being made to wait as the remaining doorman called on the intercom for a member of staff to relieve him, as he needed the loo. A fresh member of the door staff took over the duty of denying anyone entry, while the first guy went for his leak.

"Where's Dave?" he questioned.

The first member of staff, obviously senior, just touched a finger to his nose and said, "Never you mind."

The door to the staffroom quietly opened just as Dave withdrew his throbbing manhood from the folds of Natasha's sex and erupted his essence onto the smooth skin of her pubic mound.

"Perfect timing. My turn mate," the other bouncer remarked, taking up position between Natasha's thighs before pulling a condom down over the head of his engorged penis.

Dave didn't protest as his colleague thrust his hard member into Natasha's gaping sex. She was in the throes of an enormous climax and was past caring who was doing it to her.

Neil was becoming hysterical; he needed to get inside the club to see what was happening. The more agitated he became, the less likely it was he would be allowed entry. The club manager was called and threatened to call the police if Neil didn't leave the premises.

Waves of dread and panic were coursing through Neil's veins. The impotence of losing control was feeding his brain with endorphins and testosterone in equal measures.

The sorry outcome of any game played on a knife edge is that someone gets cut.

The only reason Neil was not roughly escorted from the premises was because at that precise moment, the two members of the door staff qualified to do that were busy using his fiancée.

It was sometime after three thirty in the morning that the club disgorged the remnants of the night's revellers onto the pavement. Natasha was one of the last to exit, escorted between the two burly bouncers, her breasts still swinging freely from the little pink top.

Neil felt sick to his stomach; he manhandled the uncooperative Natasha into the back seats of the car and drove off towards home. As she slept it off in the back seat, Neil was subjected to what he suspected to be the aroma of fresh sex. His head and heart were in turmoil. His little head however had no such conflicts; it was hard as a rock.

Neil couldn't control his lust any longer. He pulled into a lay-by and jumped into the back seats. He tore his erection from his trousers before plunging it into Natasha's so recently used body.

Natasha's sex offered none of the usual elastic resistance that Neil was accustomed to. The implications overpowered Neil's resolve and his own climax came immediately, causing him to nearly pass out.

If Neil enjoyed the evening, Natasha had a ball.

It turns out that she had represented a bit of a prize for the male staff of the 'Red Hen'. Most of the guys had fancied her like mad back when she had worked the bar there. When the opportunity had come their way to enjoy the ample fruits of her luscious body, they were only too happy to oblige.

Neil was not so naïve to have missed the possibility that his fiancée had been a little naughty, what he didn't know was that she had been thoroughly and emphatically shared

Neil, addicted to the powerful and inexplicable aphrodisiac effect of what he had instigated, deluded himself that this was his will, and that all was in his power to switch on and off as he pleased. Little did he realise, like every Pandora's Box, Natasha's box was not his for the closing.

In the cold light of the following day, a tormented Neil waited patiently for his fiancée to rouse before nervously asking, "Natasha, did you really go all the way last night?"

Sensing the tension in his voice and the 'little boy lost' expression, Natasha consoled, "Of course not." Seeing the obvious relief flood across his face, she added, "I pulled my jacket together as soon as I got inside, then I just headed for a dark corner of the bar where a couple of geeky guys kept buying me drinks." She could see from the way the colour returned to his pallor that he wasn't ready to face the truth, even though he claimed to want it.

A suspicious look flashed across his face and he reluctantly questioned, "You smelt of condoms, can you explain that?"

She thought fast before giggling out loud, "Master stroke, I knew that would get you thinking." A look of pure cunning flashed across her face before she elaborated, "There was an eighteenth birthday party in the club. I took a balloon into the loos with me." She met his inquisitorial gaze. "Need I go on?" she inquired.

Neil's demeanour relaxed and he hugged her to him.

Natasha felt wretched. She was well aware of her own wanton nature, especially when alcohol was mixed into the equation. Add to this Neil's foolhardy, naïve encouragement. She was appalled at how easily the lies flowed but she couldn't take a chance that Neil might not be able to cope with what he had put into motion. At least not yet!

CHAPTER 52

The lady is a tramp

The letter dropped through the door onto the mat. Neil picked it up and examined the writing. It had a variety of re-direct labels on it but it was addressed to Natasha. He thought nothing of it and left it on the coffee table before slipping out for work.

Around six o'clock, he returned home. Natasha was bustling around in a rush. "Finally, I didn't think you were ever going to get here," she exclaimed, impatiently. "Marie's getting married, and I've been invited out on her hen night tonight. Didn't get the damn letter until today, the damn thing's been trying to find us for weeks. Didn't you remember to arrange the change of address?"

"Yes I did actually," Neil defended. "The rest of our mail's got here all right hasn't it?"

"Can't rely on you to do anything," she mumbled under her breath.

Neil let out a long animated sigh, which made Natasha laugh out loud. "Oh you poor hen pecked soul you."

The dress code called for 'tarts'. After consuming nearly a whole bottle of strong red wine Natasha decided to wear a tiny low cut black dress, red stiletto shoes, ripped black fishnet stockings, suspenders, no panties and a padded bra. The bra showed a generous portion of her ample breasts. She looked every bit the tart. Out alone, you would take her for a prostitute. Just as well she would be in a group of girls similarly dressed.

She spent the next hour painting her nails and shaving her mound so that no hair remained. Any heterosexual man lucky enough to get an 'up-skirt' would surely enjoy the view.

Natasha came downstairs around eight pm. Neil marvelled at how stunning she looked. Her hair was gorgeous and her lips glistened with red lipstick. Her dress hugged her perfectly, her legs looked never ending. Five-inch stiletto shoes accentuated her slim sexy ankles. The shoes themselves just showed her toenails and Neil noticed her toenails were painted the same dark red as her fingernails. Her large breasts were pushed up showing an inviting cleavage, into which any man would love to delve. She looked cheap, every bit the low life street hooker. Neil knew no man would be able to resist removing the wrapping that covered her very sexy body.

Natasha looked at him and smiled wickedly. "C'mon Neil, I can't wait for this."

Neil picked Monica up and strapped her seat into the car. Marie's little soiree was a good 20-minute drive away.

As they reached the bar where she was to meet the others, Natasha spoke again. "Well?"

Neil answered her with a question of his own. "Well what?"

Natasha smiled, "Do you want me to be naughty tonight?"

Neil smiled; they had played this game so often. He knew this was all part of the act. "Oh I want you to be naughty all right," Neil dared her, "just you see how naughty you can be, the wickeder the better."

"Are you sure?" she questioned. "You want me to go *all* the way?"

Although Neil thought something *could* happen, he was pretty sure that she wouldn't let it go that far.

He decided to push her a little further and added, "I want you to go *all* the way and a little further!"

She opened the door of the car. "See you later," she said.

"Much later I hope," he added, unaware that he was driving home the final nail in the coffin of Natasha's conscience.

As he drove away, the street-lights illuminated the now empty passenger seat. There in the foot-well was Natasha's little clutch bag, complete with all her cash and her house keys.

Neil nearly turned around to drive back, then with a thought which made him dizzy with insane desire, he   decided   against   it.
So there it was. He had delivered his gorgeous fiancée possibly into the hands of another man. She had no money on her, but he knew she would be able to sub a little cash from Marie, at least enough for the cab fare home. Still, he couldn't help but think about what might happen if she couldn't. His manhood stiffened at the forbidden thought.

CHAPTER 53

Naked truth

As the clock showed eleven pm, Neil wondered how the party was going. He knew Natasha would behave, as she wouldn't want Marie to think badly of her. Still, it was fun imagining all the 'what ifs'. If he had the nerve, he would love to be a fly on the wall.

At around midnight and having had a few glasses of rum, Neil went to bed to await Natasha's return.

At some point he dropped off because the slam of the front door woke him sometime after 4.30 in the am.

Natasha quietly slipped into the bedroom, not noticing that he was awake. As he turned the light on, she looked like a startled doe, caught in headlights. She was very drunk and deliciously mischievous.

Neil smiled at her and asked, "Well, have a good time?"

She smiled back, "Mmmmm," and laughed.

He could see, through the transparent material of her dress, that her bra was missing. He watched as she slipped her dress down and saw she was now not wearing her suspender belt or stockings. Neil's heart nearly stopped with the excitement.

She slipped beneath the covers and straddled him with her legs. As she kissed him deeply he felt her very wet sex against him, which she clasped tightly around his thigh.

"If you're ready, you can shove your cork into my full bottle." She laughed at her cheesy comment and smiled a wicked mocking smile at him.

Neil was shocked. Waves of lust fought a rush of bitter-sweet nausea as he stared at his fiancée. Disbelief and a lack of comprehension rendered him momentarily powerless.

Natasha made a low purring sound and ground her sex hard against Neil's thigh. "Now you'd better fuck me before I pass out you bastard." Whispering in his ear Natasha slurred, "Well, ask me…"

He played dumb, replying, "Ask you what…?"

"Ask me what happened."

Neil could wait no longer and whispered, "Tell me."
Natasha rolled on top of him with the sheets wrapped tightly around her torso, pressing down on him, keeping his erect shaft tightly trapped between his legs, gently grinding her sex against his pubic mound. He gasped, desperate to hear her story.

By now Natasha's subtle undulating was leaving Neil's crotch feeling like it was smeared with wallpaper paste. Cold realisation was starting to grip him, causing his manhood to throb and pulsate.

Gently she rubbed against him and began to speak. She was very, very drunk and it was clear that Neil would have to keep her talking if he wanted to keep her awake.

"Marie and John had a huge row. The hen party was cancelled, the wedding's off too." The words were obviously taking a torturous route through her alcohol addled brain cells.

Neil pressed her, desperate for details. "What happened?"

In a moment of sudden clarity, she looked down at Neil and in a gravelly voice said, "I got *fucked.*" In quieter tones she added, "I got really, really fucked."

"Oh my god," Neil whispered through clenched teeth.

"They couldn't get in touch with me," she continued, "I hadn't sent an RSVP, so they thought I wasn't coming." Her words were coming in a clipped staccato as her sexual excitement built. "I ended up asking behind the bar 'Did anyone know Marie'. The barman knew, said she'd booked tables for the hen party but cancelled, wedding was off. I ordered a drink, lost my bag." She was breathing hard, her nostrils flaring as the arousal of recalling the night robbed her lungs of breath. "These guys started buying me drinks. I sat with them in a booth. They were all looking up my skirt, between my legs. They passed me round so they could all get a good look. It was so horny. Guy called Tony sat with me. Kept trying to lift my little dress; really flirting with me." Her breathing was becoming laboured, her speech punctuated by little moans. "Had a great time in the bar; a few sexy dances with them. They took turns buying me drinks. I'm so pissed! They wanted payback."

Neil's voice was hoarse as he asked, "What kind of payback?"

"Fuck," she slurred, and rolled onto her side, keeping the sheet around her and her legs wrapped around Neil.

"What kind of payback? he growled.

"They…I promised…" she hesitated again.

"Promised what?"

"To fuck them!"

Neil's throat began to constrict and his mouth suddenly felt very dry. "You dirty bitch," he snapped.

She continued, "We left together, all of us; this one guy holding my hand." She squirmed a little, obviously feeling self-conscious.

"Go on," Neil whispered. His voice was barely an audible rasp.

Inspired, Natasha continued in hushed, husky tones, the revelations obviously filling her with nervous excitement. "I kissed him, felt his tongue in my mouth. We all got into this van, he got his cock out."

Neil was not accustomed to her using such profanity. It heightened the depravity of the event.

"Messed about as he drove. He was swerving all over, so I thought I'd better stop. Couldn't help myself though. I sat back in my seat and lifted my dress."

"Oh my God. You fucking slut." By this time, Neil's penis was standing stiff as a post. His insults were clearly adding to Natasha's excitement as she continued her story with vigour.

"They let the seat down so that my head was in the boys' laps. They ripped off my bra and flung it out of the window. They were impressed with my tits."

"Were they touching them?"

She giggled at his naive comment. "Touching them! What do you think?" She pulled the sheet down, exposing her breasts which were covered in purplish love bites and bruising. "They really loved my tits."

The marks cemented in Neil's mind the absolute accuracy of the tale she was re-counting.

Grasping Neil's firm erection in her hand, she continued, confidence building. "You should have seen what the driver was doing to me."

"What was he doing?"

"Fingering me!"

Neil's heart was beating fast and hard in his chest. He was asking her stupid inane questions just to keep her talking, keep the buzz coming.

"Oh God," he sighed. "How many fingers?"

"His whole fucking fist!" She laughed.

Neil almost passed out.

Natasha paused recounting the night's events, her inebriation threatening to rob her of consciousness.

"Your tits are so messed up; they must have really gone to town on you," Neil prompted her, keen for the dialogue to resume.

"Oh hell yea," Natasha slurred, "you'd better believe it."

"What else happened?"

"What do you think happened?" she teased.

For Neil, the make or break moment was coming. He knew that her next sentence would seal it. For all his pushing, a little voice inside him hoped it wouldn't be true!

"They pulled over somewhere, and got me in the back of the van."

"Did they fuck you? Did you let them fuck you?" Neil asked, his voice now almost begging.

She opened her legs wide and said, "What do you think?"

"Oh god," Neil exclaimed as he gazed down at Natasha's sex, the evidence of his humiliation plain to see. "Did you let them fuck you?" he asked in a childlike voice, craving verbal confirmation.

Natasha's long lashes fluttered as her smokey eyes met Neil's with a look of lustful betrayal. "Yes, I fucked them," she confirmed. Slowly she added, her voice a low purr, punctuating every word for emphasis, "One after another, over and over, and over."

"You filthy fucking whore, how many of them?"

Natasha laughed in mocking tones, "Four. There were four of them, and I let them all come inside me. Now why don't you finish me off?"

Neil could contain himself no longer. He thrust his throbbing erection into her and felt the unmistakable touch of cool bodily fluids engulfing his shaft. He thrust all the way inside and knew the cold kiss of adultery oozing past his manhood as he made his passage into Natasha's freshly used sex. His climax followed swiftly, and he deposited his essence into the primordial ooze between his fiancée's legs.

To a normal man, this adulterous admission would be unacceptable. For Neil, as he was in a state of obscene arousal hovering around the point of losing consciousness, Natasha had temporarily been raised to the position of 'High Priestess', her sex elevated to the status of 'Holy Grail'.

Such experiences borrowed from the laws of nature and debts must be repaid. The euphoric feeling would be short-lived!

CHAPTER 54

What a difference a day makes!

"Oh dear, I really don't feel well. I think I need to stay away from the booze for a while." Natasha gently pushed back the covers. The bruises and love bites on her body made Neil wince as the memories flooded back. Playfully, she chided, "Neil, you bad boy, you shouldn't have pushed my buttons the way you did."

"What do you mean?" he asked.

"You know what I'm like when I get drunk, you're supposed to protect me, not encourage me!"

"Oh I see," he replied, barely disguising his anger. "So it's my fault that you get pissed and screw around?"

"What?" she questioned, a note of incredulity in her voice.

"You heard!" he snapped.

"No. No. No. We are *so* not doing this; you have been pushing and coaxing me for months. You practically forced me into this. Now you're going to get shitty? This is too much, you're too much Neil."

He looked at her with a look of distaste she didn't recognise. "God, you stink of sex, go and have a shower or something!"

She was too angry, too hurt to cry. She threw the covers off the bed and she stormed out of the room.

"You total fucking bastard," she shouted back at him, slamming the bathroom door.

It was a full hour later when she emerged from the bath. Her hair was bundled up in a towel turban.

She had wrapped the largest bath towel she could find around herself. Her eyes were red from crying.

Neil intercepted her on the landing. He wrapped his arms around her.

"Get off me Neil," she cried, squirming to be free of his embrace, "leave me alone."

He shook his head. "I'm sorry… I'm so sorry OK? I just don't know where I'm at with this. I'm so sorry. I know it's my fault, my thing. I'm having a hard time with it, that's all. I'm really sorry. I'm just having regrets. Oh I don't know, I'm just feeling really insecure now."

She hugged him back. "Neil, you know how much I love you. If you're not comfortable, then we don't do it. We don't need other people. I don't need anyone else. You're my world Neil. Everything I do is to please you!"

"I know. I know. I am so lucky to have you."

"Let's just concentrate on making each other happy Neil. Forget all the other stuff. Just me and you."

"And Monica."

"Of course," she agreed.

It should have ended there.

It didn't.

CHAPTER 55

Missed opportunity

Happy families proved to be nothing more than an impasse.

Two weeks later, things were beginning to settle back into a comfortable routine.

Natasha returned from a morning play group session with Monica. "Neil, Debbie and Sharon have asked me if I fancy a night out with them next week. Saturday night," she light-heartedly remarked.

"Where?" Neil questioned.

"I don't know. A nightclub I suppose. We didn't really get as far as discussing where."

"Have you said yes to going?"

"Well, yes. I suppose I have. You're all right with it aren't you?" she replied, confused.

"Are Debbie's and Sharon's partners OK with it?"

The confusion in her voice became more apparent. "Neil, what gives? Since when have you got funny about me going out?"

"Oh, no. It will be fine, I'm sure. I suppose you have me down as babysitter?" he snapped.

"No, that's alright Neil. Just forget it. I'll get Mum to sit. No better still, I won't go," she retaliated.

"No, no, it's OK. I'll sit for you, you just go on out and have yourself some fun. Don't worry about me," he added petulantly.

"Neil, for God's sake. Is this still about what happened? I thought we'd put that to bed?" she asked, somewhat subdued.

"Yea, someone was bedded, that's what I'm worried about," he snorted, under his breath.

"What?" she enquired, genuinely not hearing him.

"Nothing. No, it's OK of course you can go out. Take no notice of me; I'm just being irrational and possessive. Of course you can go out with your friends. A good night out with the girls is just what you need."

Natasha hugged him, her mood warming instantly. "Thanks. I thought you'd be OK with it!" She added, "We just need to get Deb's fellah to sit now and we're on."

Friday night. Natasha put Monica to bed early. She cracked open a bottle of red wine and consumed a few well deserved glasses.

Neil got home late. She was quite well relaxed by the time he came in the door.

Natasha was wearing hold up stockings, a backless, deep plunge front dress which left nothing to the imagination.

"Wow!" Neil observed. "What's the special occasion? Is it my birthday?"

"No," she purred, "it's your sex day. I thought you might like to choose an outfit for me to wear out tomorrow night."

Like the flicking of a switch he was frothing at the mouth. All Neil's resolutions to curb the kinky stuff were gone. By the time they had finished, Neil was pressuring her to be naughty again!

CHAPTER 56

Cracks

Debbie decided to drive as she wasn't in the mood to drink. Her car was parked up outside her house by one o'clock Sunday morning. Natasha didn't show up at home until after three!

The mind of a cuckold is a confusing place. After the overwhelming blood rush of desire comes insane jealousy. In the cold light of day, with the hormones washed from his brain, Neil would think with his heart instead of his smaller, but nonetheless influential, organ. To bring some rationale to what could never make any sound sense, he convinced himself that he was the instigator and that everything Natasha did was to please him. He knew he had to control the regrets and recriminations and view things as a new direction for their exciting, albeit unusual sexual urges.

As the weeks and months went on, Neil increasingly gave in to the rush of their lusty sessions, involuntarily pushing his emotions further and further down, as the heady buzz of the drug intensified.

Closeness in their relationship was now judged on the intensity of their angry, nocturnal activities. Family life was fading into a background of mediocrity; merely inconvenient stops between stations of lust.

If Neil was having problems reconciling his uncontrolled, sexual desires with his instincts, Natasha too was struggling to accept that Neil could love her the way he professed to, whilst wanting to share her. She couldn't take his increasingly cold attitude after her illicit sexual liaisons.

Without meaning to, Natasha was beginning to build up defences around her emotions, convinced that Neil was beginning to fall out of love with her.

Neil interpreted her barriers as confidence and arrogance. To him, she was becoming quite bristly. It seemed that their new-found erotic fantasy lifestyle was not really sitting well with either of them. Guilt and recriminations were leading to further hostility. Neil couldn't do a thing right without it causing bickering. Natasha was finding him increasingly brooding and sulky.

Communication had broken down. Emotions were being conveyed only through the medium of licentious sex.

Natasha was becoming more daring and taking greater risks in the pursuance of her liaisons.

Neil had taken to plying her with copious amounts of alcohol before dropping her off at some remote bar or club, penniless and dressed like a hooker, knowing that her passage home would depend on some sleazebag's gratitude for services rendered.

For Natasha, the alcohol numbed the depravity of the act and helped her to forget their faces. All she really craved was the attention and approval Neil showered her with in the immediate aftermath of her infidelities.

After each encounter, Neil's passion would cool more quickly, leaving her feeling more alone and unloved than at any time in her life. If Neil would only love her with as much passion as he showed her for those brief moments in bed, she would do anything he wanted.

It was all about sex, they had long since stopped making love. Natasha was rapidly becoming miserable.

CHAPTER 57

Reach out

Natasha and Star had become firm friends since the rally in Oostende. She had never had a real friend and confidante, apart from Julie, whom she loved to bits, but they had just been neighbours and intellectually they were worlds apart. Women, like her pal Sue, tended to befriend Natasha to share some of the positive male attention she attracted, or they viewed her as a threat and mistrusted her. She needed to talk to someone about the direction her and Neil's relationship was taking and the older woman had the emotional experience which Natasha lacked. They met up in a coffee shop. Natasha returned to the table with two cups of filter coffee and pushed a cup across the table to Star.

She was somewhat clumsy in broaching such a difficult and potentially embarrassing subject but Star soon sensed that she needed something off her chest and calmed her with a few soothing words. "Come on then love, it can't be so terrible. Tim and I have seen some pretty unusual twists and turns in our relationship too. Tim used to lodge with me and my husband. Try making that work! Now come on, 'a trouble shared is a trouble halved' you should know that." She added, "I can't help you if you don't let me in."

After a protracted pause in the conversation, Natasha dropped the bombshell. "Neil likes me to have sex with strangers." She blurted it straight out, then blushed scarlet. "There, I've said it. Neil likes me to dress up like a cheap whore and have sex with total strangers. He gets off on it."

"Wow," Star exclaimed. She paused awhile, clearly taken aback. She let the enormity of Natasha's statement sink in before replying, "He likes you to have sex with strangers?"

"Yes," replied Natasha.

"What, all the way, full penetration, the lot?"

"Yes," Natasha confirmed, "God knows what they do to me, I'm always so drunk. Neil's starting to really pressure me, he's not happy unless I've been out and had sex with other guys, then after he's got his rocks off, he gets all funny and sulky, like he can't really handle it."

Star sat forward in her chair, her face contorted with surprise and confusion and asked, "What do you think Girl, how does it make you feel?"

Natasha reddened up again before saying, "Oh, I don't know really. I didn't mind the sex at first; it was quite a rush really. I'd be more than happy with just Neil, but I do enjoy sex, so it wasn't exactly a chore. It's just that the whole issue is coming between us. Saturday nights are becoming almost a ritual. Neil babysits Monica. He drops me off. I have to go out alone to some club or another, get picked up, have sex with strangers then return home in the early hours. If I come home early or I don't feel like going out, he gets irritable and causes an argument."

Star sat back in her chair again, mouth agape.

"I don't think Neil loves me anymore. He gets so moody, and then he's plying me with alcohol. He knows what I'm like with the booze and there he is, pushing me out the door again, all turned on, pressuring me to perform. Just so he gets his jollies."

Despite the shock of Natasha's revelations, Star was really trying to find some sound advice to impart to her friend. "My folks experimented with free love, wife swapping and the like, back in the sixties, so I do have some insight into the lifestyle."

"And?" Natasha questioned.

"Well, they split up. I don't know. I think humans are hard-wired to be monogamous, at least, once the right soul-mate has been found. You do surprise me though. I always thought Neil was the possessive type?" Star held her hand as she could see Natasha was becoming emotional.

"He was, that's another thing which makes me feel insecure. He was apparently quite jealous of his other girlfriends and yet here he is making me sleep around as though I were a whore and him my pimp." Natasha's voice tailed off at the end of the sentence. She stared down at the table, trying hard to keep the tears at bay. "I've never told anybody this, not Neil, not even my mum. My ex used to treat me like a possession. He never loved me. He used to get drunk and violent, and then he would share me with his gambling buddies. I learned to just detach emotion from sex and make the most of the physical attention, substitute it for love. He was a control freak, he made me feel worthless. I've always been attracted to controlling men; this is beginning to feel like it's all coming around again!"

Star, having had a little more time to ponder the situation, squeezed her hand and spoke softly. "Natasha, I do know one thing, Neil loves you to bits, I'm sure if he knew how you felt it would have an effect. What about having Tim speak to him; urge him to see the error of his ways?"

"No!" Natasha replied, raising her voice slightly. "No, don't say anything to Neil; he would be mortified if he thought you knew. It could even destroy your friendship. I would never want that." Natasha cupped her hand over Star's reassuringly and said, "Thank you so much for listening to me Star, it's been so nice to share my dilemma like this, as you said, it has shared the burden." She stood up to leave and added, "I have to find a solution to this problem before it splits us up like your mum and dad."

"My mum and dad probably had a whole host of issues besides. You and Neil are such a great couple, you're perfect together. I really hope you can find a solution." Just before parting company, Star added, "Don't you let Neil push you to do anything you're not comfortable with and don't go taking stupid risks just to please him. I'm worried about you now!"

The two women hugged, kissed each other on the cheek and walked off in their separate directions.

CHAPTER 58

Sacrifice

Natasha, sat in a seedy nightclub in Exeter, dressed as usual in next to nothing, was experiencing an 'out of body' episode; as if she were looking down upon herself, observing her life. She didn't like what she saw.

"Hi," he said.

Natasha snapped out of her caustic reverie as the handsome dark skinned man perched on the stool next to her. Unusually, he was staring into her eyes. She was wearing a black see through top; most potential suitors would be staring at her chest or trying to look up her tiny skirt.

"Hi," he repeated, "my name is Isa, my friends call me Izzy. What's your name?"

"Natasha," she answered, neglecting to follow protocol and use an alias, as would be the established procedure for these frequent encounters.

"Hmm, Natasha," he pondered, "birthday of Jesus Christ. That's a coincidence; Isa is the Arabic name for the prophet Jesus."

Something about the man interested Natasha. She found herself studying his handsome dusky features and his well-toned body. Neil's rules were that she shouldn't fancy her conquests.

To hell with Neil, she thought. She liked the manner of this man; his looks were none too shabby either. "To hell with you," she re-iterated, this time, out loud.

Taken aback, Izzy said, "I'm sorry?"

Natasha let out a little squeak of laughter. "Not you Izzy, I was thinking of someone else. C'mon, dance with me," she laughed, pulling him towards the dance floor.

They made love tenderly in Izzy's hotel room that night. Natasha decided, her heart filled with sadness, not to return home as usual but to spend the night with Izzy.

The die was cast. She knew she had taken the first step in ending her relationship with Neil.

In the morning, she returned home. Neil was beside himself with frantic excitement. She couldn't bring herself to betray her night with Izzy in such a sordid way. She made up a story to satisfy Neil's carnal desires. For the first time since they had met, sex with him left her cold.

Saturday nights were now spent with Izzy. He was something in the oil business back home and was in Britain for a few months on company business, living out of a suitcase; home was his hotel room. Saturday nights, it became Natasha's home too.

Izzy, it turned out, was a Bahraini. Born a Sunni Muslim but educated in the States and the UK. He considered himself a Persian, more a God-fearing Atheist, if such a thing could exist. He had thrown off the chains of religious doctrine in pursuit of a more Western style way of life.

Natasha was now lying to Neil about her Saturday night liaisons. It was difficult for a sensitive person like her to wear two hats. She was having a hard time keeping up her double life.

The girl behind the counter was explaining to Natasha in hushed tones how to read the test results. "You don't have to use test tubes and reagents anymore, it's all quick and simple now, you just have to wee a little on the stick, give it ten minutes to react, then, you compare the colour change to the chart provided, that indicates a positive or negative test result."

Back in the privacy of her own bathroom, Natasha stared at the strip. There could be no doubt, she was indeed pregnant.

Her relationship with Neil was falling apart. The positive pregnancy test was the final agony. She couldn't face telling him. Chances are the baby would turn out to be Izzy's, in which case the skin colour would be a dead giveaway.

Saturday nights were spent with Izzy, plus the odd weekday if she could sneak away.

It was almost three months to the day that they had been secretly meeting when Izzy announced he was returning to Bahrain. "Natasha, I have been happier these last few months than I have ever been," he confessed. "I want you to come home with me to Bahrain. I want you to be my wife."

CHAPTER 59

Serendipity

After weeks of soul-searching, Natasha was on the cusp of deciding she would take up Izzy's offer to leave Neil and move to Bahrain with him.

Out of the blue, she received a call from Star.

"Natasha, I need to talk to you. I've had some thoughts about your situation; I'd like to have a chat. Meet me for a coffee?"

"I'd love to," Natasha replied, "give me an hour. Shall we meet in the same café as before?"

"Sure," Star replied, "I'll get the coffees in, see you soon."

Sat at the table, Star spoke in hushed tones. "Look, I'm no shrink, but I've had some thoughts about what's going through Neil's head. What I think it is that he needs to sort out."

Natasha stirred her coffee with a distinctly detached air and replied, "I have something to tell you too. I think it's possibly too late for me and Neil." Natasha paused before continuing, "Sorry Star, please go on with what you were going to say."

Star looked a bit deflated then said, "Neil's long-term relationships, before he met you, all ended the same way; the girls were screwing around behind his back. I think this is Neil's way of controlling his own destiny. Maybe in his heart of hearts, he thinks he's not enough for you, not worthy. Perhaps he thinks if he allows you to take lovers, encourages it even, that you will love him all the more and stay with him. It's crazy, but I know how much Neil cares for you. It's the only explanation that fits." Star looked at her friend's face, Natasha was avoiding her stare.

She looked up from her cold coffee and said, "Star, I've met someone else. I think Neil and I are too far gone." She told her about Izzy, how they met, how she felt about him. She told Star about his proposal. However, she stopped short of confessing about the pregnancy.

As they parted, Star hugged her friend close to her. Natasha could see the tears welling in her friend's eyes.

As they walked away, she wondered if she would ever see Star again.

CHAPTER 60

Confrontation

Natasha's heart was breaking. Isa had presented her with a ticket to accompany him to Bahrain; one way.

The prospect of leaving Neil was tearing her up. She had never before felt the kind of passion she had shared with Neil, in the early days. If it weren't for the baby, she would confront him. She would tell him how she felt, how she wanted him the way he was, before all the lust had soured what they had.

The date on the ticket loomed. After much soul searching, she decided to have a heart to heart with him to see if they could save their relationship. If he responded, if, by some miracle, he felt the same way, she would come clean about the pregnancy, about how there was a chance that the baby was not his, about Isa. It would be hard. With the prospect of leaving him she had come to realise that she still loved him dearly but wasn't sure they would be able to survive the revelations which were to come. If not, she would cut and run, that very same day, marry Isa and hope one day to love him the way she had Neil.

Ironically, Neil too had arrived at a similar crossroads. He knew their relationship was near breaking point. Something had to change drastically. He didn't want her going with other men anymore. It made him feel physically sick to think of what he had encouraged her to do. He had tried to stop it over the last months. Now it seemed that she was in charge.

Neil cursed the confusion he felt about the whole scene; a scene of his creation, which now threatened to destroy that which he held most dear. He cursed his perverse sex drive, cursed the way his body reacted to her indiscretions. It was like an addiction, an addiction he was determined to break. He knew that it was entirely his fault. He needed to tell her these things, let her know how his feelings had changed; tell her about the changed man he wanted to be; sit down and talk about his feelings, how he worshipped her; how he wanted to stop all this sordid stuff, get married, settle down and have a child together.

Neil was at the bike shop when she rang.

"Neil," she said, "we need to talk."

An irate customer had just walked through the door and was bending Neil's ear about some insignificant warranty issue. "Natasha, I can't talk now," he said.

Guessing he was being deliberately obtuse again she blurted out without thinking, "Neil, I'm pregnant." After a breath or two had passed, she added, "I don't think the baby's yours."

The blood drained from Neil's face; he slammed the phone down and grabbed his car keys. Mr Irate stood between Neil and the door, protesting his rights. Neil demonstrated he had the right to lie on the floor clutching his eye.

As he gunned the engine homewards he considered the ramifications of what she had said. This was fate's way of punishing him for abusing the love they had found. Payback for allowing confused fantasy to merge with the real world.

He would accept the child and love it as his own regardless of how it was conceived. He must convince Natasha of his sincerity. It would be make or break. He couldn't, he wouldn't lose her now, after all they'd been through.

Neil's thoughts were dramatically cut short as his world began to spin as if in slow motion. Cassette tapes, sunglasses and bottles of aftershave were all suspended in a bizarre three dimensional collage. Then darkness and absolute peace.

Neil had been particularly unlucky. Fate had conspired against him. A slippery road, the first icy patch of the winter season. His sports car, driven at a tremendous pace which far exceeded its abilities, had clipped the kerb upon entering a normally innocuous roundabout, spun out of control and flipped over. Neil, who in his haste, hadn't buckled up, was miraculously thrown clear of the car before it landed heavily on its windscreen, crushing the surround flat and filling the car's interior space with twisted metal and glass. The wreck ended up hidden in the thick copse in the middle of the junction, virtually invisible from the road.

It was dark by the time a confused Neil regained consciousness. In the absence of light, he didn't notice the oak tree, or the patch of fleshy, exposed wood shining with fresh sap where the bark had so recently been rent. He failed to register the viscous stain on the frozen moss and roots at the foot of the tree; an inert clue to the seriousness of his plight.

The house stood deserted. The interior was lit only by cool reflected light from a single streetlamp. Neil stumbled inside. The usual conversation of the TV was missing. It sat there in the corner; a lifeless black screen where the reflection of Monica's laughing face would normally be etched, staring in wonderment at animated characters of one or another of her favourite Disney films.

He called out, "Natasha." Striding to the stairwell he called again, "Natasha, are you there?" He noticed the chill in the air. The heating was off. The timer was playing up and they were turning it on manually when they were in the house. *Damn,* he thought, *where the hell is she?* He considered going into the kitchen to switch on the boiler. Thinking better of it, he tried to run up the stairs, tripping on the steps as his leaden legs refused to keep synchronous time, anxious to see if she was in their bedroom. "Damn," he thought again, aloud this time, "why is it so damn cold in here?"

The letter was lying on the pillow, as usual wrapped in a delicate ribbon with an intricate bow. His hand was trembling as he withdrew the letter from its silky prison. Despite his chill, he felt sweat on his brow and wiped it away with his shirt sleeve.

As he focused on the paper, the blood-soaked arm of his shirt went unnoticed.

"Dearest Neil, I am so sorry it has come to this. I can't live like this any longer, I am leaving you." The words began to fade out and blur; the floor came rushing up to meet him as he lost consciousness.

Just as the life blood of a candle pools to extinguish its own flame, Neil Curland slipped into a coma, an internal bleed threatening to snuff out his life force just as surely as the charred remains of the candle's wick.

As Neil's awareness faded, he silently mouthed Natasha's name.

At that precise moment, a hundred miles away, Natasha's plane was taking off towards a destiny across the other side of the world, her mind focussed on the new life which lay ahead of her, and the new life growing within. As life ends, so life begins.

CHAPTER 61

Worlds apart

The first weeks in Bahrain were wonderful. Izzy, it turned out, was an extremely wealthy man. Being a Sunni Muslim, Isa's family were part of the ruling elite and wealth and privilege came hand in hand.

They were living out of a posh hotel while their living quarters were prepared in Izzy's family home. Izzy let her in on a rather disappointing revelation when he told her they would have to pretend they were married, as his family's religion would prohibit them from co-habiting unless they had tied the knot.

Since his return to Bahrain, Izzy had started visiting the mosque twice a day to pray. He told Natasha that it was expected of him and as long as they were living in a Muslim country, it would be better for them to observe their host culture.

He was beaming with pride as he introduced his young attractive 'wife' to his family. His mother, obviously the matriarch, was the one member of the family who didn't speak a word of English. Once an extremely attractive woman she had been married off to Isa's father to cover some sort of family debt. Quite ill-educated she spoke only her native Urdu. Living under the same roof were Isa's younger brother, his wife, their two children; two girls of five and six, and Isa's teenage son by his previous wife.

Demonstrating his westernised attitude Isa's brother, Jalil, offered his hand to Natasha for a handshake. His wife Aalia, however, stood waiting her husband's approval before coming forward in greeting.

Natasha moved forward to shake her hand, only to find the woman pulled her close in an embrace and whispered in her ear, "I am so pleased you are here, my sister." In innocence, Natasha went forward to hug the old matriarch the same way. She was rewarded with a sharp rebuttal as the woman spat on the ground and shouted something in her mother tongue, which subdued everyone in the room. Isa retaliated with a raised voice. A heated exchange in Urdu followed. The old woman, clearly reminded of her place, spat again and stormed out of the room.

"I am so sorry," Isa offered, "my mother is old, she expects to remain the boss of the household. I have told her that as a Westerner my wife will be the head. I will not tolerate it any other way."

Natasha put her hand on his and said, "I don't want to usurp your mum's authority Izzy, as long as she lets me look after you and Monica, everything else can remain as it is. You don't need to make changes for me."

"I have spoken," he replied curtly. "She will have to accept that change occurs."

Hanging back out of the limelight was Isa's son from a former marriage. Izzy introduced him. "Natasha, this is Mahmood, my son." The teenager hung back, he struck Natasha as sullen and petulant. She mouthed a hello to him. His eyes cast across her face then down to his feet. Obviously uncomfortable, he scurried out of the room.

This was just one of many things Natasha was to find strange here. She was naturally unaccustomed to the culture. The country was strictly divided; rich and poor, men and women. In the early days, she was treated well, more tourist than Bahraini woman. Things would change when she moved in with Izzy's family.

Finally, the preparations were complete and Natasha and Monica moved into their new family home.

Izzy proudly showed the living arrangements to Natasha. Their quarters were palatial. "First, I'd like you to see our bedroom. Just to spoil you, we have an en-suite and a hot tub." Connected to the master bedroom, separated by just a door was a small room which Izzy declared was the baby's room. "Just for when my son is a baby and needs his mummy close to hand," he announced. "Once he is a little older, he has his own suite of rooms along the hallway." Just off the corridor from their room was Monica's room. She had a bedroom and studio to herself. "Once my son is old enough to sleep in his own room, I will use the small room as my study." Across the quadrangle was a pool-house with a full-sized swimming pool.

"Where does your son live?" she asked Izzy.

"He has his quarters with my mother." Izzy's face took on a serious expression. "Listen Natasha, my son is a little disturbed. My former wife had an opium addiction, the boy was born 'troubled'. He lives with my mother, it is like he is her son. He will not bother you. We do not ever mention his mother." He looked her in the eye and said, "We would like to keep it that way, if you don't mind. I'm afraid that I won't be here to help you settle in," Isa confessed. "I have to pop away on business. I won't be gone long, just a few days."

"Can't we come with you?" Natasha implored.

"I'm afraid not," he replied, "it's going to be a bit of a whistle-stop tour, just meetings, contract signings and moving on to the next meeting. It will be far too hectic for Monica."

That night, in a freshly painted palace, in a strange country, thousands of miles from home, Natasha was dreaming of a humble fishing village on a Greek island, with a little motorbike outside and Neil lying by her side.

CHAPTER 62

The gilded cage

Natasha decided to have a wander round her new home town. She prepared herself for the heat of the Bahraini sun, tucking her hair into a headscarf as Izzy had advised her to do. Western women were free to wear what they pleased, but as the wife of a senior Bahraini businessman, it was advisable for Natasha to observe the dress code of her adopted culture. Keen not to offend, she wore a long cotton skirt and a blouse covering her shoulders. With her dark features, she could easily pass for a native Bahraini.

The sheer size and layout of the family home was confusing to Natasha. Despite finding her way into the courtyard via several entrances, she was unable to find the door that led to the outside world. Eventually, she found herself in the quarters of Isa's family.

Seeing the familiar face of Aalia, she asked the other woman, "Aalia, it is Aalia isn't it? I hope I'm pronouncing your name correctly."

"That is correct; Ahleeha, you say just right." Her English was slightly broken but nevertheless very good, hinting at an expensive overseas education.

"I would like to visit the town today." She looked somewhat embarrassed before adding, "I can't find the outside door!"

Aalia put her hand on Natasha's and said, "The door for outside is past the old lady's quarters." She looked worried as she added, "You must seek her permission before you may go to outside!"

"What?" Natasha exclaimed. "You are joking? I need the mother's permission to go outside?" She continued angrily, "I thought I was the head of the household now, not the mother."

Aalia answered, "When your husband is away, his mother is head. You must respect her rules or she can make big trouble for you!"

Natasha angrily retorted with, "We'll see what Izzy has to say about that when he gets back."

Aalia caught hold of both her hands, she made sure she had Natasha's full attention before saying, "He is a Bahraini man, it does not mean anything that he takes for him a Western wife or makes himself a Western man. He is a Bahraini, a Muslim. He will respect and obey his mother over all!" She drew Natasha by the hand and said, "Come, we will speak with her."

Aalia spoke to the old woman. The exchange was in the old woman's native tongue. Natasha, not comprehending a word, stood back and observed the conversation. The younger woman obviously both feared and respected the matriarch as she ended each sentence with a gesture not unlike a bow, keeping her eyes upon the floor the whole time. The old woman barked and cursed back in her guttural, primitive language, clearly not happy about being challenged.

Aalia quickly broke off the exchange and drew Natasha to a side room, away from the angry surveillance of the old matriarch.

"She says it is too dangerous for you to go into the town. She says you must wait for your husband to escort you if you wish to go." She giggled a little, embarrassed and elaborated, "She asks why you would wish to expose your daughter to the outside when we have servants to run such errands."

Natasha decided not to confront the old woman, better to wait until she had Isa on her side.

"What did she mean, too dangerous?" she asked Aalia.

The Arab woman looked contemplative and answered, "We have some problems here, some social, and some religious, maybe political. There is some tension between Sunni and Shiite peoples. It is not safe for wealthy Sunnis to venture out alone, especially women and children, there have been some kidnappings, not many but it is a worry."

"Well Aalia," Natasha said, "if I can't go out, perhaps you could show me around the grounds, then perhaps later we could let the children have a paddle in the pool."

Aalia smiled, "I would like that very much." She added with a beaming smile which showed her sincerity, "I am so pleased Isa has brought you here, I feel like you will be my sister."

Natasha put an arm around her waist and said, "I am relying on you to show me the ropes here Aalia before I do something I shouldn't do. Now then, first off, are we allowed a drink, 'cause right now, my feet in that pool with a large glass of red in my hand is as close to heaven as I need!"

Aalia nodded. "Yes, in Bahrain, with a husband's permission, we are permitted alcohol in moderation."

"Good," Natasha replied with a laugh, "because I haven't had a drop in days and I intend to get moderately drunk."

Monica was settling in nicely to her new surroundings in the dayroom, supervised by a full-time live in governess. The two older girls were vying for the attention of their younger 'sibling' and were relishing the opportunity to help her with learning English.

Natasha, bereft of the responsibilities of mother and 'housewife' for the first time in her life, was revelling in the 'me' time with her new sister beside the pool.

Empty wine glass in hand, Natasha called out to the servant, "Fill me up." Aalia watched on nervously as the servant topped her new friend's glass up for the third or fourth time. Natasha was becoming more and more relaxed with every glass.

Izzy walked into the bedroom. Aalia had supervised putting the inebriated Natasha into bed. As Izzy pulled back the covers to climb in Natasha stirred. Seeing the masculine shape of her naked man, back from his travels, excited her and through her alcoholic haze she growled, "Come here hunky." In the half light of the room and through her bloodshot eyes, Natasha failed to see the look of shock on Isa's face. Missing the signals, she threw the covers off, opened her legs and whispered just loud enough for Isa to hear, "Come here and fuck me!" Isa slapped her hard on the face before throwing the covers off and storming out of the room!

Over breakfast, Izzy sat with his newspaper open, blocking him from Natasha's questioning gaze. Eventually, she could stand no more and slapped the newspaper from his hand.

"What is this, have you taken leave of your senses woman?" he shouted.

"What is going on Izzy, what the hell happened last night?" She paused, giving him a moment to reply before continuing, "You hit me Izzy, why?"

He flicked his newspaper back into its fold before shouting back at her. "You are supposed to be my wife, I don't expect you to come on to me like a drunken whore." He lowered his voice and added, "You are six months pregnant with my child, what sort of woman is drinking alcohol and acting like a prostitute when they are heavy with child?"

"For God's sake," Natasha retorted, "you buggered off and left me on my own. I wasn't expecting to be held prisoner here. I'm sorry I had a drink or two and it went to my head, I haven't had a drink in months. You think it's easy for me? I've left everything and everyone behind to be with you. I don't know how I fit in here. I feel like a stranger in my own clothes!" He just stood impassively, seemingly void of emotion. She burst into tears and ran out of the room.

Izzy didn't touch her sexually again for the remainder of her pregnancy.

CHAPTER 63

Original sin

In the balmy heat of the mid-afternoon, an overheated, heavily pregnant Natasha was sitting by the pool, reading a story to Monica who was cheerfully splashing water at Aalia's daughters.

"Monica," she said, "go and get your big super squirter and I'll let you squirt me with it."

"Mummy gets it," Monica replied. Natasha stood to retrieve the gun herself. As she stood, she clutched at her stomach as her waters broke and the pain of the first contraction came. Within the hour, the contractions settled in to a fast and regular routine. The physician was summoned. In contrast to labour with Monica, Natasha was blessed with a swift labour and an undramatic delivery. As expected, the newborn was a boy, with a healthy birth-weight of 8 pounds and 3 ounces.

Even in birth, the little boy was the spitting image of his dad. Unfortunately, he looked nothing like Izzy.

It was pure good fortune which saw Natasha give birth while Isa was on another of his business trips, giving her time to rest and recuperate before facing the music.

Izzy had expressed a wish for the boy to be given a Muslim name. Natasha thought that would change when he saw the child. Anyway, she had already decided to have him Christened David.

She was dozing, having just finished feeding the baby. Izzy walked in the door, having just heard the news that his wife had given birth. He walked into the room, saw mother and child asleep on the bed.

Natasha awoke to see his angry face gazing down at her.

"Slut!" he shouted, followed by, "Whore, you are dead to me, gather your things and get out of my house."

"Izzy, I'm so sorry," Natasha protested, "I swear I didn't know the baby wasn't yours. I hardly got together with Neil after we met. I promise you, I didn't mean to deceive you. I thought the baby was yours!"

Isa seemed slightly moved by what she said, then he turned to her and said, "Gather your belongings. Tomorrow, I will arrange for you to be taken to the airport and flown back to England. You can return to your whore-master. I should never have brought you here."

Natasha was in floods of tears as he turned once more in the doorway and with a stoic resolve on his face, said, "You will not speak again to my family members. I will confess to them that we were never married and that you are to leave. Let that be an end to it!"

That night, Natasha slept through sheer exhaustion. David, after his middle of the night feed, had settled and was fast asleep in his cot beside her bed.

She woke with a start as a dead weight fell upon her. Her sleep befuddled mind took precious seconds to react to the unfamiliar smells and sensations pervading it. When her senses finally focused, she realised, too late to react, the dead weight belonged to Mahmood who was on top of her, forcing her legs apart with his knees. The last thing she remembered was his evil face leering into hers as his hands tightened around her throat and she lost consciousness.

CHAPTER 64

Indecent proposal

When Natasha woke up, Isa was standing next to her bed. He spoke to her in hushed tones, so as not to be overheard. "I have made arrangements for you to leave Bahrain as soon as you are well enough to travel." His voice was matter of fact, bereft of any compassion. "I have organised comfortable accommodation for you and your children in Saudi Arabia. You will have a bank account in your name. A deposit of five hundred thousand pounds has been made at your disposal. I ask only that you do not report this unfortunate incident."

Natasha stared into his eyes and wondered how she could have ever felt anything for this man.

Isa continued, "My son's crime will not go unpunished, I assure you. He will find his father's punishment will be every bit as severe as he would have had from the courts. I ask only that you allow me to protect my family from the dishonour and shame that this would bring.

Although she felt the prospect of being 'bought off' abhorrent, Natasha knew that she was in a strange country with two children to protect and that, if he so wished, Isa could be a formidable enemy. Nevertheless, she felt a desire to twist the knife a little and finding her mouth dry she moistened her lips from the glass by her hospital bed and replied with, "Seven hundred and fifty thousand pounds is my price, take it or leave it."

He looked down at her prostrate form on the bed. For a short moment, she thought he might hit out at her, then his features softened to a resigned look before turning to leave. With a wave of his hand he said, "It will be done," before walking out of her life for good.

Natasha was collected from the hospital by members of Isa's staff; she would not be given the opportunity to return to the palace. The children were already in the car, in the care of a young English au pair, which Isa had arranged. Natasha felt a deep pang of regret that she would not be able to say goodbye to Aalia, her one friend and the only person who had made these last months bearable.

"Where are we going?" she asked the driver, whom she recognised as one of Isa's bodyguards.

"I am to drive you to Dhahran, You will have a modest apartment at your disposal. You will also have the nanny to live with you. She has bankbooks, papers and everything else you will need. You are not to attempt to make contact with Mr Hashim Al-Kooheji or any member of his family again." He beckoned for Natasha to lean forward, his lips close to her ear, so his words were not overheard by the au pair. He whispered, "Mr Hashim Al-Kooheji is a powerful man, he could have chosen many ways to cover his little," he hesitated, searching for the right words to convey the way he saw the situation, before adding, "his son's little indiscretion." Turning back to face the road, he concluded, "This scenario has the happiest outcome for you, I think."

Natasha felt it best to leave it at that and settled back to continue the journey in silence.

For the next three months, Natasha lived the life of a virtual recluse. Her body was fully healed. Having a new born baby and Monica to attend to helped to heal her mind and her heart.

She successfully weaned the baby onto bottled milk and decided the time had come for her to venture out into the world again. Time to put the horrors of the last year behind her.

Monica was now attending an International Kindergarten pre-school in Dhahran, this gave Natasha a chance to interact with the other mothers, many of them also Europeans and British ex pats.

She became friendly with Sheila, a woman in a similar situation to herself who had studied fashion design at university before meeting and marrying an Iranian man.

Sheila's marriage had broken down and she was forced to flee Iran with her child to get away from him. She had found passage from Iran, across the Gulf, to Oman before fate had taken her across the border into Saudi.

Unlike Natasha, Sheila was living on the poverty line and had found a job at the local golf course doing a menial cleaning job in the mornings while her child was at kindergarten to pay her way.

Sheila overheard Natasha conversing with one of the Italian mothers at the day centre and approached her.

"You should come and work at the golf course where I clean, they have a pro shop there and are always on the lookout for multi-lingual people." She laughed and added, "With your looks, it wouldn't be long before one of the pros snapped you up!"

Natasha modestly replied, "I don't think they would be interested in a woman with two kids in tow," then added wistfully, "besides, I think I'm off men for good!"

Sheila said, "Why don't you at least come over and have a chat with the management, you said you were thinking of looking for a job, you wouldn't have to look very far!"

Natasha contemplated it for a while and said, "OK, why not? Like you said, I do need something to occupy my time and at least I'd be able to keep an eye on you!" She gave Sheila a little wink as she finished the sentence. The two women laughed.

CHAPTER 65

Fore!

Monday morning saw Natasha dressed in a sharp business suit of knee length skirt, long-sleeved blouse, jacket and colourful headscarf, just modest enough to appease the radicals but cosmopolitan enough for the liberals. Everything was about striking a healthy balance between fashion and culture, politics and religion. Natasha had learned her lessons well and was offered the post of pro shop manageress there and then.

Natasha's days were quite full. She was really enjoying the work at the pro shop. A large percentage of the clientele were local dignitaries, wealthy oil sheiks and travelling foreign businessmen. Her favourite clients by far though were the visiting American film stars. She found them particularly amusing with their swagger and their huge entourages. Many had found Natasha a particularly pleasing distraction, but she had so far managed her resolve to avoid liaisons with members of the opposite sex, despite some tempting propositions.

The American film star Warren Bateson was in town, he had starred in the majority of teen angst movies that Natasha had seen in her youth. He was now one of the biggest names in Hollywood with both directing and acting blockbusters to his credit. Warren, it was rumoured, commanded the biggest pay check in the industry.

He had wandered into the pro shop and was looking at golfing gloves. Walking over to where Natasha was standing, he said, "Miss, can I get anything done with this glove? It's my lucky glove so I don't want to go changing it. It's just that the damn poppers won't stay done up and the palm is wearing a little." He turned to his entourage and quipped, "I don't want to go getting a blister on my palm, there's no telling what the paparazzi would accuse me of." His entourage exploded into paroxysms of sycophantic laughter, far in excess of the joke's merit.

He leant into Natasha and, cupping a hand around his mouth, whispered, "Sheeples." She smiled back at him.

After examining the glove for a while, she said, "We have a tailor at the course. If you like, I could get him to have a look at it, see what he can do."

He replied, "You'll need to make it *tout suite,* I have a game this afternoon with Derren Nicklaus which I simply must win. We have a five dollar wager on it."

Natasha left one of her subordinates in charge of the shop while she took a short buggy ride to the outbuilding where the Iranian tailor 'Daggy' had a small workshop. She walked into the unit and called out, "Hello?" There was no response. "Hello, Daggy?" she called again, still no response. Behind a long, low, white draftsman's table she saw the old Highlead Industrial sewing machine. The same model she had used, at home, a lifetime ago.

She looked at the piles of old gloves, leather off cuts and Velcro. As she rested her foot on the worn treadle switch, the years rolled back and she was once again back in Copper Road.

She took a couple of pieces of Velcro from the pile and started work on the glove.

Replacing the feeling of nostalgia was a stronger feeling of homesickness as she remembered the day a tall handsome stranger had walked up her path. She realised just how much she missed Neil.

Warren Bateson, having just played the most outstanding round of golf in his life, was ecstatic. He positively floated into the pro shop, his feet a good six inches above the surface of the floor. He rushed over to Natasha, a smile beaming across his handsome face.

"Ma'am, I want to take that tailor of yours out for a hearty lunch, he worked miracles with my glove. The man's a genius. I've been waiting to trounce Derren for ten years and have never come close before."

Natasha blushed and said, "Actually, the tailor wasn't around earlier so, knowing you needed the glove, I took the liberty of mending it myself." She coloured up even darker as she confessed, "I trained as a glove feller years ago so I had a good idea what to do."

"Young lady," he replied, "I don't get much of a chance to do as I please these days. One of the few pleasures I have is my golf. You've helped to make me a very happy man today, now I'm taking you out to lunch to celebrate and I ain't taking no for an answer."

Natasha stammered, "I'm sorry, I have to work, I can't possibly leave the shop now."

"Young lady," he replied, "me and my associates spend more money in this shop than they see for the rest of the year. If Warren Bateson says you shut up shop and come for lunch, you shut up shop and come for lunch!"

Natasha glanced over at the club chairman for approval; he was nodding his head like some demented duck.

"In that case Mr Bateson," she replied, "I cannot refuse."

"Damn straight," he replied, "and from now on, it's Warren; Mr Bateson was my dad!"

That afternoon and into the evening, Warren bombarded Natasha with compliments about how her changes to his glove had worked a therapeutic effect on his game. He insisted that if she were to go into business making golfing gear, he would be the first to endorse her products and that all his wealthy friends would follow suit.

Natasha found Warren to be an empathetic listener despite all his Texan bluster. There was a strong attraction between them, symbiotic rather than sexual. They discovered in each other a shared need. Natasha found Warren's exploits a constant source of amusement and encouragement, while Warren's interest in her was as an oasis of calm in his otherwise bombastic lifestyle. His attention had a sublime, cathartic effect on Natasha as he listened intently to her life story leading up to her present situation, here in Saudi.

"God damn girl," he replied, "I could turn your story into a Hollywood smash, people would fall over themselves to tell a story like yours."

"Oh please no," Natasha laughed, "it's been stressful enough in reality without re-living it in celluloid."

By the time his short stay in Dhahran was up, he and Natasha had become firm friends.

He left her with a short statement; "Now Natasha, I have coursed around this globe like a rolling stone, without managing to stick to anyone or anything apart from my work. I can count the number of real friends I have on one hand. There's my family, my wife, bless her, and now you." He held her hand as he delivered the last of his parting speech: "I know you ain't got any money worries, but I think you need direction in your life, sooner or later the kids will be all grown up and you'll wonder where your life's gone. Take me up on my offer, you get some designs for golf gear up and running and I will endorse it. Pretty soon you won't have time to be sad and your life will be filled with the excitement you deserve." He paused, reading her eyes for a reaction. "It may not be too sexy, but darlin', sexy's what got you into this mess! No girl, you lay the foundations of a good venture and just watch if your life don't just go right on and fall into place. Shore up your kids' future too." He squeezed her hand.

"You mark my words, I'm a pretty shrewd businessman as well as a damn fine actor you know!"

CHAPTER 66

Neil

It was the postman that alerted the emergency services; finding the front door open he had followed the trail of blood up to the bedroom.

Lying unconscious overnight, Neil's bruised brain had swollen up. He was virtually flat-lining when he got to hospital. His heart stopped beating several times. Initially, his head injury was missed, further exacerbating the prognosis.

Neil was confined to hospital for a long spell. He had suffered blood loss from severe lacerations, a broken collar-bone and more worryingly, brain trauma, meaning that although his skull had not fractured, his brain had been sufficiently churned around in his head to have done serious damage.

Natasha's mum had brought flowers to his ward. He refused to see her. He refused to even see his own parents. His brain was not firing on all cylinders.

His neurosurgeon described it to him. "Neil, imagine your brain is like a telephone exchange, connecting all the phones in the world with all the other individual handsets anywhere and everywhere simultaneously, except it's millions of times more complex. Now imagine someone ripping all the wires apart and throwing the wiring diagram away. What your brain is trying to do is find a way to re-connect all those phones. It will do it, but it may end up wired a little differently than before." The surgeon looked around the room wistfully. "When you were found on the floor you were stone cold, hypothermic; that almost certainly saved your life, at the very least, saved you from a permanent vegetative state. If the door had been closed, the heating on, you wouldn't be here." As he left the room, he turned and added, "You're a very lucky man Neil."

Neil wasn't sure whether he felt lucky or cursed.

After that pep talk came nearly a year of gruelling rehabilitation. Neil was strong; he managed to regain all his faculties and a new appreciation of life, of what he could have lost.

A TV company had approached him to follow his progress. For Neil it opened up a brand new chapter in his life, filled with endless opportunity.

The healing process had been long and hard. He had heard nothing from Natasha. He couldn't forgive her for that. He had made no attempt to track her down after his discharge.

CHAPTER 67

Expansion

The pro shop management were fully behind Natasha's venture into the sports apparel market. With Daggy and Sheila now in her employ, Natasha soon had a range of design samples ready to go. True to his word and always no more than a phone call away, Warren was full of support and helpful suggestions; his intimate knowledge of the game was hugely beneficial in the design stage.

By the time of David's second birthday, Natasha's initial investment had been paid back over and over. Sheila's flair and enthusiasm had found reward, with Natasha taking her on as a full partner. Daggy had gone to Pakistan to oversee quality control in the garment factory.

Sheila's awesome eye for design had picked out a plethora of other improvements to be made in myriad other sports. This, combined with Warren's continued exposure and the endorsement of a few of his celebrity friends, elevated their company to the position of near market leader.

Some nine months later, after a particularly successful new product launch, Sheila and Natasha had arrived back home to Natasha's roomy apartment. As the au pair put both sets of children to bed for the night, Sheila, now a frequent overnight guest, was channel surfing the obscure English programs on cable TV, hoping to pick up some inspirational tips from London high street fashion.

She surfed onto the documentary following Neil's accident and subsequent recovery. She was just about to flick over the channel when the name 'Neil Curland' aroused her curiosity.

She watched for a few moments before calling out, "Natasha, quickly, come here, there's something you need to see."

Natasha hurried into the room and enquired, "What…." The sentence tailed off as she saw the bruised and battered face of her former love on the TV screen. By the end of the program, Natasha was in tears.

CHAPTER 68

Guardian angel

Over the next few weeks, Natasha made a number of long distance phone calls, starting with the cable TV company. She found out the production company behind Neil's documentary was a UK-based independent TV company. She spoke with a very friendly and indiscreet young lady on reception duty at the firm's Portacabin in Reading.

"So you handle other projects for Mr Curland?" Natasha questioned.

"Oh yes," the young woman replied, "we have a fly on the wall style documentary set at Mr Curland's business premises, it's called, 'Copper Road Choppers'." She added, "It's one of our more successful ventures, we have a number of specials and one-off projects involving Mr Curland too."

"Is it possible to purchase the 'Copper Road Choppers' series on video, then have it shipped out to me in Saudi Arabia?" Natasha asked.

"Yes of course," said the girl, "I will put you through to distribution. You can get the specials from them as well, if you're interested."

A few days later, Natasha had the large brown paper package lying on her desk. That evening, in the privacy of her apartment, she pushed the first of the tapes into the hungry mouth of the VCR.

As the first couple of tapes were devoured, Natasha found the feeling of melancholic nostalgia replaced by an overwhelming feeling of admiration for her former love.

Neil's TV series was really good, more than that, it was TV gold. She knew she had a friend that just had to see these tapes.

In the morning she put a call through to Austin, Texas.

Eventually, she managed to track Warren down in his office in New York where he was currently working. "Warren, hi it's me, Natasha," she sang into the receiver.

"Natasha, hi girl, how the hell are you? When are you coming to visit me?"

"Warren, I have something here that I'd really like you to take a look at," she said.

"Shoot girl, I'm all ears!" he replied. Natasha ran the gist of Neil's series past him. "Hell," Warren said, "sounds like a lot of fun! Harley Davidsons and British humour, that's got to be a recipe for success, I know some shakers and movers who would be looking to network that sort of thing."

"So would you like me to send the videos to you?" Natasha asked.

"No, I would not lahke you to send the videhoes to me," he said, doing his best to mimic Natasha's English accent, "what I would like you to do is grab those two little ankle snappers of yours and fly over to my ranch in Austin for this weekend. It's time you paid me a visit and met the wife and family." He gave a belly laugh before adding, "Mrs Bateson is desperate to meet you so she can see for herself what all the fuss is about. My daughters will love you too!" He added, "C'mon over, we'll show you a true Texan welcome, then you can show me these tapes and we'll find out what it is that makes our Mr Curland the custodian of your heart!"

Natasha laughed and said, "Well, I suppose Sheila can cope without me for a few days. OK Mr Bateson, we will take you up on your offer. See you this weekend."

"Hold on Natasha," Warren added, "I'll send the studio Lear for you. Give me a tinkle when you're ready, I'll have my PA set it up, pick you up, take you to the airport. Your little girl will love it. I'll see you get the full studio hospitality treatment."

"Thank you Warren. We'll see you on the weekend." As she put down the receiver, Natasha felt a little glow inside her. She would give the sales pitch of her life for Neil's show. Warren would love it and anything Warren loved would be loved by everybody.

Neil would be loved by everybody.

CHAPTER 69

Winners and losers

The desk diary on Neil's desk showed the date: Friday, March thirteenth, nineteen ninety two.

Neil smiled a wry smile and thought, *Friday the thirteenth, what horrors do you have in store for me today?*

His PA called through. "Mr Curland, don't forget you have a twelve o' clock with the RFD Media people."

"No problem Janice," he replied, "I've got my suit in the car."

"It's on a hanger in the bathroom," Janice corrected, "can't have you pitching the new show in a creased suit. I am hoping for a pay rise when we renew the contract."

Neil smiled to himself and thought, *If you only knew, you're worth twice what I pay you.* Neil considered his middle-aged, slightly round and frumpy personal assistant one of his most valuable assets. Since her own family had grown up and moved away, she had kind of adopted Neil as her personal challenge. Janice had been his rock since the business had taken off.

Neil decided to take the BMW, he looked on it as one would a smart business suit; not too flashy but with just the right amount of maturity and commitment.

Usually, when Neil turned up at the offices of the media company, as one of their many clients he would wait in the waiting room before being called through for his appointment with whichever of the freelance production teams he was working with at the time. Today seemed a little different. He was ushered straight through, into an office in the main building.

"Neil, hi, I'm John Carstairs, chief of production."

The suit was one of the company big-wigs, one of the few permanent members of staff. So far he was the highest ranking member of the company Neil had met.

"Pleased to meet you John," Neil replied, politely. "For what do I owe this honour?" Neil joked.

"Well Neil," John said, "I don't really know where to start, this is quite unprecedented for a small independent company like ours."

Neil was puzzled, intrigued; he wanted to shout, "Get on with it," but felt that good manners prohibited. Instead, he said, "Well, I usually start at the beginning John."

"Yes of course," John continued nervously. "Well Neil, it seems that our little show has been seen by someone across the pond who has considerable influence in the American TV networks."

"Wow," said Neil, "I take it that's good?"

"Neil," he replied, "this is massive, the networks are like all the little production companies put together. They have the ability to syndicate your show and air it on just about all the major TV channels in America. Potentially, we could be looking at getting your show into most of the homes in America. Money wise, we could be talking telephone numbers."

CHAPTER 70

The postman always rings twice

Back at the office, Neil was still trying to come to terms with the day's bizarre events. He had put a call into his agent, brought them up to speed with the developments and left it with them to act for him. Thrash out the details.

Sat back in his big leather chair, the one he jokingly referred to as his 'second hand car salesman's chair', Neil's consciousness was out for lunch, leaving his subconscious to 'man the guns'.

His thoughts were interrupted by the shrill tone of an incoming call. He left it for Janice to pick up and started absent-mindedly flicking through his week's appointments.

Life was good for Neil. Since the 'Copper Road Choppers' TV series, work had come in fast and furious. The business had moved premises twice to bigger and better locations. Most of the work now was consultancy, TV and feature film prop work. They didn't really need the reality TV shows any more but Neil still loved getting his hands dirty and it kept his profile high. Now with the potential of this new American deal on the table, the only things missing in his life were Natasha and Monica.

The intercom snapped him out of his thoughts. He picked up the receiver and stabbed the 'Int' button.

Janice's voice sounded anxious. "Mr Curland, there's a lady on the phone, long distance. She won't give her name, she insists on talking to you."

"Hang up," said Neil, thinking it just another intrusive telemarketing call.

"I think you need to speak with her Neil," Janice insisted, a marked departure from her usual professional manner.

"OK Janice, put her through," he winced, conceding defeat.

"Neil?" the voice in the receiver said. Neil's head spun; for a moment, he thought he would pass out.

The disembodied voice was Natasha.

"Neil?" she repeated. "I have to talk to you." Neil couldn't speak, he was confused, just couldn't seem to process the information coming in. "Neil," the voice implored, more desperate, "please Neil, I need to explain. I need to talk to you."

Finally, the power of speech returned. "Natasha," he stammered, barely an audible croak.

"Neil, I'm so, so sorry, I didn't know. There's so much to tell you. I hardly know where to start."

"Where are you?" Neil asked, almost on automatic pilot. His voice sounded detached to him, distant; his emotions were in free fall.

"Saudi Arabia," she answered.

Neil was in turmoil. He hadn't had to deal with this emotion since his accident and clearly, the healing process was still incomplete. He was unable to correlate his thoughts and had to steady himself against his desk for fear of collapsing.

"Natasha," he stammered, "I can't, I can't...." he was unable to finish the sentence.

Natasha, fearing he was about to shut her out of his life completely, became anxious. "Neil, I didn't mean to abandon you, I had no idea about your accident. My situation here was so complicated, I can't explain over the phone." Her voice was breaking, filled with emotion. "Neil, please, can I phone you again later?" Neil dropped the receiver to the ground and stumbled from the office into the restrooms where he collapsed against the sinks, splashing his face with cold water to try and restore some clarity.

Janice picked up the receiver and said, "Hi Natasha. My name is Janice, I'm Neil's PA. Please don't read anything into Neil's reaction, he is still on the mend. Could you ring him at home tonight? His head will be clearer and he will be more able to cope with your call."

"Oh God," Natasha cried, "how bad was he hurt? Does he even remember me?"

"Natasha," she reassured, "Neil most definitely remembers you, he is extremely well, almost one hundred percent healed." She lowered her voice, hoping that Neil didn't overhear in case he considered her interference an indiscretion. "He hasn't had any emotional attachment since the accident, since you left. If you ask me, the rush of emotion has overwhelmed him."

Natasha replaced the receiver; her hand involuntarily went up to her face as floods of tears engulfed her. How could Neil ever forgive her abandoning him?

CHAPTER 71

Tickets please

Neil cleared his diary of appointments for the following week. "Janice, could you find out the flight times to Jeddah Airport in Saudi Arabia please?" he called through the intercom.

Janice rapped on the door and walked in without waiting for a reply. "What day were you thinking of travelling Mr Curland?"

"I'm not sure, I haven't decided yet." He seemed distracted. "Could you just get me flight times, airports, connecting flights etc. so I can make up my mind?"

"Mr Curland," Janice said, unsure if she was talking out of turn, "Neil, wouldn't you be wise to let things take their time? Don't rush the girl. I know how much she means to you. You must let her do this her way and in her own time. Wait for her to call again before doing anything hasty." Janice considered her next words carefully, in case she was overstepping the mark. "I've arranged for her to call you at home tonight, now I suggest you calm down and collect your thoughts so you know how to handle it when she does."

A flash of indignation flared in Neil's eyes for a second, and then subsided. She was right, this was Natasha's call and he had to let her proceed in her own time.

The phone was ringing as her turned the lock on his house door. He rushed in the door and managed to lift the receiver just before the final ring.

"Hello?" he questioned.

"Neil, it's me," she replied.

"Natasha," he said, "I love you."

"Oh Neil," she sighed, "I love you too, I've never stopped loving you. I need to see you. Can you come over for a few days, take a short holiday? I have so much to tell you. I need to see you face to face."

"I can be over tomorrow," he replied. Natasha was so relieved she burst into floods of tears again. The rest of the call was light and chatty, avoiding any serious issues. There was so much pain and angst between the two of them, the time for a detailed autopsy would have to come, but not now, now was just the chance for them to enjoy the soothing familiarity of each other's voices.

CHAPTER 72

Distant shores

Despite the waves of happiness coursing through Neil, he couldn't help becoming irritable at every little delay or inconvenience. He hadn't slept a wink. Janice was quite glad she was dropping him off at Heathrow. She would have peace and quiet for the drive home.

"Bloody regional airports, why couldn't I fly from them? I can't believe that we have to drive all the way to bloody London to fly to Saudi, what's the matter with this godforsaken country?" Neil was really getting on Janice's nerves with his pointless impatient moaning.

"Those airports don't fly to Jeddah," Janice re-iterated, through gritted teeth. "If you had been willing to change at Frankfurt you could have flown from either but you could only fly direct to Turkey or Egypt."

"Well what about Bournemouth? Why couldn't I fly from there? It's a god-damn international airport. Saudi is an international destination. Honestly, London. You'd think the country's a bloody collection of uninhabitable planets all orbiting round London." He put on an annoying Mockney accent: "*Lahndahn.* I hate Lahndahn and I hate Lahndahners. Chests all puffed up just because their ex council house is worth a million pounds."

"Stop being such a petulant child," Janice scolded.

Neil looked at her down his nose, with his mouth puckered in a Jaggeresque pout and chided, "Oooh, Ark at you Mahrm," then burst out laughing. The tension dispersed, his happy mood was restored. Janice's recent concern for Neil's personal life had changed their dynamic. She had, he felt, become a friend.

Six hours later, Neil's plane touched down on the tarmac at Jeddah, a Red Sea resort in Saudi Arabia.

He passed through customs without any difficulty, clutching as he was only a small overnight bag he was the same as any other business traveller.

His eyes scoured the arrivals lounge. A bizarre side effect of his injury was that his vision had altered. From needing glasses to read and for long distance, he now only needed glasses for close up. His short sightedness was gone. He spotted her outside customs, staring towards the baggage carousel, expecting him to be collecting luggage.

Her mane of dark curly hair cascading down across her exotic features caused Neil's pulse to quicken. Her skin was a few shades darker than he remembered. It suited her. She was breathtakingly beautiful. Her dress sense had changed, matured; still sexy as hell but more sophisticated. The trademark miniskirts replaced by a pure silk, figure hugging, Chinese style pencil dress.

He snuck up behind her and slipped his warm hands around her eyes; she turned in surprise. Their eyes met as hers began to well up with tears.

The make or break moment arrived. The tension was palpable.

"Don't cry," he whispered, "I won't be able to look into your beautiful eyes and I've waited so long to do that."

Her full lips parted and she whispered his name, "Neil." Her voice was filled with emotion. He interpreted her feelings and swept her off her feet in a passionate embrace.

"God Natasha, I've missed you so much." Their lips met and two became one.

CHAPTER 73

Tee off!

They sat in an outside café overlooking the fabulous Red Sea beach. They were holding each other's hands, afraid that if they let go, the other might disappear like a mirage. Natasha explained that Monica was with her au pair, a live in nanny who the girl loved dearly.

Neil thought he had better start things off and said, "I have very little recollection of what happened the day you left, I only know that you had phoned and I was driving like an idiot, obviously in a mad rush to get home."

It dawned on Natasha that Neil didn't remember the substance of that fateful call. She decided that it wouldn't be the time or the place to drop such a huge bombshell on him.

"We were having such a hard time," she said. "I don't want to go into sordid details but I had met someone. He wanted me to marry him and move to Bahrain to be his wife."

Neil's hands were trembling. She quickly added, "I didn't marry him Neil. I phoned you because I wanted you to talk me out of it, I phoned you because I still loved you and hoped we could still make things right. When you didn't come home, I thought you didn't care anymore, so I left.

He sat quietly for a while before asking, "Why didn't you call me? How could you just walk away and never look back?"

She looked wistfully towards the shoreline. "That's where things become duplicitous. The man I trusted, the man I came over here to be with, turned out to be a lying, controlling bastard. He lied to his family, told them we were married. Shortly after we got to Bahrain, he started attending Mosque about a million times a day. After a while, he started getting nasty, his family kept me a virtual prisoner." She saw the look of horror on Neil's face. "Don't panic," she reassured him, "this was Bahrain, not Iran. No, I was kept a virtual prisoner but in a very gilded cage. Isa is a very wealthy man; virtually an oil sheik."

"How did you get away?" Neil questioned.

"It wasn't difficult, something happened which would have caused disgrace for Isa's family. He paid me to disappear." She left it hanging in the air.

"Well?" Neil said.

"Well what?" she answered, evasively.

"What caused the family disgrace?" he asked, emphasising each word slowly, sounding mildly sarcastic.

"I can't discuss that Neil," she said with a serious tone. "I'm sorry, you'll have to cut me some slack and just trust me on that. I can't discuss it at all."

"Secrets, already?" Neil enquired.

She laughed, trying to make light, "I will tell you Neil, I swear, just not now. Not yet." she continued, "Anyway, my mum is also a villain of the piece. She was the first person I called when I left Isa. I asked her how you were. She told me you were fine, getting on with your life. That you'd moved on." She looked incredibly sad. "I don't know if I can ever forgive her. She thought you were going to be crippled, didn't want me to feel obligated, for you to be a burden to me." She swore. "Self-centred bitch."

"Wow," Neil answered, "and I thought she liked me."

Even now, Natasha's sense of family duty prevailed as she defended her mum by saying, "She nursed her own parents for years Neil. She didn't want the same fate for me."

"So what prompted the phone call?" Neil asked, intrigued.

"I saw your documentary on the TV. I couldn't believe it. I cried myself to sleep for days." She looked down at her nails as her lip quivered and tears threatened to well up again. "I phoned Mum, I think I burst her ear drums."

She erupted with laughter, Neil joined in before hugging her to him and gently rocking her, in his strong reassuring way.

God, thought Natasha, *how much I've missed this.*

CHAPTER 74

Big shot

"I hear you're a big TV star?" Natasha chided, before adding, "I've seen your show on cable."

"Really?" Neil questioned. "So, what did you think?"

"I think it's absolutely brilliant, your natural wit really shines through. In fact, it really makes the show!" Her face took on a melancholic air for an instant as she said, "I was touched by you calling the series, 'Copper Road Choppers' after my old street." She gave him a grave look and added, "I am not best keen on all the swearing and bullying though!"

He laughed and said, "It's all for show really. I'm never there as a rule. The boys run the show themselves and they get paid handsomely for doing it." He added, "I'm a pussy-cat really."

"Oh, you've changed then?" she ribbed.

"You cheeky mare," he laughed, tickling her ribs and making her twist and squirm to escape his clutches.

She looked at him seriously. "You're not going to believe this Neil," she paused a little for dramatic effect, "you're not the only successful business person here." She could hardly contain her excitement. "I have my own factory in Pakistan. Or at least, I am a partner in a factory in Pakistan." Neil's mouth was agape like a hungry dog.

"What?" he exclaimed. "What do you make in this factory?"

She was beaming with pride. "Gloves." She elaborated, "I make my own golfing apparel; 'Globe-Trotter', it's my brand."

"Oh my God," he exclaimed, the pitch of his voice rising hysterically, "I've worn one of your gloves."

He remembered when a client had taken him to a driving range in Southampton. He had thought about Natasha and her hours sat at the sewing machine. That was back when they had very first met. "Where on earth did you come by the means to open a factory?" Neil questioned.

"Now, don't shout at me," she warned, "I know how funny you men get about money. I had a very large pay out from Isa, he wanted me to get out of Bahrain in a hurry. I guess he thought it was pay me off or kill me. Luckily for me, he has more conscience than money worries." She laughed; he could tell it was more out of embarrassment than mirth. "Anyhoo, I met some people, got a job at a pro golf shop at a top course in Dhahran. I started off mending the pros' gloves on a machine at my work. I changed a few things here and there, added a few little changes I'd considered back when I sewed for Titleist. Long and short of it, they loved the modifications and I was up and running.

"The world of pro golf is a small, very, very wealthy world. Once you're in, you're in. Help, finance, advice, connections; it's all at your fingertips. Getting the gloves made in Pakistan was the master stroke though, labour and material is so cheap." She clapped her hands. "So there you go Mr Curland, we both turned out to be proper little entrepreneurs. We're richer than our wildest dreams."

"Woo hoo!" Neil exclaimed.

That night, in Neil's hotel room, they made love. It was both tender and passionate, filled with all the pure emotion they had been unable to find in the dying months of their former relationship.

Lying together in the warm afterglow of their lovemaking, Natasha turned to face Neil and said, "Maybe the old Gypsy woman was telling the truth after all."

"Huh?" a sleepy Neil replied.

"The old Gypsy woman in Hunstanton. She told me we would have two children together; a boy and a girl, making three children and that it would complete our family."

Her talking about the future gave Neil a cosy feeling inside. He would dearly love to have children with Natasha.

He smiled as his battery level began to nudge the fully charged mark again! "Best we get started then if we've two new lives to create," he sniggered to her, pulling the quilt down and exposing her naked breasts.

"You haven't changed much, horny bugger," she giggled, then pulled him close.

With their passion spent, the couple lay back exhausted. They slept with her snuggled into his armpit, like a lifetime ago. He wanted to stay awake all night just to feel her chest rise and fall with her breathing, to feel her heart beat softly against his chest. The feeling of utter contentment drifted over him and his eyelids fluttered closed as sleep overcame him. He didn't dare to dream, as dreams could not hope to compete with this reality.

CHAPTER 75

Money matters

The short break in Jeddah convinced the couple that their future lay together. Long telephone calls between the two continents kept them on the boil. Eventually, Natasha decided that she would sell up and move home to be nearer to Neil. It made more sense to bring the children up in England.

Besides, Natasha thought, *if all goes well, I hope to be home, bringing up a new baby before too long*.

Sheila, her business partner and close friend, had noticed how preoccupied she had become since she had re-kindled her relationship with Neil.

Sheila took the initiative and invited Natasha out to lunch for a chat. They splashed out and took a limo ride across the causeway into Bahrain so they could enjoy a nice sociable drink without worrying that the Mutaween[3] might raid.

They chose a quiet Italian bistro in Al Jasra old town, a place which recognised them as regular clients. After whetting their whistles with a full-bodied Italian red, they ordered their mains of pasta and meat.

Sheila decided to get straight down to it and lay her cards on the table. "Natasha," she said, "I

---

3   Secret Police

couldn't help but notice how distracted you've been since you've been back in touch with Neil."

Not sure where this was going, Natasha nodded the affirmative and said, "Yes, I have been, I must admit."

Sheila went on, "Look Tash, you know I value you as one of my dearest friends. You aren't happy here anymore. I know you want to be with Neil and I think it's only the business that's holding you back. That's why I have decided to make you an offer."

Natasha looked on with intrigue and surprise.

"If you want to take a sabbatical, that's OK by me, you can take as long as you need." She hesitated, not sure how Natasha would take her next offer. "Tash, if you want out, if you think your future lies back in England, with Neil, we can work something out. I can either pay you a retainer and you become a sleeping partner, or I can buy you out completely. Make you a very handsome offer for your share of the business." She put the ball into Natasha's court with, "What do you think?"

Natasha, somewhat taken aback said, "Do you want rid of me Sheila, am I not pulling my weight?"

Sheila caught hold of her hands and looked into her eyes. "Tash, as far as I'm concerned, this is your business, your name; I would have nothing if it weren't for you! I don't care if you just stop coming to work but keep taking a wage." She squeezed Natasha's hands hard, emphasising the sincerity in her words. "I think what you need is back home in England. Don't let the business be the millstone which holds you back! I just want you to be happy Tash. Follow your heart."

Natasha felt the tears welling up in her eyes when she replied, "I do so want to be back in England, I would give everything to be back with Neil, bringing up our son and Monica together." She continued, "My heart's not been here since I saw that documentary and discovered the truth. To be honest, I would have bailed out straight away if it hadn't been for you and the business."

She put her shrewd business head on and said, "Speak to our solicitors and put a deal together. Don't make it too generous. You know, your designs have become the mainstay of the business. I just want out!"

Sheila's offer was generous and it would secure Natasha and the children's future come what may. She agreed the deal.

That night she telephoned Neil. Natasha felt bad about keeping his child a secret but she had missed her chance in Jeddah, through insecurity. She still wasn't sure how he would react and couldn't risk telling him whilst the miles lay between them.

The shrill of the phone cut through the hush of Neil's solitary existence. His heart fluttered as he lifted the receiver. His day-to-day routines ceased to bring him any fulfilment, despite numerous exciting projects in the pipeline; his whole life revolved around the nightly phone calls.

"Hello?" he said.

"Neil," Natasha asked, "you remember the question you asked me when we were in Hunstanton?"

"Of course I do," he replied.

"Does the offer still stand?"

"Natasha," he said, "I would be thrilled, honoured, if you would be my wife."

"In that case," she said, "I will."

Neil was ecstatic; the next news she would impart would just blow him away.

"Neil, I'm coming home, I'm coming home to you, to be your wife. I'm coming home tomorrow."

CHAPTER 76

Confession

The vending machine headline announced that, the previous day, a well-known British actor had sadly passed away. The newspaper was dated 5th June 1992. Neil perused the headline and then tucked the paper under his arm with a casual deference; simply killing time.

At a little over six feet tall, he cut an impressive dash; dressed in expensive, Western style, tooled leather boots, dark, well-cut denim jeans, black shirt, a thin bootlace tie at the collar and a long dark leather coat. His full head of dark, wavy hair was pulled back into a smart ponytail. It was this meticulously groomed look and solitary stance that singled him out from the casual, gregarious crowd, moving quickly with purpose or just chatting, enjoying the company of friends and family. Only his thick, rough, calloused fingers showed him as a man who made his living with his hands.

Outside, in the short stay car park, a meter was ticking away in front of a brand new hire car, a people carrier, chosen for this trip over his favourite Ferrari because of the need for rear seats.

With the great British weather blowing rain sideways down the glass of the airport arrivals lounge, it was all but impossible to observe the take-offs and landings of the aircraft arriving or leaving every few minutes, taking their precious cargo to myriad destinations and adventures across the globe or bringing them home to their loved ones.

Neil was only interested in the safe arrival of one particular plane.

He hadn't been so nervous since his first tentative trials without stabilisers on his bike, a lifetime ago.

The monitor screens announced that flight SA3002 from Saudi Arabia had arrived. Snapped from his reverie, he began to stride purposefully towards the relevant gate.

Some half an hour later, he caught sight of her, standing surrounded by luggage to the side of the restrooms. Dressed impeccably, she was staring down, scrutinising the expensive designer luggage noisily abandoned around her feet. He broke into a run in his haste to be close to her. As he approached, she sensed his presence and glanced up, her beautiful eyes shaded by long dark lashes. She mouthed his name silently as the pressure of his hug stole the breath from her lungs, spinning her around in the joy of their embrace. His lips found hers. The kiss conveyed a thousand words.

He gently returned her to her feet as the bathroom door opened. The au pair was holding a pretty young girl with one hand and dealing with something behind the door with the other. Monica, with her mother's spectacular dark looks and long curly hair, hung back shyly keeping the door between her and the tall stranger.

"Hi Monica, do you remember me?" he enquired.

She shook her head, one hand holding a thumb up to her mouth as a pacifier.

As she came out of the door, she broke off contact with the au pair and made for the safety of her mother's coat tails.

Neil noticed the au pair's other hand was securely holding onto the tiny arm of Monica's younger brother.

"Who's this then?" he stuttered, somewhat surprised.

Natasha replied, "Neil, I would like to introduce you to your son, David."

The shy little face peered out from behind his nanny, caution losing the battle against infant curiosity. The little boy's eyes met Neil's incredulous stare. Comprehension usurped disbelief as the marvel of his own creation forged an instantaneous bond.

"I'm so sorry I didn't tell you Neil," Natasha whispered, "I needed to know that you still loved me for me, not out of duty."

CHAPTER 77

Revelations

A phone call ahead saw Janice organise a travel cot to be set up waiting at Neil's home when they arrived back from the airport.

Natasha had a lot of explaining to do but realised that, for now, the most important thing was to give Neil some time to bond with his son.

That evening, with the bags unpacked and the exhausted little ones asleep, Natasha sat down with Neil and said, "I have plenty to fess up to. I only hope that your love is a strong as you say it is and you can forgive me for all my mistakes?"

Neil just held her hand and encouraged her to go on.

"I met Isa about three months before I left you. We were seeing each other regularly; I guess it was an affair." Her eyes were puffy, tears were welling up but she was determined to come clean. "I missed my period after we had been seeing each other for a while. You and I were having problems, we weren't getting together much. I thought the baby must be his. When the baby was born, Isa was beside himself with rage. He didn't know that you and I had been sleeping together while I was seeing him, so naturally, he'd assumed the baby would be his.

"His family were beastly; they scratched and spit at me, called me a whore. Isa had to tell them we weren't married to save face. He had told them I was a widow, that's why Monica was accepted." She looked down at her hands. "What a web of lies. Anyway, it was clear that I wouldn't be welcome there any longer so just a few days after giving birth, I gathered my things and was preparing to leave." She looked to her hands again and began to tremble. "That was when it happened." She paused for a few moments to gather her thoughts, and then continued. "Isa had a teenage son by a previous marriage. I noticed the way he watched me all the time but thought nothing of it. Anyway, not to put too fine a point on it, that night, he attacked me, beat me and raped me. Left me in quite a bad way."

Shock registered on Neil's face as he squeezed her hand tightly, reassuringly.

"Rape of a foreign national is a serious crime in Bahrain so Isa begged me to keep quiet. To be honest, I just wanted to be away from them, I didn't care what happened to the boy."

She looked up into Neil's eyes and the look of pity those deep brown pools conveyed.

She tenderly tapped the back of his hand with hers and said, "Well that's me pretty much a cleansed conscience. Isa offered me a very large sum of money to disappear and keep my mouth shut, I agreed. Life goes on."

"What about the boy?" Neil enquired. "What he did shouldn't go unpunished."

"And it won't have," she replied, "what he did dishonoured his father and the household. Isa will see to it he gets a far stiffer sentence than any English court would hand down. I can assure you of that. It's over Neil. A horrid chapter in my life, behind me now, forgotten."

She took a deep breath and continued, "I'm so angry at my mum for her lies, I would have come home straight away had she told me about you. I thought there was nothing back here for me, so I moved to Saudi Arabia and started a new life."

CHAPTER 78

A bright new future

Natasha's reconciliation with her mum was not as difficult as Neil had imagined it would be. Despite his obvious anger, Neil convinced Natasha that her mother acted in her best interests. When she had spoken to Neil's parents, had acknowledged how close to death Neil had come and the terrific battle he had fought to get well, she realised that her mum probably made the wrong choice for the right reasons. *Besides,* she thought, *if Neil can forgive, then I should too.*

It was the right decision; her wedding day would have been tarnished if her mum and stepdad had been absent.

"How about the honeymoon?" Neil enquired. "We can go anywhere in the world; Las Vegas, St Lucia, Miami Beach…Where do you fancy?"

Natasha screwed her nose up. "I want to go to Crete, just as we planned. I want to go to Crete, stay in a crummy single room apartment, hire a motorbike and make love on the sand." She was adamant. "That's what I want to do." She added, "And it's non-negotiable Mr Moneybags."

Neil smiled. "If that's what the lady wants, who am I to argue?"

Neil's parents decided that they would look after the children so that Neil and Natasha could go on their honeymoon. The au pair had decided to move back to her parent's house and return to university, which suited Natasha fine, as she wanted to go back to being a full-time mum.

It would be their first chance to be completely alone together since Natasha's return. A fortnight in Crete would prove just what the doctor ordered.

They were married in the autumn; Monica looked the picture of beauty and innocence resplendent in her flower girl flowing dress with a garland of wild flowers in her hair. Her brother, finally officially christened David Neil after Natasha's father and his own father, not to be left out of any adventure, was delighting in his role as a pageboy.

For early autumn, the weather was unseasonably favourable; the temperature, hot and dry, the leaves were just changing colour. The trees, resplendent in their burgundies and browns, were the perfect accompaniment to the sand and flint stone hues of the sixteenth century village, and to the spacious sixteenth century thatched cottage which Natasha and Neil had bought together as their first marital home.

Whichever way you approached the village necessitated a drive through narrow steep-sided cuttings lined with trees, giving the illusion of enchanting tunnels through the woodland. Experiencing it for the first time, many of the wedding guests were captivated by the beauty and tranquillity. As the tunnels opened out to the majesty of the ancient village, one received the impression of entering Valhalla, or the village that time forgot.

Neil waited patiently at the altar while Natasha kept him waiting a fashionable ten minutes. It was the longest ten minutes of his life. The church was filled to capacity with locals, friends, family and colleagues.

Brin, Neil's sister and his nieces had made the trip down. Sat side by side with them in the congregation were all the old faces too.

'Lost Bob' was sitting when everyone else was standing. He had turned up at the wrong church, in the wrong village, three days too soon. Fortunately for him Neil and Natasha had a certain 'celebrity status' locally and he was soon pointed in the right direction, otherwise he would have missed the service. Jimbo, Tim and Star were also present.

Many of Neil's customers from all over the country had travelled down to share in the couple's happy day. Not a chance they were going to miss this occasion. Neil had made it clear to all and sundry that this would be Natasha's fairy-tale day and not a 'biker' wedding. Obligingly, the bikers had travelled down with their best attire concealed under their leathers, gear normally reserved for funerals and court appearances.

Neil, naturally fidgety, kept turning to his best man: Goose, of course. "Can you see her yet?"

"No mate, stop panicking," Goose replied, "she'll be here, she loves you." As the familiar opening bars of the wedding march rang through the ancient village church, little David shook loose of Neil's mum's restraining grip and ran over to his dad, before holding his tiny arms out, hands opening and clenching, beckoning to be picked up. Neil's heart soared with emotion. He picked the little chap up and hugged him to his heart. Since Natasha's return, the two had become inseparable. Neil's mum ran up to relieve her son of the errant toddler. Neil waved her away and held his son firm.

The whole congregation turned towards the side entrance as the beautiful, radiant Natasha floated into view in a gorgeous ivory wedding gown, just the right blend of natural understated modesty with a figure hugging cut at the waist and a plunging décolletage to hint at the hidden treasures awaiting the groom's pleasure.

"Wow," exclaimed Neil.

"You lucky bastard," Goose whistled through his teeth.

Natasha's heart was fit to burst as she saw her two favourite men in the world sharing such a tender moment. As she came close, Neil handed the now placated infant to the waiting safe embrace of his mum, so the ceremony could commence.

She kept the veil over her face throughout the service; Neil could barely see the coy expression her eyes conveyed. His anticipation of lifting the veil and exposing her beautiful face to his kiss, sealing their marital bonds, made him dizzy with excitement.

Welcome guests in the congregation included Colin and Katie. Colin, who had as predicted made a full recovery after the savage beating from Brian a lifetime ago, had volunteered to carry out a reading.

Conducting the ceremony was a picture perfect clergyman, in his late sixties, bearded and eccentric as they come. He wound up the service with, "You may now kiss the bride."

Ever the comedian, Goose stepped forward, as if to perform this task.

Neil put a friendly arm on his friend's shoulder and laughed, "Excuse me old friend, I think this one is mine."

Neil lifted the veil from Natasha's face. Hanging from a silver chain around her neck, he recognised the tiny silver key.

"I've put the lock back where it belongs," she whispered, "don't you ever take it off for anyone but yourself."

Before Neil could answer, she kissed him with such passion the vicar had to let out a few discreet coughs to censor the proceedings.

As they broke off, Natasha whispered in Neil's ear, "I can't wait to get you home later. You may need to lubricate the lock a little, it hasn't seen action in a while," she giggled.

"I'll be sure to bring a can of WD40," Neil joked sarcastically, referring to industrial penetrating oil. She let out a hiss and play cuffed him round the ear.

As the bells chimed out in celebration of their joyous union, the congregation filed out into the church grounds. The official photographer led Neil and Natasha out into the secluded garden to the rear of the church where an ancient weeping willow tree provided a romantic backdrop for some private wedding photos. The photographer had a few unorthodox ideas for the happy couple's private album.

"Neil, how about a picture of you down on one knee, holding Natasha's hand as if you are proposing to her." Neil obligingly knelt in front of Natasha. "Now Natasha," he added, "let's make it a little naughty, show off your garter belt."

Neil was facing the camera. As he felt Natasha lifting her wedding gown, he couldn't help but turn towards her. The photographer was preoccupied;

faffing about with his camera gear. Natasha, the saucy minx, lifted her gown way past the garter, exposing her freshly clean-shaven sex, resplendent with the little silver padlock, to her new husband.

Natasha whispered to Neil, "I hope you've still got the key?"

With a wink, Neil pulled his shirt buttons to one side, exposing his chest. Hanging from a chunky silver chain was a tiny silver key, identical to hers.

The wedding day was a whirlwind of dreams and activity from the horse and carriage bringing the bride. The beautiful garlands of flowers, the quaint little church, the sumptuous banquet in the ancient monastery.

The first dance of the radiant bride and the handsome groom was naturally the couples 'special song'. Surrounded by their nearest and dearest.

At the ritual cutting of the cake, Natasha surprised her new husband by unveiling a little extra something she had added to the cake herself. Riding high on the top tier, was a Knight, seated atop a white charger.

"That's you Neil." Natasha whispered, her voice exposed, filled with sincerity. "That's what you are to me; my Knight in shining armour."

Holding her hands in his, Neil looked into her eyes and said, "Natasha, five years ago, I didn't know you existed. Now, I couldn't exist without you."

She hugged him close, the tears flowing freely down her cheeks. "Now you've ruined my make-up silly."

The rest of the day passed without the usual hitches, thanks to the expert organising skills of

Neil, with a little help from Janice. Apart from 'Lost Bob' tripping over the disco lead, blowing a main fuse and plunging the whole venue into darkness that is.

CHAPTER 79

Honeymoon

Two weeks later saw the couple breezing around Heathrow departure lounge without a care in the world. A squirt of this designer perfume, a squirt of that one. The call for their flight had gone out a couple of times but Neil and Natasha were in a world of their own, oblivious to the time or the tannoy.

"Could Mr and Mrs Curland flying to Crete at eleven forty-five flight TU 3003 kindly make their way quickly to gate fourteen. The plane is waiting to take off."

Finally, the penny dropped and Natasha relinquished the designer purse she was contemplating buying and they rushed to the gate with only moments to spare.

"We were just about to take your baggage off the plane," the steward chastised.

Neil and Natasha giggled with embarrassment as the passengers on board tutted at them as they bustled past.

Once seated, Natasha giggled to Neil, "Are we joining the mile high club?"

Neil smiled and said, "You are just too much Mrs Curland, have you seen how small the loos are?"

Natasha replied, "I'm game if you are."

The plane touched down at Heraklion airport. In the future Chania would be the arrival airport for the North West of the island, at present though it was still a NATO air base.

The trip from the airport to their apartment would take over two hours. The coach was pitching and rolling over the narrow cobbled streets as it wound its way from one apartment complex to another along the ancient northern coast towards Kalyves.

Outside a modest apartment block, a little 125cc motorbike was waiting, tank full and primed with the promise of adventure.

Natasha had one last secret she was keeping from Neil. She would share it with him after the honeymoon was over. She knew what a fuss pot he could be and she didn't want him treating her as if she were a delicate flower in need of protection.

No, she would wait until they were home to tell him that he was to be a father again!

They sat in the back row of seats. Natasha, lying against Neil's broad shoulder, was sleepy. The coach lurched sideways, negotiating a particularly bumpy set of curves. Her face was pitched into Neil's lap.

"While you're down there," he joked.

He felt her hot little hands fumbling with the front of his jeans.

It occurred to Neil that marriage to Natasha was never likely to be boring.

EPILOGUE

Vengance

On another island in the middle of the cold Atlantic Ocean, a lifetime away, the climate was considerably less accommodating.

After the debacle at Cherry Tree Farm, He'd been picked up by his handlers, driven to a remote barn, and strapped to a chair. A car tyre stuffed with newspaper had been placed over his head. He'd witnessed such executions before, as well as removing a troublesome irritant they served as a powerful deterrent to persuade any potential dissidents to toe the party line. Only his stoic defiance had saved him; his arrogant refusal to show weakness persuaded his handlers to call in before carrying out the sentence. Mr Doherty had rescinded. True psychopaths were hard to recruit. This time the errant rabid dog would escape with a severe beating, but his chances were running out.

Outside, morning had just broken on a grey dismal day, the rain running down the outside of the filthy window of the dingy one bedroom flat in Belfast, distorted the view of the cobbled street below. Off in the distance, a tyre fire was still smouldering; remnants of a weekend of sectarian violence. The lone figure in the upstairs window did not seem to notice as he stared blankly into the middle distance.

Behind those eyes was only one thought, one searing desire; Brian Dix wanted revenge!

About the author

Nick Boyland grew up on a British army Garrison in Western Germany.

He restored and built his first motorcycle at the tender age of 16, a Triumph tiger Cub, lapping in the valves on his dressing table, using grinding compound he made himself from toothpaste and emery cloth, and re-winding the alternator with copper wire scavenged from old transformers.

The Amal carburettor, scavenged from an old BSA Bantam, had the jets braised up and drilled out on the patio with a 12 volt drill until the mixture was, 'just right'.

Nick developed a strong empathy with old British motorbikes which saw him, as a young man, riding a hard tailed, Tribsa (Triumph/BSA) hybrid chopper across much of mainland Europe.

He enjoyed the hospitality of numerous European bike clubs in his extensive travels, which brought the adventures and experiences he interlaces into his fiction.

Now living in rural Somerset with his wife, children and dog, he is the proprietor of 'Rhino Trikes': motorcycle trike conversion specialists.

Nick has appeared on TV a number of times as engineering expert 'Rhino' in the popular Channel Four programme 'Scrapheap Challenge'.

Nick's company Rhino Trikes has a credit on the International Movie Database for supplying vehicles to Northern Girl Productions for use in the feature film 'The Zombie King' starring Corey Feldman and Edward Furlong.

Still working with trikes and custom bikes, Nick now rides a customised Harley Davidson 1450 Dyna-glide sport.

More about the author can be found at www.nickboylandauthor.com

Further titles in the Bittersweet Series

Bittersweet Humiliation

The second book in the Bittersweet series.

Published December 2013

Paperback ISBN 978-0-9576285-5-7

Ebook ISBN 978-0-9576285-3-3

Recently reunited. Wealthy beyond their wildest dreams. Newly-weds Neil and Natasha Curland are enjoying the romantic honeymoon of their dreams in a modest coastal town on the sun drenched island of Crete. Back home, business is booming. Exciting new opportunities loom on the horizon, in America: the land of opportunity. As if the future could possibly get any brighter, Natasha is quietly confident that she is expecting the couple's third child.

Just a short three hour flight away, a storm is brewing deep within the troubled mind of a vicious psychopath. Unbeknown to the happy couple, their lives lie directly in the path of the storm.

The next few months will see the beautiful Natasha physically and mentally destroyed, reduced to a base human being; stripped of her freedom, her dignity, and everything she holds dear, even escape may not release her from her torment.

The clock is ticking, the death toll is rising.

Bittersweet Retribution

The third book in the Bittersweet series
Published: November 2015
Paperback ISBN Number: 978-0-9576285-7-1
EBook ISBN Number: 978-0-9576285-6-4

"Neil, would you mind dropping the kids at mum's on your way to work, I'm running late for an appointment to get my nails sorted. I'll take the Beemer, it'll be easier to park," Natasha said, her face flushed from rushing about.

"Of course, no problem. Are they ready to go? "

"Yes, all ready, don't forget David's booster seat, you left it in the garage when you had the seats down."

Neil remembered, she was right, he'd used the family car to drop some rubbish at the tip. He would have to put the back seats back up too.

"Got to rush love, catch you soon." She pecked him on the cheek and darted out of the front door, BMW keys in hand.

Neil observed Natasha as she gently wheel spun on the gravel of the drive; hard to fathom what she'd been through, what she'd survived. Just a short year before, Natasha's psychotic ex-boyfriend had kidnapped her, abducted her to Ireland into slavery, then subjected her to a lifestyle of drugs and prostitution, destroying in the process the little life growing inside of her and her body's ability to reproduce. Mentally, she had made an almost full recovery; the only thing missing from their relationship was the physical side. Those scars would take longer to heal. Neil could feel the recoil of tension through her skin whenever he touched her. Fearing rejection, he had stopped trying. Therapy had helped at first, but now it just seemed like so much 'jaw jaw'. Only time could heal these wounds. His love for her was so strong; he would wait forever if that's how long it took.

The children were sitting at the dining room table working their way through a small bag of Jelly Tots each. Neil decided to leave them there while he went out to the garage to sort out the car.

His sensitive nose registered the faint smell as he entered the garage; it was somehow out of place. As he righted the back seats, his subconscious continued scanning an invisible database, trying to place the familiar aroma without success.

He returned to the dining room and gathered up his charges, not before time as little David was about to attempt a daring raid on his sisters sweetie bag!

"Hey, hey Master Curland, less of that, you'll end up in a life of crime! Now c'mon you two, let's be making tracks to Nannie's. No doubt she'll have you loaded up with sugar and E numbers the moment my back's turned," he laughed.

He strapped the children into the sumptuous rear seat of the Range Rover and turned his attention to the garage door. The motor clicked and whirred as he pressed the button to raise the door. With it fully elevated, he looked down at the dashboard, the nagging voice in his head was still quizzing him over the peculiar smell as he pushed the ignition key home. *Pears,* he thought. *Acetone?* He was thinking of Natasha's false nails, *did she use acetone to remove them?* He turned the key from park to the first click, the ignition lights burned brightly, briefly then extinguished.

ALMONDS! The thought from his subconscious was like a warning shout from his past. Turning in his seat, he said to Monica, "Honey, unbuckle your seat belt, then unfasten your brother's belt, then take him out of the car. Run as fast as you can down to the paddock and hide, Daddy will come and look for you."

"Like hide and seek Daddy?" the little girl replied.

"Exactly Hon'. You and David go hide, fast as you can, don't come back until you hear me calling that I give up!"

"You'll never find us Daddy!"

"I know that, you're a clever girl, now off you go, hurry!"

Neil watched the two innocent children run through the open doorway, away from the garage. He gave them ample time to be well clear of the vicinity before attempting to follow. He had no idea what would set it off, the door light circuit? Perhaps the seatbelt circuit? He needed the children clear before he attempted any escape.

Leaving the ignition as it was, he reached into the glove box and produced a Swiss army knife he kept there for emergencies. Withdrawing the sharpest blade, he cut through the belt and gingerly opened the door.

He was running flat out as soon as his feet touched the floor of the garage, sheer terror adding fuel to his muscles and propelling him towards the paddock faster than he'd ever moved before.

The blast lifted the Range Rover up and through the roof of the garage. Simultaneously the shock wave expanded through the roomy four car garage before ripping through the open garage door, giving Neil time to cover about 20 feet from the opening.

The energy from the blast picked him up and threw him into the air landing him softly into the bushes which lined the drive. He looked back at the garage, the house was engulfed in an enormous dust cloud, but there was no sound at all. The pressure in his ears was unbearable, and he pressed his fingers into them to relieve it. Without fully comprehending what had happened, he starred in shock at his bloodied fingers and the sounds of the blasts aftermath slowly penetrated his stupor.

The smoke and flames had set the sophisticated sprinkler system off and the fire alarm was wailing out its tortured cry. *The children!* Neil thought, and ran down the garden towards the paddock.

The children were standing at the entrance to the stables, in shock, staring back towards the remains of their family home. Neil stooped down and gathered them into his arms as the magnitude of what they had just survived sank in!